Advanced Reviews

"Dunne's character work is the highlight of this novel; Jim and Karl both feel realistic, three-dimensional, and intriguingly flawed...the writing is clear and concise throughout, and Dunne's descriptive imagery is often compelling..."

—*Kirkus Reviews*

"A thrilling, heart-pounding ride--climb aboard Ladder 57 and feel what it's like racing through Manhattan and the rush of responding to an "all-hands" fire. Dunne has done it again, this time taking you outside the firehouse and into the pressure-packed world of the FDNY as only a 33-year veteran can share."

— Lucas Tomlinson, *Fox News* correspondent

"Tom has now shown, once again his "way with words" in this wonderful story full of relatable characters...A fascinating read that I just could not put down."

— Dan Nigro, former Fire Commissioner, New York City Fire Department

"*A Moment in Time* explores the personal and professional issues in the life of an FDNY firefighter as he struggles to come to terms with his impending marriage and a career which doesn't seem to be going anywhere fast. Dunne has created characters who are instantly believable, wholly realistic and the firefighters could have been picked straight from just about any firehouse. It had me gripped right to the very last page and the door has been left open for the story to continue - I want more!"

— Duncan J. White, group dditor, MDM Publishing, Retired UK Fire Officer

"Dunne shares insider details that bring the firehouse and its inhabitants to life: the relationship of the "probies" and the old hands who mentor them; the dangers--physical, psychological, and emotional--that firefighters face as a result of their profession; even the minutiae of the sights, sounds, and smells of a twenty-first century firehouse in the heart of Manhattan... A fine read for anyone wanting to know more about the lives of firefighters from an expert practitioner and observer."

— Matty Dalrymple, author of the *Ann Kinnear Suspense* novels

"A vivid, touching behind-the-scenes look at the life of a New York fireman – the gripping drama of the fires; the vital, sometimes annoying firehouse relationships; his own puzzling affinity for an older New York and hesitancy to commit to his fiancée."

-Triss Stein, author of *Brooklyn Legacies*

A
Moment
in Time

A Moment in Time

Thomas Dunne

Apprentice House Press
Loyola University Maryland

First Edition

Casebound ISBN: 978-1-62720-416-3
Paperback ISBN: 978-1-62720-417-0
Ebook: 978-1-62720-418-7

Printed in the United States of America

Design by Sienna Whalen
Editorial development by Carlos Balazs

Published by Apprentice House Press

Apprentice House Press
Loyola University Maryland
4501 N. Charles Street
Baltimore, MD 21210
410.617.5265
www.ApprenticeHouse.com
info@ApprenticeHouse.com

To Suzanne. For steering me straight in this lifetime.

The past is not dead. It's not even past.
—William Faulkner

Chapter 1

5th Street Tenement
Lower East Side, New York City 1883

He was about to reach for the door handle when he first saw them. It was hard to see much of anything in the dim light that filtered through the glass transom above the doorway, but he could just make out the tiny nicks and scratches that covered the door knob. How many times had he stood in this very spot and not noticed those imperfections? The air in the hallway was stale and hot. He could hear fragments of muted conversations and blaring arguments echoing from the stairway below, all of them resonating in gruff German accents. For long moments he just paused and stared at the door knob and considered its worn appearance. He had been here many times, always with a sense of joy and excitement as he eagerly waited to enter the small apartment. But that was in the past. Now he was burdened with a sense of dread and a part of him knew that he was staring at that knob to delay the inevitable, to hold off for just a few more seconds and cling to distant memories before he must face what awaited on the other side.

He finally summoned up the will to knock. A few gentle taps with his right hand shook a loose panel on the flimsy wooden door and made a hollow sound that announced his presence. When it creaked open an equally fragile looking man stood there facing him. Helmut Kohler was in his fifties but he looked much older. He had thinning gray hair and a lean body and he bore the worn-down look of a man who had dealt with much in life. The white shirt he wore beneath his dark vest had long ago lost its texture and looked about as damaged as the man. But it was his deeply lined face that most showed the strain of his life. Years ago he had been drawn to New York for a fresh start, for the opportunity that always seemed just beyond reach back in Wurzburg. And that opportunity had planted him and his family in a world of tenements that often didn't seem very different from his previous life. German was the language of Klein Deutschland, his lower East Side neighborhood, where the scent of cooked sausage and the aroma of sauerkraut competed with the smell of the garbage cans that lined the cobblestoned streets. Helmut had struggled with the language of his new land but managed to find work in a brewery where English was the foreign tongue. He worked long hours for meager pay but always provided for his wife and daughter. And they had always been there for him.

Helmut looked at the young man standing before him in the doorway, paused for a moment, and in a gravelly voice said "Karl, come in."

Karl Bergman was 23 years old and had known Helmut for some time although the man he saw in front of him was very different from the one he had first met two years ago. Now a somber presence clung to the man as tightly as the buttons on his faded shirt. But he did seem genuinely glad to see Karl, or perhaps just relieved to have the presence of someone's company.

It had not always been that way. When Karl first met Helmut's daughter, Anna, he had not been welcomed with open arms. Helmut had not been thrilled that an uneducated man who made his living delivering coal was interested in his only child. He had wished for better things for her, for some kind of path that would lead beyond the life experienced in this crowded and confusing city. But he eventually developed a grudging respect for the young man. He worked hard and his interest in Anna seemed sincere. Despite the essence of coal dust that never seemed completely removed from his clothing, Karl made Anna happy. And, like Helmut, he was Bavarian. A Prussian background would have been a real challenge to accept.

Karl nodded an awkward "Herr Kohler" to Helmut and entered. The room was small and congested but well organized and packed with items that reflected the life of a family that had always patiently dealt with any challenges New York City threw at them. A tiny cast iron stove sat in one corner, covered with heavy pots and pans and showing every bit of its thirty years of use. Above it a narrow, handmade shelf held the small collection of plates, bowls, and cups that Helmut's wife, Grete, used to present the meals she fed her family. A few items had accompanied her on the long journey from Wurzburg, carefully packed in suitcases and padded with clothing. Her neatly framed needlework hung from one of the walls, but it was difficult to see the details since the only source of light came from a window overlooking a shaft way that narrowly separated the building from the tenement next door. The walls themselves were a faded white and the woodwork an indeterminate shade of dark brown. The place had not been painted in years and despite Grete's constant cleaning efforts everything looked somewhat faded.

Karl knew this space well but it was more like he *felt* the place. It was here that the initial, uneasy meeting of Anna's parents had gradually grown over time into a warm intimacy with the family. He had sat at that table and shared meals with them and he built the shelf that held the dishes they ate from. On holidays he shared steins of beer and, as the alcohol relaxed his normally stiff reserve and loosened his tongue, Helmut would tell long stories of a Germany he was only too glad to leave but on some level still deeply missed.

But that was all in the past for the small apartment had taken on a new essence; an air of fear and distress had entered the home along with the tuberculosis that had stricken Anna. Karl could see her lying on the bed in the farthest corner of the room, her mother seated in a chair right next to her, grief projecting from her hunched body almost like it was a physical presence. Twenty years prior she had given birth to Anna in a different bed in an equally tiny tenement room. Her torment then had only been physical. Now it reached right down into her soul as she watched her only child languish in a quiet, faltering sleep. He went over and put his hand on Grete's shoulder. She gently placed her own hand over his without looking away from her daughter.

When Karl glanced at Anna he noted that not much had changed since he last saw her. Her thin, delicate body was partly covered by a light blanket but he could see that she was wearing a different gown and her dark hair had been carefully groomed, no doubt by her mother. The thick, dark curls flowed onto both sides of the pillow. The same curls that hung from the large bonnets she wore in better times when the two of them would walk and explore the streets of the neighborhood. He recalled watching those curls as they teasingly bounced from beneath her hat and gently moved as they caught the breeze. Like they were a part of her but with a life of their own, so light and so free.

Karl had always looked forward to those walks. Often, in the middle of an exhausting work day, as he poured yet another load of coal down into a tenement basement, he would think of being with her. Their time together always seemed to go by too quickly. They usually strolled along Avenue B just glancing at the wares on display in the stores and markets. In flush times they might stop at an oyster saloon on Avenue A or maybe even see a show over on Bowery. She always moved with a light touch of grace, her long dress sweeping just above the sidewalk as if she were not walking but somehow gently gliding along. He most cherished those moments they shared in the Weisse Garten when they enjoyed the cool shade of the park on warm summer evenings.

But that was in the past, in a happy time that seemed so recent and yet at the same time so painfully distant. Now, as he watched over Anna's troubled breathing and fitful sleep, he remembered what was most absent. Her eyes, those pale blue eyes. Perhaps more than anything that is what he remembered, what he missed most. As often as he saw them Karl never failed to be captured by Anna's eyes. They were pale blue and they were happy. It was like she could smile with those eyes even if you couldn't see the rest of her face. As if such a thing were even possible. Now he couldn't see them at all. He could just imagine them as he glanced at the dark circles below her closed eyes wondering when they would open and hoping they would not lose their luster.

Karl felt uneasy as he stood by the bed and struggled for something to say to Grete that would somehow ease her pain. But he could not find the words and with a quiet "Take care Frau Kohler" he leaned down and again placed his hand on her shoulder. Grete responded with a sad, silent nod. Somehow he knew that he would always remember that nod and the defeated look on her face. It was as if a milestone had been reached and the gesture measured a point at which both had been forced to accept a harsh reality. Anna was not going to recover and this precise moment would always be etched in their memories as a turning point in their lives.

Karl moved from the bed and as he scanned the room around him he looked at it as though seeing it for the first time, as if the walls and the window and the furniture were not real objects but images that would be seared into his mind and always remain to haunt him in the days to come.

Helmut met him at the door as he was leaving and said "Thank you Karl. You will come again soon?"

"Of course, Herr Kohler" he responded, but even as he spoke the words he felt a deep level of sympathy for him. For he knew that he too was struggling to hide from the gravity of the situation, to cling to even a brief fragment of hope however unrealistic that might be.

Back out in the hallway Karl paused for a moment, relieved to be out of the apartment but at the same time frustrated by his inability to alter fate in any way, to change what was happening inside, or to at least provide any kind of reassurance to Anna's parents. He turned toward the narrow wooden stairs that led down to the street. When he had walked up these flights just a few minutes ago he was still clinging to an illusion, or at least still hiding from reality. Now he was being inexorably forced into a new path, one he resisted and could not even comprehend, for Anna would not be on that path with him.

The wooden steps squeaked like cracking bones as he moved down the tight stairway, each one responding noisily as he stepped on it and issuing a relieved groan as he moved on to the next one. The sound masked the conversations in the apartments that he passed, each one harboring its own desperate existence.

It was a relief to finally reach the street. The fresh air and open space were an abrupt and refreshing change from the stagnant atmosphere of the tenement. Karl walked along the sidewalk, unmindful of the crowd of pedestrians who surrounded him. Sadness clung to him and weighed him down. It slowed his normally brisk gait, as if he had a heavy, wet coat draped over his shoulders. He stopped at the first empty tenement stoop he spotted and abruptly sat down on the warm concrete. He suddenly became aware of the street life that moved before him and watched it all in a detached, dazed manner. Snippets of conversation emerged from groups of women who walked past, their broad hats shielding their heads and long dresses flaring out from tightly tailored waists right down to where they almost swept the sidewalk. Several of them were carrying baskets of produce and items purchased from street vendors who stood nearby hawking their wares and eking out a living from their fragile push carts. Karl could smell the oranges that sat in one of the nearby carts, a sweet aroma that briefly worked its way through the odor of horse manure. Through it all the chorus of voices blended with a constant rumble of noise in the background. A wagon lumbered down the street laden with scrap metal, steel rimmed wheels rattling on the cobblestones and horses hooves clopping with every step. Children ran and laughed in a raucous game they played at a nearby hydrant. The laundry that hung from clothes lines strung between tenement windows and fire escape railings swayed in the breeze like flags on a ship.

As he sat on the stoop Karl watched an existence that stood in vivid contrast to the world of the decayed tenement he had just left. Here there was activity and movement, a flow of energy and of life. How could such a world continue to go on oblivious to what he had seen, to what he was feeling?

A large draught horse stood by hitched to an old wagon, its face immersed in a feed bag and eyes covered with blinders. Karl watched the animal as it quietly and slowly chewed. He had handled horses when he delivered coal, prodding and directing them for hours through the congested streets as he worked his way through long, exhausting days. But those horses were just accessories to his job, a means of moving heavy cargos, creatures that required food and rest and care, but basically tools to accomplish a goal and somewhat taken for granted. He had never really looked at one in the way he regarded the horse that now stood impassively in front of him. As he observed the horse he noted how the muscles in its huge flanks flexed when it whipped its tail to ward off flies and how the thick veins in its head pulsed with the flow of blood that pumped through its body. He watched its massive ribs move as it gave off a huge sigh and looked at the long tendon that flexed in its leg when it repositioned a hoof, seeming far too delicate to support such a massive load. And always the scent, an earthy essence of work and sweat and warm flesh that radiated from the animal. There was life in this creature and there was energy, pulsating and mixing with the warm breeze and the hanging laundry and the ceaseless drone of the peddlers. And soon, very soon, this horse would still be alive, still be a part of the life that flowed through this street. And Anna would not.

Karl lowered his head as he sat on the stoop and stared at the flagstone sidewalk.

Chapter 2

Astoria Queens
New York City, Present Day

It was the phone answering machine that woke him up. He should have turned the damned thing off. "Are you there?" she asked. Yeah, just barely, he thought as he struggled to gain some level of consciousness. The digital clock on the night table flashed 10:35 AM in bold, red numerals like it was scolding him for sleeping so late.

"If you are, please pick up."

He felt like he'd have a hard time just picking himself up right now. He was exhausted and abruptly ripped out of a deep dream state, still recovering from the previous 24 hour work tour, his circadian rhythm once again shot to shit. He managed to just lift his head, and glanced at the one white sweat sock that was lying on the floor next to the bed. Where the hell had he put the other one? And why did he still keep this answering machine when he had a perfectly adequate cell phone? He knew why. He could turn the thing off, though this time he had forgotten. Turn it off and escape from all the intrusions of the world. Then the only paper trail leading to him would be a series of unanswered emails.

"Just want to remind you we're having dinner at my parents' house on Wednesday."

It was Laura, his girlfriend of three years, or more precisely his fiancée, but that was a word that did not slide easily from his tongue or a concept that rested easily in his mind. He sat up in the bed and glanced at the full bottle of beer that lay next to the alarm clock. He had opened it up last night, tossed the cap, and then decided that he really didn't want to drink it after all.

Wednesday, parents, dinner. Yeah, he had forgotten. He wasn't even sure what day *this* was. Weekdays, weekends, holidays, they all blended together in his line of work. The phone call had abruptly ended an intense dream that left him dazed and confused as he fought his way into a new state of awareness. He tried to remember the dream and its vague images of people, places, and intense emotions, all of which seemed so very distant and at the same time hauntingly familiar. He recalled walking on streets he did not recognize toward a destination that held some vital importance. He strained to remember the details, but it all remained just beyond his reach, clinging to the fringes of his consciousness. And the harder he tried the more distant it all seemed. Like a tiny light in a dark room that you could see in the periphery of your eye but would disappear the moment you looked straight at it.

"They'll be expecting us around seven so if you can get me about six that should be good."

He pictured the dinner, and the parents, in an expansive house up in Westchester County. Fastidiously groomed lawn, gravel driveway raked to perfection, trimmed hedges rigidly adhering to sharp geometric shapes. Her mother, warm and welcoming. The dad, not a bad guy but a bit more distant and a lot more opinionated. The food, a tasty and exquisite work of art but certainly not prepared by the parents. They hired people to

10

do that.

"Jim, you there?"

He thought of attempting to force his way from the comfort of the blankets and grabbing the phone but he just couldn't get his body to face the blast of cold air that had built up over night by the air conditioner that sat rattling in the window. When he slept he liked it cold and dark.

"I've got a meeting in a few minutes so I'll have to call you back later."

Laura attended a lot of meetings. It seemed to Jim that her hard-earned MBA had led her into a world of endless meetings and he often wondered if the comfortable salary she earned was really worth all the hours and commitment her work required. But it certainly seemed like she ate it all up. Laura Whitacre was a lot of what Jim Hanley was not. And that was one of the things he liked about her. She was tall and bright, blond and attractive in an all-American way, and spawned from a background that contrasted sharply with his. Her family boasted a long Princeton tradition but daddy's wealth and connections could have landed her at any Ivy. Not that she had needed it. Her resume spoke for itself. Her position as the captain of her high school volleyball team along with her numerous advanced placement classes and stratospheric SAT scores could have written a ticket to any college. Harvard had been her safety school for goodness sakes.

Jim had ridden the subway to a community college where he had been a somewhat disinterested history major. His mind easily wandered as the lectures droned on about esoteric topics like who held the Spanish throne in the 15th century or the significance of the War of the Roses (which from the name of it certainly seemed to him like quite a wimpy war). For Jim real history was envisioning the taut sails of wooden ships as they made their way over vast oceans or pondering how constipated the sailors must have become after weeks of a diet consisting of dried beef and stale biscuits. When his name finally came up on the civil service list for a job as a New York City firefighter he put his academic pursuits on hold and jumped at the opportunity.

But despite their differences they had established a real connection. They met, of all places, at a church social although a church was the last place either of them would normally prefer to be in unless it was for their own funeral. And then they wouldn't have much of a choice in the matter. Jim worked in a male dominated job, a reality that had limited his social connections. He quickly tired of standing in bars, nursing a drink, and trying to conduct some kind of conversation with a woman in the midst of ear blasting music. The strained "where do you live, what you do" banter led to the occasional short-lived relationship and to the not so occasional sex which ranged from just "ok" to "oh my God that was great, let's have a cigarette" -and Jim didn't even smoke.

Although he kept busy there was no permanence in his life and Jim was always left feeling somewhat unfilled by it all. One evening as he was reading the paper he saw a small notice that a midtown church had posted about a social gathering for "young urban professionals". He knew that group was unlikely to include guys who carried axes on their jobs but, figuring at 29 years of age, he at least qualified for one of the parameters. And he *was* an urban person though a lot of Manhattan residents might question whether Astoria was actually a part of the city or even know where it was. The borough of Queens was indeed part of New York but despite the presence of the art museum in Long Island City and the sculpture on display in Socrates Park it was not considered a hip place to live in.

So it was with some trepidation that Jim took the train to Manhattan to check out the event. He thought the church had a most appropriate name. Our Lady of Solace, perfect label for a place designed to ease the social pangs of young people who worked in demanding New York City jobs that offered impressive salaries, inadequate free time, and the likelihood of communal alienation.

It wasn't until he actually got to the site that he realized it was a "members only" affair. Membership in the organization was accomplished through an application process designed to weed out any inappropriate candidates. Jim couldn't help feeling he might just fit into that category and was about to leave when he spotted the young woman sitting by the table at the entrance. She was collecting the $10 dollar entrance fee and he was lured over by her inviting smile.

"Hi! Welcome to the party" she offered in a bright, perky voice.

"Glad to be here" he responded, thinking he just might fake his way inside and not totally blow the evening after having trekked all the way from Queens. Thankfully she didn't ask for any form of ID as Jim laid his ten dollar bill down on the table, all the while making eye contact with her and trying to appear that he was not only a member but a long time, well established one at that and flashing his "of course I'm sure you recognize me" smile. Jim had learned much from his seven years of working in the fire department. He could BS with the best of them.

"Thank you so much, have a good time!" signaled that the gate was indeed now open for him and he again noted her welcoming smile and desperately tried not to glance down the ample cleavage that peeked out from her blouse as she leaned over the table.

He started walking toward the large room where people were gathering when "Just a minute please" stopped him dead in his tracks. Caught in the act! Exposed! Jim felt the same nervous guilt the nuns in grade school had evoked when they uncovered some perceived malfeasance on his part. He turned to the woman at the desk, somewhat embarrassed but knowing that he had at least given it a shot.

"You forgot your drink tickets." Again with that affable smile on her face. Jim took the tickets feeling relieved and guilty at the same time.

Once he started walking around the room he wondered if it had been at all worth it. He was sporting one of his best dress shirts but clearly the rest of the room had gotten the memo about wearing more formal business attire. He got into a conversation with a few guys but they spoke of little else but stock prices and he quickly lost interest. One woman engaged him with a very polite but very predictable dialogue about politics. When she asked him what he did he said he was a firefighter and she responded with "but what do you do for a living?" and he knew it was going to be a long evening. He managed to politely escape from her and for a long time just stood by himself feeling some-what awkward and out of place and wondering just why the hell he had even come here when it would have been a lot easier to stay at home and catch the Knick game. It was at that precise moment that he had caught Laura's eye.

Laura fit in perfectly and looked like the life of the party. She was impeccably dressed and moved around the room with an air of confident grace, like someone who could hold her own in a debate and then kick your ass on the tennis court. It was she who took the initiative and came over to introduce herself. They quickly got into an easy conversation and when he mentioned the kind of work he did she really did seem interested and pro-ceeded to ask him a lot of questions about a job she knew noth-ing about. They hit it off right away, in part because they shared an equally sharp sense of humor, but also because Laura fell for what had always proven to be a classic misinterpretation of what Jim was all about. With his casual dress and solitary manner Jim gave the appearance of being a real challenge. He looked like someone who had a lot of friends and many connections in life and who was not desperate for company but would be a most interesting person to be with. In fact he had few real friends and moved through the world always feeling somewhat like an outsider, forever trying to fit in but always with a sense of belonging somewhere else.

"You don't have to get dressed up."

Laura's voice on the answering machine roused him back from the mental funk he had drifted into, his head again lowered onto the pillow and the warm comforter now pulled up all the way to his chin. Not only had he left the machine on but the volume was set to max. Another plus for Laura though. She had always accepted him for what he was, which was quite an accomplishment considering her background. Jim had a couple of sports coats he could whip out in an emergency but a vast part of his wardrobe consisted of fire department sweats and tee shirts that he had accumulated over time.

Laura's comfort with him went beyond the essence of her generally tolerant nature. On some level Jim offered a sense of liberation for her, a reminder that life offered the possibility of paths that existed beyond the most obvious ones. In at least one small corner of her mind she sometimes wondered exactly what all the competition eventually led to. College, the MBA, the struggle of the corporate boardroom, where exactly were you at the end and how did you know when you got there? Laura was bright and curious and grew up always wondering what life was like on the other side of the fence. And that fence was not in Westchester. It could be in the Bronx or Nebraska or anywhere that might offer an escape from the safe but predictable life she had always known. Jim offered such a possibility, one she found both captivating and frightening.

"Ok I'll speak to you tomorrow. Hope you have a quiet tour tonight. Love you!"

There it was again, the L word. Jim had no doubt that Laura did in fact love him and he felt a real attachment to her. But he always found himself analyzing what it meant, how it was really supposed to feel, wondering if what they shared was the same thing that the married guys at work had or what the couples on the cover of *People* magazine experienced. Was Laura "the one" or was it all just subject to chance? Of all the millions of women in the city he happened to stumble upon her at the party. What if he had stood inside that room just a few feet further to the right or remained at the entrance flirting with the woman collecting the entrance fee or perhaps not even gone at all but stayed home to watch the game? Would he have eventually crossed paths with some other woman and felt the same with her? Jim knew he was unfairly comparing Laura to an ideal, to an image of the most perfect woman and recognized that it was not only an exercise in futility but also a threat to the intimacy they shared. But always there were the questions, the fantasy of someone else out there existing in some vague, ethereal reality.

And therein lay a basic difference between Laura and him. She seemed so sure of herself, sure of everything and able to commit to things without worry. The MBA, her job, their life together, whatever doubts existed were never sufficient to diminish that commitment. Jim was sure of nothing. Engagement, marriage, his job in the fire department, it all seemed appealing but could he really say with absolute confidence that he anticipated those prospects as definite, decades long experiences, or were they paths that would eventually feel stagnant and confining and leave him pondering if he had missed out on some other ambiguous possibility? He wondered if these were normal concerns or if on some level everyone felt the same things and just didn't verbalize such thoughts. Jim was deep and insightful, qualities that had served him well in many ways, but at the same time always held him back as he constantly examined the world at a distance, observing and probing, looking for some place that felt like a natural fit, but much like the details of his vivid dreams, always appeared to lie just out of reach. Laura seemed able to commit to so much. He couldn't even commit to drinking that bottle of beer that had sat, open and stale, on the side table since last night.

However such thoughts required far more energy than he possessed at the moment. In just a few hours he had to return to the firehouse and work another night tour. He would be earning overtime pay for this one but it wasn't the money he sought, it was freedom. Jim's base salary was more than enough to sustain his somewhat frugal lifestyle but he didn't want to wait until the real heat of summer set in. Guys would be less willing to do the extra tours then and the chief would be ordering men who were low on overtime hours to come in to work. And that was yet another commitment he didn't relish.

He pulled the plug on the answering machine, rolled onto his side, and quickly fell back into a deep sleep in the comfort of the dark, cool bedroom.

Chapter 3

Jim stumbled out of bed several hours later still feeling somewhat groggy. He pulled up the window shades, squinted at the bright sunshine, and proceeded to his kitchen to prepare a strong cup of coffee. Only a firefighter would have his morning wake up brew at four in the afternoon but he savored the rich aroma coming from the old Mr. Coffee machine as he dressed and prepared for work. The small, first floor apartment was still cool from the hours of running the air conditioner at full blast. As usual it was very quiet since the Greek couple who lived on the second floor of the two-family building were at their jobs, he a cab driver, she a teacher's aide at a local school. They had been somewhat uneasy when they first rented the apartment to him since in the past they only had female tenants and weren't quite sure what to expect from having a man living in their house. But they quickly grew to like Jim. He was always available to help with minor repairs and he paid his rent on time. And it was nice to have a firefighter in the house, like it was a bit safer just having him there.

Jim picked up the one white sweat sock he found lying on the floor, folded it with its mate and placed both in the large dresser that sat in the bedroom right next to his weight bench and desk.

Various sized dumbbells laid scattered about and the glowing computer screen on the desk displayed a number of recently ignored emails. The room served as a combined sleep, work out, and entertainment space, not to mention as an escape from the intrusions of the outside world.

In a few minutes he was ready to head off to work and he buckled into the white Toyota that sat in the narrow driveway just outside his entrance door. The driveway was one of the advantages of living in the apartment since parking spots were at a premium in the neighborhood. Jim had spent far too many hours in his adult years participating in the traditional New York City pastime of hunting for a parking spot.

Soon he was driving over the 59th Street Bridge and working his way towards Manhattan. Officially it was the Ed Koch Bridge, named after a long time city mayor. But Jim refused to call it that. After all, it had been called the same thing for 111 years and it seemed to him that changing the name reeked of the elitism he always objected to. Like there were different rules for different people and all of it depended on just how connected you were in life. He sometimes wondered if there might eventually be a Kardashian Tunnel or perhaps a Jay Z Memorial Highway. Nonetheless he always enjoyed this part of his commute since it allowed him to peek down at the East River that flowed steadily beneath the bridge.

Jim had always been fascinated by the river and spent many lazy hours just watching it flow by, intently observing how it was pushed by the tides and parted by the boats that slowly strained against the powerful currents. There was a certain timelessness to it all. In a city that was in an endless state of change the water was a constant. This same river, these very waters, were the one natural element that had ignored all of the enormous transformations the city experienced as it evolved through the years. 19th Century sloops, World War II barges, and Circle Line tourist boats had all come and gone without influencing it in any way. When Jim jogged through Astoria Park he often stopped to view the Hell Gate section of the river, a frightening spot that had sealed the fate of many vessels including, the story went, an old English sailing ship laden with gold that had been overwhelmed by the ripping currents. He often pictured the wreck, buried somewhere deep in the riverbed, hidden far below the dark threatening waves that were in relentless motion on the surface. The river had an essence and a power that could not be constrained by any concept of time.

His view of the river and thoughts of its past history abruptly ended once he arrived on the Manhattan side of the bridge. He tightened his grip on the steering wheel the moment he faced the maelstrom of rush hour noise and traffic. Manhattan was both a fascinating place and an assault on the senses. There were cars everywhere, many of them honking their horns. High rise buildings blocked out any view of the sky and layers of pavement hid any indication of the meadows and streams that had once meandered through the borough. Jim turned left on Lexington Avenue figuring he'd work his way down to 34th Street, a wide block that might allow for an easier flow of traffic. The drive from the bridge to the location of his firehouse on the West Side was always the most trying part of the commute.

It had not always been that way. Jim thought of a time not long ago when the city had become a ghost town and the normally packed streets sat empty and quiet with just the occasional solitary pedestrian passing by, face shielded by a mask and mind shrouded in fear of a deadly virus. Unlike the flow of the East River that was a side of nature that even New Yorkers couldn't ignore. Many of them had rediscovered the pleasures of quiet suburban houses and escapes to remote lake and beach communities whose populations suddenly swelled with frightened urban refugees. Most had abandoned those safe retreats and returned to a buzzing city with its offerings of fine wines, Broadway plays, and pastrami sandwiches at one in the morning. The pandemic was now a sad memory, a nightmare implanted in the collective mind of the city spoken of in hushed tones of fear and with an awareness that any sense of order and control could suddenly prove to be an illusion. But now the faded remnants of graffiti that still peeked out from some of the monuments and public buildings were the only physical reminders of that disruptive era. The city had come back and so had the traffic and congestion.

It was a relief to finally arrive at the firehouse. Jim parked his car across the street, grabbed his bag of freshly laundered work clothes, and paused to look at the building. That was always a reassuring sight. The three-story structure was over one hundred years old, built in an era when civic architecture was still accomplished with a sense of art. Not like the soulless concrete monstrosities of the 60's and 70's with their industrial facades and stainless-steel interiors. The front of Ladder 57's quarters was done in classic, freshly repointed red brick. A limestone arch curved over an old overhead garage door that looked barely wide enough to allow the truck to pass through. The bright yellow markings painted on each side of that opening were free of any scuff or dent marks and gave evidence to the skill of the chauffeurs who drove the enormous rig through it dozens of times each day. A plaque on the front wall recorded the date the firehouse was built along with the names of those who had served as the mayor, fire commissioner, and building architect. All of them were now long forgotten, their names just faint green letters engraved on the oxidized bronze. Jim felt a connection to this building. He sensed the history that emanated from the place and appreciated the classic style that stood in such contrast to the stale sheetrock walls of his Queens apartment.

As he approached the firehouse Jim saw two men working on the front sidewalk. They were busily engaged in sweeping up the bits of debris that had been blown there by the wind along with the used condoms left by men who had been blown by the local prostitutes. Dave Wozniak and Tyrone Hillman were the two newest men assigned to the company. They were probationary firefighters, both just a few months out of the fire department training academy on Randalls Island. As new "Probies" they faced a full year of being the low man on the totem pole until, finally, they would get off probation and be accepted as permanent members of the FDNY. Until that happened it was expected that they would be in constant motion, cleaning the firehouse, polishing the brass, and taking a lot of shit from the senior members. So far both had accepted that role and fit in pretty well with the company. But both were anxiously waiting for the day when another probie would be assigned to the unit. Then there would at least be another guy to share their burden, someone who sat even lower on that totem pole.

Dave looked up from his broom and greeted Jim with a quick and loud "Hey man, how's it going!" Tyrone just offered a shy nod. Both felt a level of comfort with Jim and were relieved to see he would be working tonight. He was one of the few experienced guys who was not constantly busting their chops.

"Keeping busy I see" Jim responded as he paused to gaze at the two of them.

Dave Wozniak was built like the proverbial brick shit house. He was immensely strong and would often be found in the weight room once he finished his firehouse chores where he'd slap 250 pounds onto a barbell and knock off an impressive number of bench presses. He had all of the strength and endurance the work called for but was very much a work in progress and tended to move about in an abrupt manner that exuded a constant state of expended energy. But much of that energy was raw and misdirected and expressed in his nearly violent technique of scrubbing pots in the kitchen or in his frantic style of mopping and sweeping. Dave was a guy who would eventually evolve into an effective firefighter but his current state called for close supervision by the senior guys and company officers. Such frenzied activity on the fireground could prove to be dangerous to himself or someone around him. There were subtleties in firefighting, ways of thinking and conducting yourself that had to be learned in order to survive in such a dangerous occupation. Dave also had a way of incorporating the "fuck" word into most of his conversations, artfully wielding it as a noun, verb, or adjective, his dialect as raw as his physical presence.

In contrast, Tyrone Hillman was a quiet individual and Jim found it more difficult to get a read on him. Tyrone was about the same height as Dave but built much leaner. His eyes peered out shyly from behind the round gold rims of his glasses and made him look like someone who was distant and holding himself back from his surroundings. Which he was. He was one of the few black firefighters in the company and didn't fit the mold of "firefighter" they were accustomed to. Even though the department had made sincere efforts to increase the number of minorities on the job, its basic essence was still influenced by its Irish Catholic roots. Italian, German, Polish, it didn't matter much what ethnic background someone was from, they all tended to become some form of "Irish" in an institution that had chaplains, religious societies, and traditional values. All except the black guys who were coming on the job in increasing numbers but had not yet reached a level where many could boast of having fathers or even grandfathers who had been in the FDNY.

Like all new probies Tyrone had been quite nervous when he

first reported into the company. Some of the older black firefighters on the job had mentioned rumors of the "black bunk" that was said to exist in some of the firehouses in the 1950's. It was, they claimed, a bed that was reserved exclusively for the few black guys who were on the job back then. He also realized that many of the people he would be working with would probably have nothing to do with him if he hadn't become a firefighter. A lot of them were from the suburbs. It's not like they had attended the same schools or would ever even think of going to the Brooklyn neighborhood where he had grown up. But much to his relief, Tyrone had been treated like every other probie when he started working, which is to say harshly but fairly.

To some extent it was his insightful nature that made him feel like an outsider. But there was another issue that influenced his situation. Tyrone was burdened by the fact that he was more intelligent than many of the men he worked with, including some of the officers. Though he never verbalized it, a lot of what he heard and saw seemed to him like adolescent nonsense.

Jim watched as Tyrone swept the sidewalk, noting how he worked his broom in a manner that was so different from Dave's robust but clumsy efforts. He moved with grace, each sweep carefully planned and efficiently pushing the debris, like he had sized up the challenge before starting each stroke. And he was accomplishing a lot more than Dave.

"Hey Tyrone, did you get your helmet fixed?" Jim inquired.

"Yeah, I went out to the Quartermaster on Randalls Island and they fixed it right away," he responded.

That was why he felt comfortable working with Jim. He didn't enjoy harassing the probies like some of the other guys and he actually took the time to teach the new men. Like how to get your gear repaired, or how to force your way through a difficult door at a fire. He recalled how awkward he had felt on his very first day in the company. Jim had been the only veteran to step up and give him a tour of the tools that were contained in many compartments on the rig. Right away Jim seemed like a decent person who would be good to work with, maybe even become a friend. A white guy no less.

On a more basic level Tyrone also sensed that Jim held back very large parts of himself. He often observed him sitting at the kitchen table just monitoring the banter without comment and listening to the raucous laughter without joining in. Tyrone suspected that, for some undefined reason, Jim felt like just as much of an outsider as he did.

Jim left the two probies and entered the open bay doors of the firehouse. He glanced to the right and could see Anthony Faiella sitting at the house watch desk, deeply immersed in a conversation on his cell phone. The house watch area was the nerve center of the firehouse, the place where all phone calls and alarms were received from the dispatcher. It was a small space, tightly enclosed by well-constructed walls that were covered with framed copies of unit citations that the company had earned for past actions. Faiella's gangly 6 foot 3 inch frame barely fit into the area and with his long legs awkwardly sticking out from the chair it kind of looked like a clean shaven Abe Lincoln was manning the watch desk. Jim nodded a greeting toward Faiella who in turn completely ignored him.

Faiella was often on his cell phone. He fancied himself a writer and for as long as anyone could recall he had been hard at work on a novel. He was currently working his way through a third rewrite of the book and twenty seventh rejection from a literary agency. Late one night, after returning from a "good job", which was firehouse speak for a tough fire, the guys were sitting together in the kitchen charged up on caffeine and adrenaline. They actually got him to talk about the storyline of the book, which he was normally reluctant to do. Something about a main character who was suffering through a deep conflict and sought redemption by traveling through Europe on a bicycle. The men nearly pissed their pants laughing and that was the last time they ever heard about the plot. Jim didn't laugh at all, in part because that wasn't his style, but also because on some level he kind of identified with the character.

The incident was soon forgotten but it did lead to yet another firehouse nickname. For a while Faiella became the "Redeemer" which for a brief time evolved into "Jesus". But in an institution with such traditional roots that was considered too sacrilegious and quickly dismissed. Eventually Faiella simply became "Shakespeare" and the moniker stuck.

Shakespeare was not a popular man in the company but it had nothing to do with his writing. The men just didn't like his approach to the job. It seemed like being a firefighter was just a sideline to his main calling in life, a temporary state to pay the bills until he found his way onto the *New York Times* best sellers list. And those long, intense cell phone conversations didn't help. The men assumed Faiella was talking to literary agents or guys in Hollywood. Jim thought he was talking to his shrink, or should be.

Jim left the house watch desk, walked past the truck, and headed toward the kitchen. The rig sat there quietly parked in all of its polished red splendor, a precise "Ladder 57" shining from the side door in a brilliant display of gold leaf lettering. He was hit by the familiar scents of his work world, sweet aromas of oil and polish, bitter odors of ammonia and floor wax, and the traces of smoke that always emitted from the coats and helmets that hung on a long rack, some still moist from recent jobs. The apparatus floor was an environment of extremes, a garage where the polished sliding poles gleamed and contrasted with the coarse gray concrete floor and pockets of fresh paint stood out against an ancient tin ceiling of an indeterminate color, covered as it was by decades of vehicle exhaust and soot. And always the noise, the ceaseless drone of the department radio, the ear splitting announcements over the PA system, and the shouted comments of the men echoed against the tile walls and filled the space with a confusing and assaulting soundtrack. It was a sensual place to work in but certainly not a gentle one.

When Jim went through the metal door that led into the kitchen he entered an entirely different environment. The kitchen was much more than a place to eat. It served as a gathering place where the men conversed and debated and competed for their place in the harsh pecking order of the firehouse. Jim was always struck by the fact that just one thin door separated an area that served as a dining room from the apparatus floor on the other side and how the industrial aroma of the garage was immediately replaced by the fragrance of roast beef or chicken cutlets.

Everything in the kitchen was massive. It was dominated by a long table surrounded by a dozen well-worn plastic chairs that had seen better days. A huge stove sat on one side with a collection of pots and colanders that hung from hooks attached to the ceiling, all of them large enough to feed a small army. There was a television flickering away on a hand crafted shelf airing an afternoon news show that no one was watching. All in all it looked like the kind of kitchen you would see in a restaurant or a home unit on steroids. And there, sitting at a small round table tucked into the corner sat Sean, the senior member of the company, immersed in a copy of the *Daily News*.

Sean Walsh had sat at that same place for years, the seat becoming a spot that all knew was unofficially reserved just for him. But he didn't just sit there all that time. It was more like he held court, greeting familiar faces, teaching new probies, and verbalizing a running commentary on life. Sean was on the short side and had a sinewy build except for the slight suggestion of a beer gut, a result of his years as a strident disciple of the Yuengling brewing company. His gray hair and lined face gave evidence to the thirty plus years he had on the job but his impish smile and easy Irish humor gave off an aura that reflected his philosophy of life. And that, simply put, was that a lot of shit happens and you had to roll with the punches and stay true to who you were and never submit to any ridiculous set of rules that tried to explain it all. He was an approachable man but the newer members of the company were still somewhat in awe of him. He seldom spoke of it but Sean had actually been there when those buildings went down on 9/11 killing 343 firefighters along with thousands of civilians. For months he had spent long days knee deep in the dust searching for the remains of coworkers and finding little but a realization that life was indeed finite and had to be lived according to one's own rules.

Over the course of the following years Sean had been to many of the tough fires the company encountered. Their work was proudly remembered in the unit citations that hung at the house watch desk though the words on the neatly framed certificates could never properly convey the hellish conditions they had met and overcome. There had also been much in his own life for Sean to surmount. A few years after 9/11 his wife filed for divorce leaving him dazed and regretting whatever failings he had that contributed to the break up. There was also a son he had not seen for years. Rumor had it that he was living somewhere out West and dealing with drug issues.

Jim noted that Sean had his usual nearly empty can of Coke at his side which he knew did not contain any soda at all. Sean would purchase the drink at the soda machine, pour out the sweet contents, fill half of the can with his favorite beer, and slowly nurse the brew. Years ago, right after 9/11 when the entire job was going through an emotional crisis, the upper echelons assumed that he had a drinking problem and ordered him to the counseling unit for help. Sean dutifully went with the program but the truth was he never had an issue at all. He always sipped that beer for a while and eventually dumped out the tepid remnant in the sink. His beer wasn't a drink, it was a statement, one that said "fuck you" to the vagaries of the pain he had witnessed on 9/11 along with his divorce and the loss of his son. The only drinking problem Sean encountered was when his local supermarket ran out of his favorite brand of beer. Then he could go for weeks without that drink until they restocked the shelves. A priest probably consumed more alcohol when he performed a Mass than Sean did over the course of a tour, a thought he noted in the few times he actually went to church. His near empty can of Coke was no different than the unsmoked cigar butt that some men clinched in their jaws for hours. In a way that he himself probably didn't fully comprehend, that can was an effort to bridge the painful gap between his joyful disposition and his stark Irish fatalism.

"Hi Sean" Jim said, spotting him at the table.

Sean looked up from his paper, took one look at Jim and said "You look like shit."

"That's kind of what I feel like."

"Still tired from the last tour?"

"Yeah, kind of worn out" Jim responded, not wanting to say too much. He was tired but it felt like he was dealing with a lot more than lack of sleep. In the past he came as close as he was capable of in confiding with Sean, and that was limited to admitting that he was nervous about getting married. Sean had once met Laura when she visited the firehouse and liked what he saw. His sage advice to Jim was that Laura was a great woman and he had better get his head out of his ass and not blow the opportunity. Jim couldn't dream of sharing his intense dreams or any of the occasional strange fleeting thoughts he had with anybody, including Sean.

"Barker working tonight?" Jim enquired.

He was talking about the company captain, Julius Henderson, more commonly referred to by his nickname "The barker" or just "Barker" which described his method of communication.

"Naw, he took the tour off, that other guy is covering his spot tonight" Sean informed Jim and on hearing this a sly smile appeared on both their faces as they considered the thought of working a night tour with Captain Lopez.

Daniel Lopez was a newly promoted captain and rising star in the department. Considered one of the top students on the job, he had an amazing capacity for memorizing thousands of pages of technical material from the numerous department procedural manuals and then accurately rehashing it all over the course of a four hour multiple choice promotional exam. There was no doubt about his ever becoming a chief, it was just a question of when. The only problem being that while the civil service promotional process was good at evaluating a man's memory it failed to test his ability to deal with people or, some would argue, his sanity. Lopez's social awkwardness rivaled his retention skills. He could not comprehend that the twin silver bars of rank that sat on his shirt collar did not automatically earn respect from the men. The fire department was a quasi-military institution but in Ladder 57 the emphasis was on the quasi and Captain Lopez's rigid military manner did not sit well with the company.

"Well we've got an interesting fifteen hours ahead of us" Jim offered.

"Interesting indeed" Sean responded knowing full well that he and Lopez were the proverbial oil and water and had butted heads in the past. Jim looked at him and was hard pressed to imagine two men who were more different. It might be kind of fun to watch the two interact over the course of the night.

Jim left the kitchen and headed upstairs to get changed and ready for work. He started walking up the long metal staircase, his hand sliding along the gleaming brass railing that reflected hours of Dave and Tyrone's polishing efforts. Up on the second floor he walked along a line of beds in the dark bunk room and then past the company office where a glow of fluorescent light filtered through the pane of frosted glass in the door that separated it from the sleeping area. And then up the final flight to the top floor where long rows of metal lockers sat beneath the same kind of flaking green ceiling that hovered high above each level of the firehouse.

Jim's locker was plain and unadorned unlike many of the ones next to it which were covered with stickers proclaiming a favored sports team, or crudely labeled in magic marker with the guy's nickname. A few had photos of voluptuous nude women planted on them, their perfect, airbrushed faces peering out in permanent seductive smiles. Jim opened the metal door of his locker and began rummaging through it for a relatively clean uniform shirt. It still retained a bit of the smoky scent from the garments he had worn on the previous tour. He grabbed a blue shirt, gave it the smell test to gauge its relative nastiness, and judged that it was inoffensive enough to get him through the night. He made a mental note to get to the laundromat sometime the next day though he didn't look forward to the hour long boredom of feeding quarters into a machine and watching as the whirl of colors tumbled in the dryer.

He glanced at the work calendar that hung inside the locker door. It was a complicated chart of dates and numbers that determined the flow of his life. The days he would be working, the time he would have to be available to work overtime, the breaks of complete freedom, even the dates he could anticipate feeling exhausted and run down as he had been today were all determined by this schedule. Kind of like a menstrual cycle for men only this cycle changed every week rather than monthly, leaving Laura perpetually groping for any clarification on which days he would actually be available to do things with her. Jim gazed at that calendar as intently as if he were evaluating a car purchase. A number of significant dates were coming up. His mother's birthday was on the 6th and he had tickets for the Ranger game on the 14th, both days highlighted in yellow marker. Another union meeting he was sure to miss was listed for the 17th. A softball game on the 18th was clearly circled in thick red ink and the annual company picnic, an event he had traditionally avoided, was coming up on the 8th of next month. There was one additional date several months from now. That was his wedding day and it was only faintly marked in pencil.

Jim's concentration was suddenly interrupted by Faiella's ear splitting announcement over the PA system, "Roll call! 1800 hours. Roll call! All members to the house watch."

That's typical of Captain Lopez, he figured, demanding a formal line up in front of the apparatus floor for his roll call rather than the informal meeting in the kitchen that Captain Henderson and all the other officers favored. For that matter he thought that the whole idea of labeling it "roll call" was overkill. After all there were only five guys to account for.

He headed for the nearest sliding pole. Over the past seven years Jim had used that means of getting down to the lower floors hundreds of times, to a point where it had become an automatic routine that required no thought or physical preparation. It didn't matter whether he was rapidly responding to a fire or just casually heading down to the kitchen to check on the status of the meal, the act itself had become an ingrained response that seemed as natural as walking down the stairs. And, it was a lot quicker which was the whole point in the first place.

Jim pulled back the yellow safety gate, leapt onto the smooth brass pole, and moved down swiftly through the darkness of the bunkroom. The carefully polished brass felt cool and slick as it moved through his grip and he skillfully slowed his descent just as his feet touched the padded landing mat at the bottom. He then leapt onto the next pole and in seconds was standing right next to the rig on the brightly lit apparatus floor. He could see Tyrone and Dave standing with Captain Lopez by the house watch desk and when he walked over to join them he spotted Faiella sitting comfortably on the front bumper of the rig.

Daniel Lopez was a man with an erect posture and a tight build who exercised his body with the same frantic intensity that drove his obsessive study of fire department procedural manuals. His social anxieties stemmed in part from his stiff personality but also from the insecurity of a Bronx background of very limited means that had instilled a powerful work ethnic in him. The fire department offered advancement in salary, power, and status if one was willing to make the sacrifices that a passionate study regime required. Lopez had made that commitment but at the expense of alienating those he worked with.

Jim looked at the shining silver insignia bars that sat perfectly aligned on the captain's well pressed shirt collar. He tried to imagine what the sweat, smoke, and soot would do to that collar if they caught a good job tonight but it was impossible to picture him looking like anything other than totally squared away. Dave and Tyrone were standing at attention right in front of the captain in an admirable performance of the respectful role required of a probationary firefighter. Jim could sense that Lopez was not thrilled with Faiella's casual perch on the truck bumper but rather than address it he gruffly asked "Where's the fifth guy?"

The fifth guy? The fifth guy had a name which the captain most certainly knew since he had worked with him in this firehouse several times before.

"Call him on the PA again" he ordered Faiella who, not being that fond of Sean to begin with, was only too happy to do it again only this time in a much higher volume and a reprimanding tone. But the moment he touched the PA switch Sean suddenly popped his head out from the side of the rig.

"Good afternoon captain!" Sean cheerfully offered to Lopez, shit eating grin beaming on his face. "Just wanted to get into the proper uniform."

Sean was indeed in an FDNY uniform, a light blue buttoned shirt that was an official department issue some fifteen years ago and had since been replaced by three or four new styles. He had casually grabbed the shirt from his upstairs locker which was practically a fire museum loaded with antiquated uniforms and old cigar boxes full of loose brass uniform buttons.

Lopez glared at Sean. This roll call was not going the way he had planned. Not like the one he had recently conducted at a unit out in Brooklyn. All of the firefighters in that company were new to the job and had not yet developed the salty behavior he often noted in many of the senior members. Nonetheless he proceeded to address his small command and gave out the assignments for the tour. The two probies, Dave and Tyrone, were assigned as the forcible entry team which meant that, as new firefighters, they would work under the immediate supervision of the captain and would be responsible for breaking through doors and conducting quick searches for victims inside the fire apartment. Sean and Jim, being the more experienced firefighters, were assigned to positions that would require them to operate independently and move on their own at a fire. Their job would be to vent the smoke out of the building and to position ladders to make any necessary rescues from the exterior. That would require working from precarious positions on the rig's one hundred foot aerial ladder or from the confines of one of the ancient fire escapes that had hung for decades on tenements scattered throughout the West Side.

Despite his vast experience Sean was never assigned to drive the truck. It wasn't that he couldn't. In fact he had been officially trained as a chauffeur years ago and was indeed very capable of driving. But on some level the department just didn't trust him. The management correctly perceived him as being a very experienced loose cannon who would take his pension before he took any bullshit. With all of the recently hired personnel, the job needed men with Sean's knowledge and ability. But it also feared the independence that came with that background. Instead, Faiella would drive, a task he was generally assigned to and was surprisingly adept at. And that was fine with the rest of the crew because that meant he and the captain would be sitting up front in the cab and the rest of the guys would be granted some much appreciated separation from the two of them and their nonsense.

"All right men, check the apparatus" was Captain Lopez's final comment upon completion of what was to him a most dissatisfying roll call. He proceeded up the stairs to his office where he began to attack his beloved administrative work. At least the various written forms and computer applications were basic, black and white, entities that did not cop attitudes. Nor did they call for the more nuanced skill of managing firehouse personalities.

As the newest members Dave and Tyrone were expected to make sure that the radios were charged, the tools were clean, and, most importantly, that each man's mask had a fully charged air cylinder. Depending on a firefighter's conditioning, physical activity, and even his emotional state, the masks could provide anywhere from ten to fifteen minutes of breathing time. You didn't want to find out at the wrong time that your air tank was only half full. As always Jim was intent on checking his own gear. It wasn't that he didn't trust the probies, he just liked the predictable routine. For that matter there was a lot in the job that provided him with a much needed sense of structure. The scheduling of the work calendar, the roll call at the start of each tour, even the procedures that had been established for various types of fires, all provided a sense of order in his essentially uncommitted approach to life. Functioning in the role of "firefighter" allowed him to experience a level of assurance that he was incapable of establishing on his own. And though he was reluctant to admit it, throwing himself into that role also provided a ready escape from those distant thoughts and images he had experienced, and suppressed, throughout his life.

Jim was just "Jim" to his coworkers but, in an institution that was rife with nicknames, he also had the seldom used moniker of "Mr. Thoroughly". Whether he was checking on his gear, painting his room, or making his breakfast, Jim had a way of focusing intently on the details of the moment and on the task at hand. It had been that way since he was a boy. When he built model airplanes or hit a baseball the very act of gluing small plastic parts or focusing on a rapidly spinning ball centered him and provided a much needed distraction from the dreams and odd images that came intermittently but always left him in a state of confusion. None of the other firefighters had any idea what motivated Mr. Thoroughly to lose himself so intently in his work. And, despite his insightful nature, Jim himself was unaware of what exactly drove him to concentrate on the physical presence of the moment, nor did he care. It just felt right and made him feel more at peace in a world that he often felt alienated from.

Once all the equipment was checked out, and the captain thankfully removed to his office upstairs, everyone gravitated to the kitchen. Tyrone and Dave had peeled a large pot of potatoes and an enormous side of beef was already roasting in the oven so the guys had time to jump into one of their usual intense kitchen discussions. Those conversations generally involved sports and politics but in a tangent you could only experience in a firehouse they somehow got into the topic of the best sausages they had ever eaten.

"Kielbasa!" was Sean's strong recommendation.

"No, spicy Italian sausage with homemade sauce served with spaghetti. But it has to be the kind of gravy that sits on the stove for hours, not that bottled crap" Faiella responded, though no one could ever recall a time when Shakespeare actually made any real efforts in the kitchen much less attempted a homemade anything.

As usual Jim chose not to verbalize his preferences but if he did he would have been a bit embarrassed to admit that he really liked hot dogs. He thought of the savory, salty taste of the ones he ate on the rare occasions when he went to a Yankee game and how he always regretted eating more than one. It wasn't that two dogs and a plastic cup of beer left one twenty five dollars lighter. It was more about no matter how thoroughly you brushed your teeth the taste stayed in your mouth for hours and made you feel like you didn't want another one for at least a year.

Tyrone didn't verbalize a preference either. His favorite happened to be andouille but he felt entirely too removed from the conversation to even mention it. He couldn't believe that these guys could actually have a debate on the relative merits of wieners when there were so many more important things to talk about. Race was not the only issue he was going to have to deal with in this job.

Dave had patiently listened to the conversation and at precisely the right moment offered a very loud and confident "Bloodwurst!"

"What the fuck is that?" Sean inquired and Dave proceeded to share more bloodwurst minutiae than anyone cared to hear but, given his Polish background, it was kind of accepted that he must indeed have a fair level of expertise when it comes to the topic of sausages.

Having thoroughly debated the sausage issue the conversation somehow moved on to a discussion about Elvis Presley's greatest songs. Dave quickly jumped on the topic and offered "Forget about it, *Hound Dog* and *Blue Christmas* are the best fuckin ones by far."

Jim didn't give a damn one way or the other though he agreed that *Love Me Tender* was by far his wimpiest. Tyrone sat back in his chair desperately hoping for a run to come in and end the pain of having to endure this endless dialogue.

Faiella listened to the deliberation and then knowingly announced to all "Did you know that Elvis served with the 3rd Armored Division in Germany in the 1950's?" That was pure Shakespeare, always having to show that he possessed some special esoteric knowledge that others were not privy to. As if anyone really gave a shit.

Sean, who due to his age probably knew more about Elvis than anyone else sitting at the table, remained silent on the issue until it had been thoroughly talked out. Then, with just the perfect sense of comedic timing that he was so adept at, he sadly stated "It's a real shame that the King didn't live long enough to know that Michael Jackson was his son in law" which brought out loud guffaws from all. Jim could see from the rare smile that appeared on Tyrone's face that he too thought it was really funny.

In the middle of all the kitchen banter Jim suddenly

remembered that the power saw had been used at a fire on the previous night tour. If they caught a job tonight he would have to use it to cut a roof and vent the smoke out of a building. "Mr. Thoroughly" never wanted to leave things to chance and it occurred to him that it was possible that nobody had taken the time to check if there was enough gas in the saw. He left the kitchen and proceeded to open up the compartment on the rig where it was stored. Sure enough, the tank was only half full, a situation which would seriously limit the amount of time it would operate. He moved to a large gray metal cabinet that sat near a wall on the apparatus floor and picked up the one gallon gas can that was stored inside. The old red can was full but he noted that the hinged cap that covered the spout was thoroughly rusted. Jim thought about all the guys who had probably used this can over the past few days. Did even one of them consider replacing it with a new one? Maybe they were distracted by some fascinating sausage discussion. He knew that there were a couple of brand new cans in the basement and he headed down to get one.

The stair that led to the basement was located right below the one that went to the upper floors. But the basement stairs were not adorned with any shiny brass railings. It was just a steep black metal portal that led to the rear section of the basement and was dimly lit by a couple of underpowered light bulbs. Once Jim got to the bottom he entered the bright, fluorescent world of the finished basement area. The guys in the company had spent a lot of their own money to fix it up and, since firefighters tended to be very skilled with their hands, they had done all of the work themselves. He walked by the work out area which contained a couple of stationary bikes that had been donated by a local gym that went out of business soon after the Covid-19 crisis. Then past the bench that held a barbell with weights the size of train wheels attached to it. These were the weights that Dave often pumped so effortlessly but always seemed far too intimidating to Jim, accustomed as he was to numerous reps with a far lighter load. Most of the walls here were covered with mirrors which allowed the men to check on their form as they lifted but, more importantly, enabled them to consider the size of their biceps as they exercised beneath the bright fluorescent lights. He ducked past the heavy body bag which hung from the ceiling and provided such a great outlet for the men to work out their frustrations as they slammed into it with images of annoying chiefs or cantankerous ex-wives. The entire area seemed to retain the essence of their hard labored sweat.

Jim headed toward the front, unfinished section of the basement where the new gas cans were stored. He walked past the TV room which the guys had also built themselves. It was widely believed that Sean always had a few carefully stowed cans of his favored Yuengling beer somewhere in the room, available to him in a heartbeat in the event his Coke can required replenishing. But no one had ever actually found his alleged hiding spot and Sean was certainly not talking. The room was loaded with comfortable sofas and coffee tables and finished with dark brown panel walls. Every piece of furniture was a giveaway or second hand item that someone had dragged from home and not a single piece matched anything else in the room. But some of the couches were deeply padded and offered an inviting place to recline on as they watched the action on the large flat screen television that was mounted on the wall. And that action could range from viewing graceful hockey players slamming into each other on the ice to agile porn stars slamming into each other on some Hollywood set. Jim occasionally liked to go to this room when no one else was there. It was a quiet place and provided him with a much needed escape from the constant presence of other men which he usually found to be somewhat irritating around the 19th hour or so of a 24 hour tour. Some night tours he even slept down here. He welcomed the privacy and was certain not to miss any runs since the loud bells that signaled a response were clearly heard even in this deep cavern.

When Jim got to the section of the basement that laid beneath the street side of the firehouse the entire atmosphere changed. This was an unfinished area with bare masonry walls and an ancient oil burner that sat upon a cracked concrete floor and barely cranked out enough heat and hot water for the timeworn building. There was a distinct odor of mold and moisture from the water that dripped from above and slowly accumulated in the floor drains. In contrast to the finished basement area the only light came from a few dim bulbs that hung from the ceiling and even that glow was partially blocked by the numerous metal floor jacks that had been installed to help support the apparatus floor directly above. This was an unwelcoming area of the firehouse that was seldom used, much less visited by anyone. Once or twice a year some highly motivated chief might enter here while performing an inspection of the building or someone might come down in search of a tool or item that the unit needed.

Jim proceeded through the shadowy area until he reached a large wooden bin near the front wall of the firehouse. It was enclosed on three sides by walls constructed of old, unpainted wooden boards. They were covered by dark stains and some sections of the wood were worn smooth from decades of hard use from some distant era. Jim knew that he was looking at a remnant of the original 19th century building. This had been the coal bin for the firehouse, a fuel that had long since been replaced by the oil or gas that currently heated all New York City buildings. The bin now served solely as a place to store some excess equipment or to dump useless junk that no one could figure where else to put or had no initiative to just throw out. There was a damaged CPR practice dummy lying inside that had Faiella's name written on its head in magic marker and had for a short while been the source of great entertainment for the guys. There were a few obsolete hose fittings scattered about along with a broken step ladder, sections of old rope, and a canoe paddle. And, way in the back, was the bright red new gas can that Jim sought.

Jim grabbed the can and stepped back to survey the entire area. He could see how it all kind of fit together. To his right, beneath the front sidewalk of the firehouse, was an old metal scuttle that would have been opened to receive the coal deliveries. He envisioned how there would also have been some kind of chute in place to guide the sliding load of coal into the wooden bin he was standing in front of. Right next to the scuttle opening there was still an antique vault light built into the cement sidewalk with numerous round glass sections that allowed some light to filter into the cool, dim section below. Jim recalled that firefighters referred to them as "dead lights", an appropriate name for something built a century ago.

Though he seldom came to this spot there was something about it that always captured him. Part of it was no doubt his appreciation for old architecture and the historical aspects of the New York City Fire Department. On several occasions he had climbed up a steep ladder on the top floor of the building which led to a small storage cabinet containing company journals and records dating back to when Ladder 57 was established in 1868. Jim spent countless hours leafing through those 19th century pages, savoring the impeccable penmanship on the yellowing pages which recorded mundane items about who was on duty or the status of the horses along with significant reporting about fires, deaths, and injuries, all of which were now just distant, forgotten events.

But Jim was sensing something deeper as he stood there though he was incapable of comprehending exactly what it was. This old coal bin was something different for everyone in the firehouse. For most it was just a dumping area for seldom used gear or unwanted junk. For Captain Henderson it was another thing to handle on his checklist, an area that had to be cleaned up when the chief came by to perform his annual inspection of the firehouse. Most chiefs were ok to work with but some could be a real pain in the ass and went through the building with a fine tooth comb just looking for a dusty area or some accumulation of stuff that he would use to critique the company. The barker never verbalized it but in his mind he could just picture Lopez performing in that exact role in a few years when he would no longer be a fellow captain but a ball busting battalion chief.

To Jim the area around the old bin was both fascinating and unsettling at the same time. He had never really seen or handled real coal. For that matter virtually nobody in 21st century New York had. He remembered seeing a large model train layout in Macys at Christmas time when he was a boy. He would watch as the small electric locomotives chugged around the metal tracks pulling long lines of freight cars, some of which carried loads of what was supposed to be piles of coal in their beds. But those loads were only tiny chunks of black plastic designed to replicate the real thing. The essence of real coal was lost to most people, a memory as forgotten as those horses that were recorded in the old Ladder 57 company journals.

Still, as he stood there with the gas can in his hand, Jim was able to *sense* what it had been like. He imagined a vaguely familiar scent: crude, pungent, and dusty, like he was smelling the very soul of the earth. Aromas had a subtle but effective way of evoking memories. The fragrance of a certain perfume always reminded Jim of a girl he had really liked in high school and a pine scent brought back visions of his father at Christmas time who always insisted on having a real tree rather than one of those soulless fake ones. But where on earth did this familiarity with a fuel he had never touched come from? He could even envision the sound that a load of coal would produce as it rumbled down a metal ramp and kicked up clouds of dust that would settle in his hair and his skin and become a part of him. These thoughts evoked something inside him but it was not a familiar thing like perfume or a pine tree. It was all so fleeting and, like many of his dreams, impossible to recall and invisible the moment he tried to focus on it.

Jim stepped away from the old bin feeling very unsettled. He walked back through the bright fluorescent area of the finished basement and then back up the stairs to the apparatus floor where he would pour gas into the new can, check the saw, and hang out with the guys. Anything that would distract him from whatever the hell it was that he had experienced downstairs.

Chapter 4

The rest of the tour was pretty quiet. There was just enough activity to allow Jim to refocus on the job and to once again put any of his confusions on hold for a while. A few runs for false alarms and water leaks came in early and around midnight they responded to a minor stove fire in one of the nearby apartment houses. The guys got a laugh out of that one since the residents were a couple of young professionals from some tiny town out in the Midwest who were brand new to New York and thought they had to pay the city for the service Ladder 57 provided. Sean informed them "It will be one hundred bucks for the visit and an extra twenty-five for shutting off the gas valve." Captain Lopez looked at Sean with disdain and proceeded to patiently and professionally explain that the emergency services in New York were a 24-hour service funded through taxes.

Back in the firehouse the guys stayed true to form. Dave referred to the apartment residents as "Fuckin yuppies". Jim didn't bother to inform him that the yuppie generation had long since passed and most of them were now grandparents. Tyrone didn't add anything to that but when they were working on the stove he had spoken to one of the tenants and discovered that they had both been political science majors in college. Sean chuckled about the incident, and Faiella just took it all in without comment. Shakespeare's mind was like a sponge that constantly stored away even his most minute experiences with the hope that eventually he might be able to whip one out to help move along the storyline of his novel.

The next morning Jim sat with his coffee at the kitchen table ready for the day. He felt like he had taken the city for a ride this time, earning overtime pay for what turned out to be an easy tour, and even more important, getting in some overtime hours before the real heat of the summer set in. He felt he kind of had it coming to make up for his recent night tours, most of which had been really busy and absolutely exhausting. He needed to feel refreshed because today he was scheduled to have dinner at the Whitacre's and it might take some energy to put on a good face for them, or at least for Laura.

When Jim got home he had a light workout with the weights and then went for a long run through the park, where he watched the swift currents flowing through the river. He thought about the massive amount of water that was once again in motion, surging between New York Harbor and Long Island Sound so powerfully and timelessly while the rest of the city just went on with its business oblivious to it all.

It was late afternoon by the time he showered and hopped into his Toyota to pick up Laura in the Upper East Side. He worked his way through the traffic on the bridge and proceeded uptown on 3rd Avenue until he made the familiar right hand turn on East 80th Street. Jim had driven this route so many times it felt like the car could drive itself which, when he thought about it, probably wasn't a concept that was that farfetched given the technology they were developing. He wasn't quite sure how to feel about that. It would certainly be a convenience, especially in a crowded city like New York. But it would also represent another thing that he couldn't control.

Those thoughts were put on hold when he arrived at Laura's place. He had planned to double park, call her on his cell phone, and wait in the car until she came down but, somewhat amazingly, there was a parking space available right in front of the building. Jim liked the excitement of the city but had spent years developing the skill of maneuvering around the crowded streets. Stumbling upon a place to park right in front of your destination was something that only happened in Hollywood movies about New York, and he swiftly took possession of the spot.

Jim entered the lobby and was warmly greeted by the doorman, Adeem, who he had gotten to know well over the past three years. He was an enormous, 250 pound man and Jim always thought that his Mid-Eastern background made him look like a cross between a bar bouncer and a terrorist. But his intimidating appearance belied his warm nature and he greeted Jim his customary "How are you Jimmy! You have any good fires lately?" He liked Jim and liked the fact that he was a firefighter. For that matter he also liked Laura who greeted him every time she passed by and always remembered him very generously at Christmas even though it wasn't his holiday.

"Doing good Adeem, just the usual BS at work but I'm dealing with it" Jim said.

"Hang in there. Don't let the mayor get to you" he responded. Adeem viewed Jim as a fellow blue-collar guy he could relate to, a small player in a large system that was not to be entirely trusted whether it was the management of a building or the government of a city.

"No way he'll ever get to me, I'm too small a target. Can you buzz her down?"

"Right away my man."

As Jim waited in the lobby four or five residents passed

through leaving the building. Only two of them bothered to offer a greeting to Adeem which struck Jim as being kind of sad. Why were so many people always in such a rush to arrive at some destination? Adeem was a really decent man but to some he was invisible. Jim wondered if he ever felt as much of an outsider as he did.

It wasn't long before Laura appeared in the lobby in an explosion of flowers. She was impeccably dressed in a short, floral print dress, sported a red flower in her hair, and radiated a scent of sweet lilac perfume. Jim half expected to see butterflies fluttering around her. Her pale pink lipstick matched some of the flowers in the enormous bouquet she carried, a gift intended for both her parents but one that only her mother would really appreciate. As always Laura came prepared for things. Jim had briefly considered how the sweet essence emanating from her contrasted so starkly with the earthy coal scent he had imagined in the firehouse basement but he quickly forced the thought from his mind.

"Was I supposed to bring something?" Jim felt an instant pain of guilt at not thinking about picking up a bottle of wine or something for her family but then again he hadn't just been relaxing at home for the past couple of days.

"No, just your appetite" she responded and once again he remembered that one of the things he liked about Laura was that she always had him covered and really didn't expect much, which was really impressive considering her background.

As they waved to Adeem and headed out toward Jim's car Laura said, "My parents are looking forward to seeing you."

"I guess your father hasn't had an opportunity to sit down with a 'what' for some time."

Jim's response came out abruptly and with an edge he didn't really intend. He was referring to something Laura had related to him when they first started dating a few years ago. When her parents asked what the new guy in her life did for a living she told them he was a firefighter to which her father responded "He's a *what?*"

It's not like her dad looked down on the profession. It was just so different from the world he knew and had grown up in. He tended to place cops and firefighters into the "civil servant" category, someone who was there to help you out when you needed them but certainly not a person you would ordinarily socialize with or meet in the country club or the boardroom. Her father had actually grown to like Jim when he got to know him but wanted to steer him in a different work direction when it became apparent that Laura was serious about the relationship. His daughter was going to be well cared for regardless of who she married and in Jim he saw a good man who just needed a bit of a push. And that push could easily be accomplished toward a job in a bank or investment firm through one of his many business connections. He was somewhat myopic but genuinely sincere in his desire to steer his future son in law into a "real" job. Naturally Jim bristled when Laura told him about her dad's intentions.

"Look, he means well. He just has a different perspective on life. Just humor him, you know it doesn't matter to me what you do for a living" Laura assured him in the car.

"Yeah, I know" Jim responded, feeling somewhat guilty for his snappy comment. He had some trouble relating to the man but he didn't actively dislike him. And he really did enjoy her mother's company. Also, it was true that Laura, being the ever-accommodating person she was, had always shown a genuine ability to accept Jim for who he was and for what he wanted out of life. Which was a considerable accomplishment after years of dating men who wore three-piece suits and whose tastes ranged from squash games in stylish health clubs to double malt scotch in Wall Street taverns. On some level Jim represented a rejection of that life or at least an opportunity to delve into that foreign world that had always sat on the other side of the suburban fence. Jim's life offered an escape from the three-piece suit world she had been immersed in for so long, which kind of fascinated and scared her at the same time.

She could see evidence of that world as she slid into Jim's car. The eight-year-old Toyota had a number of significant dents which Jim never bothered to repair. When she asked why he didn't fix them he explained that if the car looked really good he'd have to worry about getting more dents and, living in New York City, that was certain to happen. Which, when she thought about it and pictured the shiny black Mercedes her parents drove, kind of made sense.

Jim started up the car and turned toward Central Park. "You're going up the West Side Highway?" Laura inquired.

"Yeah, I like that route."

"It might be quicker to just head up the FDR."

She was referring to the highway that ran along the river on the east side of Manhattan. Its official title was the Franklin D. Roosevelt East River Drive, but that mouthful had always been referred to simply as the FDR. Most New Yorkers never even thought about the 32nd president of the United States as they sat in their cars and inched their way through its habitual traffic.

"I know. I figure we've got time so we'll just ease our way on up."

Jim knew that driving up directly from the East Side was the most direct way north since they were already on that side of the city, but his choice of direction was more influenced by the scenery than the distance. Driving directly north would put them through a series of crowded highways that inched through the Bronx and only offered an urban backdrop of apartments, tenements, and Yankee Stadium. The West Side provided the stunning views of the Hudson River that he always savored.

Once they got on the West Side Highway Jim felt a sense of relief as he gazed out on the expansive river. The Hudson was much larger than the East River. It went from New York Harbor all the way past Albany and was influenced by powerful currents and tides that quickly changed the level of the shoreline. The sky seemed to open up here and that was a rare sight in New York City. He could see the graceful expanse of the George Washington Bridge and the remote shoreline of New Jersey. As they worked their way north they were treated with a stunning view of the cliffs of the Palisades which sat, distant and never changing, on the other side of the river.

Jim glanced at Laura's profile as he drove. They spent a lot of time together in the Toyota when they went on forays out of the city and there was something about the snug confines of the car that often led them into lengthy discussions about their lives. Here was where intimate chats about family or work issues often occurred. They had even come up with a name for the vehicle, referring to it as the "therapy mobile".

As he looked at Laura, he considered how in certain ways she was the perfect fit for him. She took him out of the world he had always known. Although he worked in the tough, blue-collar job of firefighting he didn't really share the style and values of that world. He had moved on from the middle income, Brooklyn upbringing of his past but wasn't really sure of exactly where he had landed. Laura's background was not an easy fit for him either. He had trouble relating to the formality and decadence that he perceived in it. In fact, Jim often felt like he was just lightly stepping through several different worlds without committing to any of them. But the warmth he shared with Laura often allowed him to put that struggle aside for the moment and to just concentrate on the reassuring pleasure of her company.

As she sat there casually watching the scenery roll past Laura was deep in her own self-examination. She was an only child and felt close to both of her parents. However, she was also a very intelligent, independent daughter of two people she truly loved but did not necessarily want to emulate. Laura was the end result of two dissimilar people. Her mother was a kind and gentle woman, but Laura had always been somewhat alienated by the passivity she sensed in her, a thought she had verbalized to Jim but never directly to her mom. And her father moved through life with the assertive approach of a highly successful business-man, traits that had also guided her many achievements but at the same time occasionally struck her as being somewhat shallow and directionless. She sometimes struggled to answer the question of where exactly all of the wealth and drive of the business world eventually led to. Laura was bright and competent. And she had already accomplished much in her life. But, much like Jim, she possessed the ability to examine that life at a distance and to straddle a world without getting hopelessly lost in it.

"What do you think they're going to have?"

"Huh?"

"I mean to eat"

Jim's question shook her out of her contemplation.

"Oh, I'm sure that Olga is going to come up with something tasty" Laura responded, referring to the Whitacre's chef, a mid-dle-aged Russian woman who she always suspected was just as capable of cooking up some kind of scheme as easily as preparing one of her meals.

"Hope she makes a lot of it. I'm starved."

Laura knew Jim had a very healthy appetite, the result of a physical job, dedicated exercise, and a metabolism that allowed him to occasionally inhale an entire pint of ice cream without putting on any additional weight on his 170-pound frame. She also appreciated the fact that he would eat in a slower, much more civilized manner at her parents' table. At the firehouse every meal was treated like it was the last one before you were going to the electric chair, in part because so many of them were interrupted by a run but largely because the atmosphere was laden with testosterone and cravings for high calorie nourishment.

They were now driving through the Inwood section of northern Manhattan, a neighborhood Jim really liked. The hills and sections of forests that still existed in the area offered a glimpse of what the city had been like in its pristine state centuries ago.

"Look at all the sailboats out there today" Jim excitedly noted as he gazed out on the river. The Hudson sprawled out beneath them far below the highway and he could see about a dozen boats in the distance. Their sails looked like tiny white kites as they raced across the glistening water.

Laura didn't look at the boats but she watched Jim and, as she often did, relished his boyish enthusiasm. When they had first met she thought of him as a solid man, a steady and reliable person who was there when she needed him. Time had only made her feel more secure, and much closer. And, though he did not totally fit the typical image of a gentleman in her rarified background, he was definitely a gentle man. It didn't surprise her when Jim related how he refused to harass the new probies like the other guys in the firehouse. He viewed the whole tradition as an exercise in pointless cruelty.

"How was work last night?" Laura inquired.

"Not bad, we had this annoying Captain Lopez again but I got to work with my regular guys and it was a pretty quiet night".

"Faiella still writing the great American novel?"

"Yeah, and still pissing everyone off."

"How about Sean?"

"He was there and so was that probie, Dave. He's a nice kid

but sometimes he doesn't come off as the brightest light. Strong as an ox but he's got some learning to do. Before he got trained at the fire academy, I bet he thought the Heimlich maneuver was something you used to pick up girls in a singles bar."

"You mean it's not?" Laura teased.

"Nah, you should know. You tried to use a version of it to meet me at that party."

"In your dreams. I just walked over to you because you looked so pathetic. Don't forget, you weren't really invited to that party. Anyway, that's history now."

"Yeah, ancient history. Can you believe that was three years ago?"

It was indeed three years that they had been together. And over those years they had grown very comfortable with each other. Their infrequent arguments ended quickly because both were capable of admitting that they might actually be wrong about whatever it was they had been arguing about, a skill Laura figured she had likely inherited from her mother. And they both enjoyed the kind of teasing discourse that often came up in the car. But there were things about Jim that Laura had still to discover. Despite their ease with each other she sensed there were aspects of him she did not understand.

"What's going on in your job?" Jim asked.

"The board sat down last week and decided they had to seriously consider diversifying. They keep worrying about market saturation."

Jim nodded but had absolutely no idea what that meant. As often as Laura talked about the meetings she attended at work Jim still didn't have a really clear idea of what exactly it was she did at those meetings. All he knew was that it was an investment firm looking to make money which was fine with him as long as she was happy working for them.

As he drove the Toyota, the coal bin episode was stewing in Jim's mind. He tried to think about what exactly he had been feeling in the basement of the firehouse last night but struggled to duplicate the experience. Just another vague occurrence in a series of elusive incidents that seemed to come and go throughout his life. Something that he would try to forget about. But the knowledge of it built up over time to a point where it found a place in his mind, a place he tried to deny. And the very attempt at denial highlighted the fact that there was indeed something there he could not hide from. He was good at hiding things from the people in his life, including Laura. But it troubled him that he had something pressing so heavily on his mind that he couldn't share with her. Kind of like the stress that a married man might feel who was having an affair with another woman. That at least would be an identifiable problem. But he had no way of verbalizing, much less understanding, the bewildering encounter he had experienced in the basement. And to tell part of it would lead to relating all of it and admitting that it wasn't just an isolated incident but one of many that had plagued him throughout his life. And what might that say about him? Would Laura accept something that even he didn't understand? So he said nothing and drove on keeping such personal thoughts within.

"We're only about forty minutes away now," he said as they drove over the bridge that connected northern Manhattan to the Bronx. Here he was treated to a final extravagant view of the river. The sight of it eased his mind a bit and he forced himself to turn off his troubling train of thought. The drive through Westchester blocked his view of the Hudson but the crowded semi urban section of the lower part of the county was quickly replaced by comforting scenes of forests and rolling hills. Jim liked the geography of this region and as he drove, he compared it to one of his commutes from years ago. Back then he had been dating a woman who lived on Long Island. He remembered that he enjoyed her company but quickly grew to despise the ordeal of wrestling with the dense traffic on the Long Island Expressway that it took to see her. Sometimes that trip took so long he felt like he should bring a few sandwiches and a change of underwear. In contrast, there was an ease to this trip due in part to the lack of traffic but also because of the rapport he enjoyed with Laura. As he proceeded further north the scenery got even more rural and the size of the houses got bigger, indicating that they were getting close to the Whitacre's home.

Jim got off the highway exit and followed what had become a familiar route to Laura's parents. It was an area of dense woods and crisp air with classic farmhouses painted in tasteful shades of barn red and woodland green, all comfortably isolated from their neighbors by the luxury of three-acre zoning. Many sat on larger plots that had once been occupied by farmers who toiled their way through the rocky soil. But they were long gone now and replaced by the bankers and stockbrokers who renovated the old houses and labored their way through the rocky economy. The twisted two-lane blacktop eased its way higher and higher up a small mountain. It occurred to Jim that geography often related to wealth and as one moved up in elevation there was a good chance that you were also moving up in affluence and power.

Finally they arrived at the intersection of a small lane which led to the Whitacre's house. Jim drove onto the property and passed through the impressive architectural wrought iron front gate which was flanked on both sides by tall, carefully groomed hedges. There were no tacky lion statues, fake marble columns, or any other attempts of faux wealth to be found here. The whole place reeked of taste and restrained dignity. Sometimes Jim felt like he was about to enter a museum rather than visit someone's home. As he drove toward the house his tires made a soft crunching sound as they rolled over a gravel driveway that was, as usual, raked to perfection. Off to the side a low hissing sound issued from buried sprinklers that refreshed the thick green lawn and left a scent of fresh, moist grass.

Jim parked the car but as he and Laura walked toward the front door he remembered the slow oil leak that had recently started dripping from a failing engine gasket. He thought about the stain he was probably going to leave on the impeccably clean driveway and hoped it wouldn't be too noticeable. Another thing to put on his to do list when he got back to the city.

People tended not to use the large brass knocker that sat on the front door of the Whitacre's home. Artfully shaped and polished to a vivid shine, it looked more like something to be observed and appreciated as a piece of sculpture rather than a tool to announce one's arrival. Jim stared at the shining brass hardware in rapt fascination. Today for the first time he noted that there was a small imperfection in it. One of the screws securing it to the door was slightly smaller than the others, no doubt an error on the part of whoever had installed it. Jim paused for a moment and concentrated on the tiny defect. This was always an uncertain time for him. He often hesitated a few seconds before entering the house to psych himself up to meet with Laura's parents. Not that they were unwelcoming to him. It was more like he felt the need to prepare himself to share in the confines of their home, a comfortable place but one that was not an easy fit for him. It always felt like he was about to make an abrupt jump between two very different worlds.

Laura pressed on the doorbell, and they heard the faint familiar chime echoing inside the house. Her dad opened the door and his face lit up on seeing her.

"Hi sweetie. How was the trip up?"

"Good daddy, how are you?" Laura responded as he engulfed

her in a big hug.

"And Jim, how are you?"

"Good Connie."

Jim stood in the doorway and regarded Laura's father. Cornelius Whitacre was tall, tan, and handsome in a "My ancestors came on the Mayflower, where the hell are you from?" kind of way. He was "Connie" to everyone except the CEOs of the many corporate boards he served on and as he shook Jim's hand he flashed a brilliant white smile that reflected thousands of dollars of dental work. But it was somewhat of a confusing smile that might be read as "welcome and come on in" or just as easily as "let's take a good look at your stock portfolio". The ludicrous side of Jim always had a playful desire to stand erect, snap his heels, and give a brisk "Herr Whitacre!" when he met Connie, an act that would no doubt leave him in a confused state but would certainly entertain his wife, Janice. But as always Jim held back, well aware of the fact that Connie was oblivious to firehouse humor.

When he entered the foyer Jim could see that Janice was smelling the flowers Laura had given her. She looked up, saw him, and broke out in a warm smile.

"And how are you dear?" she said as she engaged Jim in an earnest, matronly hug.

"Really good, hope you like the flowers" Jim responded. Laura flashed a quick glance at him, and he suddenly remembered that he had nothing at all to do with buying them and, as always, it was she who had been the thoughtful one. Another small glitch in the process of once again trying to assume the role of future son-in-law. But he found that he was much more at ease in that role with Laura's mom. There was no confusion in her smile, it was as warm and sincere as the rest of her.

Janice Whitacre was a well-bred, gentle being who was at

peace with the world and all of the people in it. And a part of that peace was her willingness to accept the quiet role of being the wife of a high profile, extremely successful man. She was dressed in a very neat and conservative pants suit, the type of outfit that allowed her to easily blend into the background of the many social events she attended with Connie. With her traditional look and quiet manner she would have fit in perfectly as a woman in the Eisenhower years. Which wasn't surprising considering that was the era she had sprung from. But her style belied the deep intellect and wicked sense of humor that she possessed. She was able to use that humor in a self-deprecating way that cut through what she viewed to be a lot of the nonsense in her life as well as the idiosyncrasies of Connie's world.

It was that very ability to see the ridiculousness in things that easily bonded her to Jim. They both shared the gift of that humor as though it were a language only the two of them understood. And it was a completely foreign language to Connie, whose straight forward approach to life often left him confused and feeling left out when his wife and Jim hit on something they found to be hilarious. It was during those few moments that Connie would retreat into being an observer of a situation rather than the man who set the tone for things. Though he did not share this characteristic with his wife the two of them had otherwise managed to establish a deep connection. Over the years Janice had outlasted all of the trophy wives that had come and gone in the lives of Connie's business associates.

Standing off just on the left Jim could see that Olga was waiting to greet them. Olga Mikhailov held the job title of cook but in reality served as the general get it done person in the Whitacre household. Olga was a middle-aged woman whose accented English, matronly build, and bleach blond hair reflected her Russian roots. She had worked for Laura's parents for so long it seemed like she was a part of the family. Her presence had allowed Laura to know someone who came from a life outside of the country club world she grew up in, a world she had always been curious about. But Jim always sensed that Olga was somewhat of a disgruntled member of the Whitacre clan. She was well treated and generously paid, but on some level felt like she had not achieved what she deserved in life. Olga was alienated by the very wealth that she served despite the benefits it had bestowed on her. She liked Jim and viewed him as someone who was different, similar perhaps to her nephew who worked as a police officer back in Moscow. Occasionally she would corner Jim and confide in him some perceived insensitivity or injustice she felt she had been subjected to. But he had the sense to politely excuse himself from such rants. There was a key difference in how they perceived life. Olga's alienation grew from a sense of entitlement, his from a state of confusion. And Jim preferred to deal with his thoughts in a much more private manner. Nonetheless he noted that at the dinner table Olga always gave him the most generous portion of food and the largest slice of dessert, an effort no doubt in favoring someone she viewed as a fellow member of the proletariat.

Jim glanced around the house as they all headed for the dining room. They passed beneath the elegant chandelier that hung from the ceiling in the main entranceway and then proceeded into the living room where their voices were muffled by a thick mauve carpet that softened their steps and caressed their feet. Here he spotted the familiar collection of plush sofas which were arranged in a circle as though intended to encourage conversation. But it seemed like it would be a real challenge to actually sit down on one of them, covered as they were by mounds of Navajo themed pillows. Two long couches sat near a fireplace which appeared large enough to roast an entire cow. Jim glanced at the collection of antique carpentry tools that were displayed on the walls, none of which had been put to actual use in decades. For that matter nobody in the house had any idea what their function was anyway since that was the kind of work they simply hired people to do. The entire living room looked like it was straight out of *Architectural Digest* magazine with its artful arrangement and tasteful furnishings. But to Jim it seemed like a living room that was not really intended to actually live in.

When they passed through the final long hallway that led to the dining room Jim noted the carefully framed paintings that were illuminated 24 hours a day by tiny lights even though no one ever seemed to take the time to actually look at them. Every time he walked through here he suppressed a desire to turn off each of the lamps that sat above the picture frames. It wasn't that he disliked art. The waste of electricity just kind of annoyed him.

They entered the dining area where a long table constructed out of stout pieces of recycled barn wood stretched nearly the length of the room. Each of the two silver candelabras sitting on it held four long stemmed white candles that, as far as Jim knew, had never actually been lit but certainly added to the elegance of the setting. Connie sat at his usual spot at the head of the table with Jim and Laura to his left and Janice on his right. Over the past few months this had just naturally emerged as the official seating arrangement. And it proved to be comfortable for all since it allowed Connie to assume the focal point that he was used to having and gave Jim the nearby assurance that Laura provided. As he sat Jim ran his hands over the fine wood grain of the tabletop. The attractive semi-gloss finish gave no evidence of its previous life as a structural element in a building that housed animals. He was struck by the contrast of this dining room and the one in the firehouse he had experienced last night. The firehouse kitchen contained Formica surfaces and plastic seats, chipped plates, and boisterous conversation that echoed off the tiled walls. This dining room was plush and elegant and reflected the lives of people who lived in a very different kind of world. Jim briefly thought about the fact that he didn't really feel at ease in either of those worlds.

While Olga poured water for everyone Janice mentioned to Laura "You'll never guess who I ran into yesterday. Carol Perkins of all people, I haven't seen her in years."

"Carol, yeah I remember her." Laura recalled a young girl she had learned to horseback ride with when they were both about ten years old. A lifetime ago.

"She's married and has a two-year-old now and she still lives nearby."

That didn't surprise Laura at all. She remembered Carol as a prim, confident girl, the daughter of a man who had made a fortune in tech stocks. Carol was a social butterfly who fit well in that world. But she never struck Laura as being a very curious girl. Just someone who was definitely content to go with the program. Probably married to some investment banker who commutes to the city and continues to generate a lifestyle of nannies and a big house in the same town she grew up in. All very nice but somewhat predictable.

Connie settled down next to Jim and said, "We've got to get you out on the DJ one of these days soon." He was referring to the *Dhow Jones*, his trim 36-foot sailboat which was docked nearby on the Hudson. If a boat was a hole in the water that sucked up a lot of money this hole was an especially big one. Replacing one broken fitting or frayed piece of rigging on the DJ would cost about as much as Jim could earn from three or four overtime tours. But Connie handled it all in stride for the DJ was much more than a boat. It was also a meeting place, a deal maker, a forum for the heavy-duty financial transactions he made on it with investors who were well lubricated with martinis and anxious to scoop up a share of the profits he always generated in his investment firm. The *Dhow Jones* was a floating tax shelter that Janice had named. Connie first offered to name it after her but in the end his wife's sense of humor won out.

"Yeah, that sounds good Connie" he responded, although it wasn't really high on the list of things he'd planned on doing in the near future. In fact it might not even earn a pencil mark on the calendar that hung from his locker at the firehouse. Also, Jim had a boat of his own that he occasionally enjoyed sailing on. He had purchased an old beaten-up Sunfish that someone had been looking to get rid of for $200. The small fiberglass hull and its slightly bent aluminum mast sat under a musty tarp at the same marina that was home to the *Dhow Jones*. Billy, the Puerto Rican grounds keeper who worked there, had offered to allow Jim to store it free of charge because of his connection to the Whitacre family. But he refused the offer. Jim didn't want to accept anything that might compromise his highly valued sense of independence. Instead, he found out how much they would normally charge for storage and made sure that he took care of Billy with at least that amount at Christmastime. Some part of that money would be spent on the six pack of beer that he occasionally shared with Billy. But more to the point it eliminated any sense of obligation on his part. Obligation was a form of control and loss of control scared him whether it sprang from Connie or from one of the strange dreams and images that plagued him.

As Janice went on about Carol Perkins Connie leaned toward Jim like he was about to share an important but personal message. "By the way, I was approached by one of my brokers the other day. He's expanding his operation and will be looking to hire some new trainees. No pressure mind you but if you're at all interested in looking into something new I can put in a word for you."

Here we go again Jim thought. He knew that Connie meant well but he had heard things like this a few times over the past year and that 'no pressure' was a relative term. Connie was a master salesman. He never went for the big push but in business and in life he had a subtle approach that was designed to slowly wear you down. He did in fact like Jim. But there was a reason behind his efforts to steer him in another work direction. Connie was a very pragmatic man who had made full use of rational decisions in accomplishing the success he had achieved. And he knew full well that firefighters got injured. Some even died or got very ill from the work and slowly wasted away on disability retirements. He didn't want Laura to ever be subjected to such a possibility. Connie viewed Jim as a good man but one who, in his current state, represented a bad investment. And he wanted to turn that investment into "triple A" security for his daughter.

"Daddy, he likes what he does" Laura suddenly interjected. She had heard snippets of their conversation as she was listening to her mother.

Way to go Laura, to the rescue again. Jim had to hand it to her, she was always willing to go to bat for him.

"Sweetie I'm only running some ideas past him" Connie responded with his hands raised up in a poise of self-defense. He backed off on the issue, but Jim knew it was only a matter of time before it would come up again.

"So what's going on at work?"

"Oh the usual. A ton of meetings about raising some fresh capital" Laura responded. Janice quietly listened in as Connie and Laura discussed the intricacies of stocks and bonds and risk assessment, topics she had observed from the sidelines over the years as Connie rocketed to success. She held a master's degree in art history but the role she had assumed in life as a mother and as the steady wife behind a successful husband had kept her from pursuing a career of her own. But she lived vicariously through her daughter and was relieved that Laura had been able to carve out a path she could call her own.

"Are the men at work still treating you fairly?" she asked Laura.

"They're fine, mom. But of course Richard is still there." Richard being the one employee of Turner Associates who treated Laura like she was invisible.

"He thinks the world revolves around him and he dismisses a lot of my recommendations like they're meaningless trivia." Laura went on to tell her parents how much she despised the man and how she sometimes went for a long run in Central Park when she got home to rid herself of the stress he caused her.

As he listened in to the conversation Jim was again reminded of how amazed he always was by the simple fact this family actually talked to each other. They shared an open ease and conducted real conversations that revealed the details of their lives and their feelings. Were most families like this? He couldn't help but contrast the free-flowing table talk that surrounded him with the restrained home life he had experienced growing up in Brooklyn.

Jim had also been an only child. But it was his parent's style rather than a lack of siblings that had often left him feeling cut off from them and, to some extent, from the world. Not that they were bad people. In fact, he thought of them as being the salt of the earth. Dan Hanley was a solid man who worked for decades as a supervisor for Con Edison overseeing gas emergencies throughout the city. It was a hands on, blue-collar job with a very stable company that took care of its employees, almost like a civil service position. He was thrilled when his son became a firefighter since the job provided the same kind of job security. His father was always kind and patient with Jim but he generally held back large parts himself. He was a Vietnam veteran who had seen a lot but seldom spoke of the terrors he had witnessed. As far as Jim could ascertain there had been some kind of incident in a rice paddy that haunted his mind. But there was no doubt that it was Agent Orange that eventually ravaged his body. Jim watched as he slowly wasted away in a nursing home where he silently accepted his suffering until the end.

Jim shifted his attention from the painful memories of his dad and gazed at Janice who sat opposite to him on the other side of the table. He observed how she deftly managed to interject small comments into the conversation while, at the same time, kept her distance from it all, almost as if she had other things on her mind. In reality she was sincerely interested in hearing what both Jim and her daughter had to say. But she was essentially an introspective person and the decades of a relationship with an opinionated, high-powered man had taken a toll. Her basic DNA and her marriage had shaped her into being more of an observer of life than an active participant. And they had also nourished both her sharp sense of humor and appreciation of art.

It occurred to Jim that, despite their obvious differences in wealth and education, there were some similarities between Janice and his own mother. Both tended to be quiet "background" people who listened but kept a lot of opinions to themselves. But Laura's mother was not afraid to actually discover Jim as a person. Their shared humor had helped to create an easy rapport between the two of them. When she asked Jim a question about himself he was generally comfortable speaking to her as long as it didn't intrude on the forbidden topics that even he shied away from.

It saddened him to know that Janice knew him better than his own mom did. Beth Hanley was an unassuming woman who still lived in the same Brooklyn neighborhood she had grown up in. Since her husband's death she basically went through life looking to avoid any unnecessary problems. Nor did she especially want to hear about negative things that might be lurking out in the world. It was as if you didn't discuss something that was troubling it wouldn't prove to be significant, or perhaps not exist at all. She felt a deep love for her son but there was an equally deep gap between that love and her knowledge of exactly who he was. She was very pleased to see that Jim was going to settle down with Laura and, though she hoped for an eventual grandchild, she dared not to ever mention it. Jim made sure to visit her regularly but over the course of those visits he always felt the strain of the severely restricted limits of their conversations. There was a sort of unspoken arrangement between them that, aside from the safe topics about how things were at work and how Laura was doing, there were huge aspects of his life that were off limits. Jim could not express to her any discomfort he might be feeling about the upcoming wedding. And any mention of the incident in the coal bin, or the other confusing images that came and went in past years, was unimaginable.

"Asparagus?" Connie's voice snapped Jim out of his thoughts as he raised a large bowl in his direction. Jim looked at the offering and spooned a small portion onto his plate. Normally he didn't like asparagus and thought its overcooked, mushy consistency tasted more like a bitter paste than a healthy vegetable. But it looked like Olga had performed a slight miracle. The fresh green stalks were lightly coated with olive oil and a touch of seasoning and actually looked quite appetizing. The asparagus sat well next to the delicate sea bass that was carefully arranged on his fine china plate. Although the portion sizes were not up to Jim's normal capacity he felt uncomfortable asking for more when Olga offered. But he did have seconds on the coffee which came from an enormous stainless steel machine that sat on a side table and looked like it was capable of brewing espresso, frothing your milk, or reading your horoscope. It produced an exquisite beverage, smooth, dark, and rich, completely unlike the acid that generally sat in the coffee pot at work.

"A toast to the soon to be newlyweds!" Connie said with a smile as he held up his glass of wine. His bright smile and perky tribute interrupted Jim's moment of caffeinated serenity.

"Thanks daddy" Laura responded, and she flashed a quick glance at Jim who had a distant look in his face as he joined in lifting his glass. She understood that her father meant well but also knew that Jim was uncomfortable with such verbalized sentiments. She said as much to him in a quick meeting of their eyes. For all of his neurosis and worry about making significant changes in his life she knew that Jim had made a deep connection with her, the kind of connection that allowed for a great deal of communication without any words being spoken.

When it was time to leave Jim was in the familiar "coming back to earth" mood that he generally felt after visiting the Whitacre's. In part it was a sense of relief to be returning to his own world. But it was also a return to the comfort of just being himself without having to perform in any kind of expected way, like raising that glass to Connie's toast, or not accepting second portions of food he normally would have happily gobbled down.

The drive home was quieter than usual. They were both tired from a long day and their fatigue encouraged a pensive mood in the car. As he headed south on the highway Jim thought more about the course his life was taking than on the direction he was driving. He looked over at Laura and wondered what she might be thinking as she sat gazing out the window. Laura always seemed very self-assured. Was it possible that she harbored any doubts about her own life?

But he said nothing. The nuns in grade school had taught

him that silence was golden. As an adult he learned that it was better than gold. Silence was a refuge, a safe place where he could hide his most intimate thoughts and fears.

Chapter 5

Jim felt somewhat out of synch when he returned to the firehouse for his next tour. He had been off for three days and was physically refreshed. But he often found that after a few days away from work he had to reset his mind to both the job of firefighting as well as the world of the firehouse. Sometimes, when he had not been to a fire for a while, the thought of exactly what he did for a living seemed kind of absurd and the danger of that work was more obvious to him. Firefighting was like that. If Jim went through a period where he went to a lot of jobs it seemed like he couldn't wait until the next one came in. It was like he got addicted to the adrenaline rush. But when he thought about what the job actually entailed- hanging onto the top of a 100-foot ladder, climbing up an ancient fire escape of questionable stability, or crawling down a burning hallway, it did seem like a strange way to make a living. Not at all like the "normal" jobs people had. People like Connie for example. As he sat alone in the kitchen nursing a tepid cup of bitter coffee he thought about the tasty brew he had enjoyed at the Whitacre's. That was three days ago, forty miles upstate, and on a different planet altogether. Jim could hear the roar of trucks and honking car horns from where sat in the kitchen and thought about the quiet pastoral scenes he had just shared with Laura.

It was a warm morning and the apparatus doors were wide open. The guys scheduled to work were standing in that opening waiting for the start of the tour and watching the parade of people as they walked past. These were the daytime people of Mid-Manhattan, guys in sharp suits who clung to their attaché cases like they held state secrets and women in sneakers burdened with large shoulder bags that held the fashionable but uncomfortable shoes they'd wear once they got to the office. All of them were moving in that tight, rapid city pace that said, "Don't mess with me, I'm on my way to something important". In contrast, the firefighters watching them stood by casually and leaned against the warm masonry beside the door, a few holding their own cups of strong firehouse coffee. Some tried to catch a glance from the women as they walked past. Occasionally one would pleasantly nod to the men but most just moved on and ignored them. The commuter crowd contrasted sharply from the street people of the night. It was during the nighttime that the abandoned West Side sidewalks changed character altogether and the doors to the firehouse doors were closed to the solitary prostitute or homeless person that might pass by.

Jim looked up from his coffee and saw Captain Henderson enter the kitchen. Julius Henderson had been the regularly assigned Captain in Ladder 57 for six years. He stood a shade over six feet tall, was powerfully built, and had a comb over hairstyle that just barely managed to cover the bald spot on his head but could not cover the rage that always seemed to be seething within him. Henderson was very experienced, decidedly high strung, and viewed with a mixture of fear and respect by most of the members of the unit. He wielded his powerful voice like a weapon when he supervised the men at a fire, lashing out at them in a manner that definitely motivated but at the same time put everyone on edge. Like he was not speaking, but barking. Only Sean seemed to have an immunity to the Captain's volatile nature, enabled as he was by his hard earned philosophy and life experiences.

Unlike Captain Lopez there were aspects to the "Barker" that the men did appreciate. Over the course of his 35 years on the job Henderson had stepped up a number of times to help out his share of drunks. And he had balls, which was a vital necessity on the fireground but also in the day to day operations of the department. On a number of occasions he had shown that he wasn't afraid to stand up to some difficult chiefs. And, unlike Faiella, he actually was an accomplished writer. A few years back he had published a technical book about firefighting that had become a kind of a bible for both firefighters and officers and offered practical lessons drawn from his extensive background.

Jim had mixed feelings about Henderson. He admired his grit but was never quite sure of what to expect from him. There were times when he was actually approachable and friendly. And others where he seemed to be on the verge of exploding.

"Hi Jim, how are you this fine morning?"

"Doing good Captain," Jim replied, feeling relieved that it looked like he was in one of his good moods.

"Let's get the guys in the kitchen."

Jim walked out to the front of the firehouse to get the men and as they gathered around the long kitchen table Henderson gave out the assignments for the tour. Sean and Dave were working today and the two open spots were being covered by Williams and Scanlon, two guys from nearby firehouses who were working overtime. The captain informed them that they were scheduled to go out on building inspection in the afternoon. That would involve spending three hours evaluating the fire safety of nearby buildings, an important aspect of the job but one that many firefighters were not that thrilled with. They much pre-ferred the intense, adrenaline inducing work of actually going to a fire over any kind of administrative duties. Jim could see from the expressions on the faces of the two overtime guys that they weren't thrilled about how their overtime money would be earned. But Henderson was too intimidating a person for them to say anything.

After the roll call and the usual equipment checks and house cleaning were completed the men scattered to different parts of the firehouse and Jim was on his own again in the kitchen. He thought about going to the basement for a light workout with the weights but after his experience down there on his last tour that was the last place he really wanted to be.

Sean suddenly entered through the kitchen door. He was not carrying his usual can of Coke, a decision made out of respect for the Captain. Not that Henderson wasn't aware of his act, Sean just didn't want to push it in his face as the two of them actually shared a bond in their years on the job. They had been to many ass kicking fires together over that period and the Captain was well aware of Sean's steady reliability. The numerous close calls, the occasionally frightening moments, and the devastation of 9/11 had cemented that bond. Both had learned what was really relevant in life.

"How was your time off Jim?" Sean asked.

"Interesting, I went up to Laura's family for dinner. It went ok but every time I travel up there I'm kind of amazed at how some people live. Definitely not a small house on the Jersey Shore. I guess there's people out there making a lot more money than we are."

"I know, I'm surprised my ex isn't living like that after all the fuckin' alimony I've sent in her direction," Sean responded with a grin on his face.

Jim watched Sean as he opened the refrigerator door hoping to scrounge out a bit of whatever leftovers remained from last night's meal. Sean's humor and smile seemed ever present but as Jim stared at his lined face, he wondered just how much inner turmoil he might be hiding given all he had been through in life. Were there things that haunted him? Perhaps he was just better at turning it all off, something Jim desperately wanted to be able to do. He knew that years ago Sean had been ordered to the department's counseling unit for a short time and thought about what that experience must have been like. He wondered if they had helped in any way or if it was all just a bureaucratic walk through.

"Ah! Bats and balls," Sean declared in triumph. He had found a Tupperware container in the fridge that was full of the sausage and meatballs left over from the spaghetti dinner the guys enjoyed last night.

"Looks like Faiella must have been working. This is exactly the kind of meal he would want, not that he'd actually cook it himself, the lazy bastard," Sean carried the container over to the microwave oven with a hungry look on his face.

Jim enjoyed seeing the straightforward joy on Sean's face as he uncovered the tasty snack. And on some level he also envied that joy. Sean's contented smile seemed so basic and untroubled despite all the curve balls that life had thrown at him. But Jim turned off such thoughts by jumping into the normal routines of the firehouse. It looked like the kitchen floor needed a good mopping. After he accomplished that task he proceeded to clean the tools on the rig. He found comfort in performing the familiar chores. He concentrated on the texture of the wood grain on the six-foot hooks as he washed them and then savored the fine balance of the steel Halligan. Jim had always admired the simple design of the Halligan forcible entry tool. It was about three feet long with a sharp metal point at one end and a bent fork at the other. It looked practical and primitive, like something a Viking warrior would carry. Firefighters carried a lot of tools in their work and the physical aspect of the job appealed to him. Tools, smoke, and fire were clearly defined realities, things he could see and touch and smell. Dealing with them kept him grounded and occasionally exhausted him to a point where he wouldn't think about the future, or the past, and he could just exist in the present moment.

When he had finished his work Jim placed all the tools back in their assigned places on the truck. He admired how clean they looked and then considered how filthy they'd soon become when they were put to use again at the next fire, for there would most certainly be a next fire and it probably wasn't that far away. This line of work took a toll on both the tools and the men. But until that fire came, the men would continue to cling tenaciously to their firehouse traditions. And the ritual of preparing and sharing the meal was an important part of that tradition. That simple task always evoked a healthy debate on what exactly that meal would consist of. The discussion started early today since they had to go out for fire prevention activities in the afternoon and they wanted to make sure they could fit lunch in on time. Williams and Scanlon suggested cheeseburgers, a firehouse staple. But they were outsiders and it basically came down to what the guys assigned to Ladder Company 57 preferred. Jim had once enjoyed quiche at the Whitacre's but he knew better than to even suggest that given the general meat and potatoes style of the firehouse.

"Surf and Turf!" was Sean's recommendation. But both Jim and Dave knew that was just his much overused joke about eating tuna fish and hot dogs.

"Sausage and Peppers, that's always good shit," Dave offered, but Jim had heard just about enough sausage talk recently and Dave's choice of works did not exactly encourage an image of culinary delight.

Eventually they agreed on shrimp parmigiana heros and they headed out on the rig to a nearby supermarket. When they arrived there, Captain Henderson sat in the truck and monitored the radio for any runs that might come in while the men shopped. And they were very particular in their food shopping. The supermarket had a good fish counter but it required two additional stops to complete the grocery run. A small Italian deli provided the fresh mozzarella and the rolls could only come from an old West Side bakery that emitted a mouthwatering scent of baked bread they could smell from a half a block away. There would be no cheap white bread carbohydrates for this crew.

The company managed to get back to the firehouse and have the food ready just a few minutes before noon. They had run out of paper napkins and forgot to pick them up at the store so Sean placed two rolls of toilet paper on the table.

"There you go guys. Irish linen to wipe your hands," he said with a smile on his face.

Jim regarded the massive sandwich that sat on his plate. The foot long hero was dripping with tomato sauce and smothered in a thick layer of cheese that hid any evidence of the crustaceans that lied within. It looked like the kind of sloppy meal that would require ample use of Sean's "linen". Jim liked shrimp and in order to actually taste the delicate flavor he proceeded to remove half of the bread and most of the cheese, an act which earned suspicious glances from some at the table who couldn't comprehend why he wasn't just chomping it all down like everyone else. Firehouse meals were frequently interrupted by emergency responses. You didn't savor food, you ate it, knowing that your next bite might be your last at least for a few hours.

True to form, just a few minutes into the meal they heard in the background chatter of the fire department radio that "all hands were going to work" at a location just beyond the normal response area of Ladder 57. The men knew that they might be called to the fire if it went to a multiple alarm, a possibility that made it even more urgent to inhale a few more calories.

When he heard the job announced on the radio Dave dropped his hero and excitedly said, "All right! If that goes to a 2nd alarm we'll definitely be going there," his appetite suddenly deadened by the prospect of working at an actual fire. He was new to the job and hadn't yet been to many fires. Dave was at that early stage in a firefighter's career where the excitement of the work far surpassed a true appreciation of the dangers involved.

"Tell you what probie. If they need help, why don't we just send you over there in a taxi and leave the rest of us in peace" Sean replied. Over the course of his long career Sean had been to more multiple alarm fires than he could count. This was just another one to him, one that was going to interrupt yet another meal. Williams and Scanlon actually perked up at the thought of going to the fire. They'd both much rather earn their overtime doing that rather than inspecting buildings for the rest of the tour.

Within minutes the announcement of a 2nd alarm screeched out of the radio and was instantly followed by the loud buzzing of the computer at the watch house desk. Ladder 57 had been assigned to the fire and the men instantly transitioned from kitchen mode to a "let's go to work" mindset, their bodies charged by the sudden jolt of adrenaline. Sean put down his sandwich in disgust and the men quickly covered their food with plastic lids in the hope of at least keeping it relatively fresh. But Sean had been through this routine enough to know that by the time they got back from the job his sandwich was going to be a coagulated mess of hardened cheese and mushy bread that even the microwave couldn't salvage.

The truck was out the door in a heartbeat and started heading toward the East Side carefully weaving its way through the congestion of Mid-Manhattan. It was the noon hour, and the streets were packed with the usual double parked delivery trucks, lines of taxis, and crowds of people. Ladder 57 forced a path through the throng with the help of a piercing siren and an ear-splitting air horn. Every so slowly the rig made its way as pedestrians covered their ears, truck drivers cursed, and taxis scooted out of the way, all of them fully engaged in the relentless dance of New York City traffic.

Each officer had his own personal style of using the sounding devices. Some used the air horn intermittently and only stepped on the floor mounted button in particularly jammed areas. Others used it almost as a weapon and laid on the horn as if it were capable of dissolving any person or thing that happened to have the audacity of standing in front of the rig or failing to immediately move out of the way. Captain Henderson was decidedly in the latter school of thought. From his seat in the back of the rig Jim could see the veins sticking out the captain's neck as he tightly gripped the handset of the radio to his left ear and engaged in a continuous barrage of curses directed towards the traffic. Here was the side of Captain Henderson that many feared. But in a way his explosive nature was made for just such moments and his pent-up rage found a much-needed means of release in the vitriol he projected from his elevated seat in the front of the truck.

Seated right next to the captain was Williams, who was assigned to drive Ladder 57 for the tour. As he skillfully maneuvered the truck through the chaos of the streets his quiet concentration contrasted sharply with Henderson's agitated state. Jim watched as he artfully navigated the rig through the swarm in a sort of urban version of the parting of the Red Sea. The guys knew they were going to work and that eliminated their usual banter about the attractive women they passed in the street. Gone too was any exchange of the sharp humor they normally shared in a ride to the supermarket. Instead there was no conversation at all as each of them strained to hear the dispatcher's radio voice over the intense noise for any updates on the fire.

Each of the men dealt with the excitement and anxiety of responding to an emergency in their own way. Jim had a good body of firefighting experience but for him the nerve-racking minutes of riding on the truck before he actually arrived at the scene of a fire was always the most apprehensive time. It was the unknown that unnerved him, the uncertainty of just what challenges he would be facing and how much he could control. Once he got there and could physically see what was going on he was able to size up the fire and calmly go to work.

Sean put all of his usual kitchen humor on hold and was very quiet when he responded to a fire. He could play the role of a clown in the firehouse but was a seasoned pro when it came to actually performing the work of firefighting. He had seen a lot and much of what he had experienced was bad. As he sat on the rig he looked relaxed, but Jim could see the concentration in his face as he monitored the messages from the radio trying to pick up any information about the fire or the building they were going to be working in.

Scanlon was having second thoughts about this overtime tour. Scanlon was a man who enjoyed his comforts and now he was going to a fire. That meant a lot of sweat and dirt and he had not brought a change of clothes when he left his assigned firehouse this morning. He knew the guys assigned to Ladder 57 would let him borrow some dry things to wear when they returned from the job but the thought of hanging around in his sweat-soaked jockey shorts was a definite turn off. Maybe, if Captain Henderson was in the right mode, they could stop by his firehouse on the way back from the job so he could grab some things from his locker. He made a mental note to evaluate how approachable the captain appeared to be after the fire. His volatile nature was common knowledge to all the companies in the battalion.

Of all the guys on the rig it was Dave, the most untried man, who was most at ease as they responded. It was his very naiveté and inexperience that shielded him from any sense of nervousness. To Dave this was still a very new and stimulating game and his adrenaline was provoked more by his tremendous sense of excitement about going to a fire than by any fear about the things that could go wrong once he got there. That's what the officers and senior men like Sean were for. Their years of seeing people getting injured or killed in this line of work gave them a perspective that a new guy like Dave could not possibly have. Men in their 30's and 40's had long outgrown the initial adolescent excitement of the work and developed a middle-aged appreciation for the realistic dangers of the job.

"There it is!" Dave said in an excited voice when the rig made a right onto 5th Avenue and the fire building came into sight. It was as if he had just spotted a celebrity or the President of the United States.

"Make sure you bring your hook, probie," Sean calmly responded. The fire had largely been extinguished and he knew that they would be doing a lot of overhauling work and the 6-foot hook would be needed to pull down the ceilings in the building to expose any hidden pockets of fire.

The fire had started in a shoe store on the first floor of an old four-story building. Captain Henderson checked in with the chief in charge who assigned Ladder 57 into the store to complete the search and overhaul work. As they approached the building, they could see the first due companies coming back out to the sidewalk. They looked beaten up and filthy. Their sweaty faces were streaked with soot and strings of white building insulation hung from the shoulders of their drenched coats like tinsel on a Christmas tree. The face pieces of their air masks swung loosely from their sides as they walked past and the continuous vibrating sound that emanated from those masks showed that they had used up most of their air supply over the course of the firefight.

Jim paused for a moment on the sidewalk and looked at the store. This was no *Famous Footwear* outlet with the usual inventory of inexpensive shoes built out of "man- made" materials by some underpaid worker in a third world country. On the contrary, this 5th Avenue merchant specialized in pure bred leather beauties that were imported from Italy and started at $500 dollars a pair. Jim spotted a number of shoes scattered about, their stylish elegance just a distant memory as they laid on the floor all soaked in water and covered by debris. The entire store was in shambles and the men stepped carefully over piles of stock, fallen shelves, and shattered counters as they worked their way into the building. Residual water from the hose lines still drained from the store and the air was thick with a post fire scent of moist soot that would become embedded in the men's hair and their skin and remain a part of their essence long after they showered. Light tendrils of steam still rose from the sodden contents, twisting and dancing like ghosts of the flames that had just been extinguished. And now all of it was strangely silent, a stark contrast to the intense noise of the shattering glass, roaring saws, and booming shouts of the fire fight that had just occurred.

This was an old structure that had been extensively renovated to fit in well with the upscale nature of the neighborhood. The modern, fluorescent sign that sat above the entranceway artfully concealed numerous layers of paint that remained from decades of previous store occupants. Inside the store a clean acoustical tile ceiling hung from above and sheet rock hid the old brick and plaster of the original walls. Each detail had been added to mask the antique essence of the place. But beneath the fashionable front, the old elements still remained. The building was like a chubby man who held in his gut on the beach or an older woman who still dressed like she was stepping out to some disco. For many of the stores on 5th Avenue much of what was visible was merely a façade.

"Get this ceiling down!" Henderson barked at Dave, the Captain's intense voice adding to the probie's adrenaline fueled energy level. He proceeded to attack the light acoustical ceiling tiles with rapid jabs of his hook, each piece falling quietly at his feet.

"No, not that stuff. The tin you see above it!" the Captain corrected. He was referring to the old tin ceiling which Dave could see sat about a foot above the acoustical tiles he had been working on. The darkly painted tin was embossed in intricate detail and, like the other architectural remnants, it had been hidden for years by the clean white panels that hung beneath it.

Dave proceeded to attack the tin using his hook in powerful upward strokes. He worked rapidly at first but within minutes he was totally exhausted and could only manage a few feeble thrusts with the tool. His efforts had produced a few small openings in the ceiling but most of the tin was still in place and hiding small remnants of fire.

"Kid you'll never last twenty years on this job if you keep working like that" Sean said as he watched Dave's efforts. He took the tool from him and aptly demonstrated how it was far more productive, and much easier, to just insert the hook into one of the holes he had created and then to pull down on the tin to slowly peel it off in large sections.

"You see, it's like opening a sardine can. Even an old guy like me can do it." Sean may have been somewhat of a loose cannon, but he knew his job and was willing to pass on his knowledge to others.

Jim helped Dave in the task of pulling down the tin and within a few minutes they had managed to open up a large section. When they stepped back to examine their work they noticed an old pipe in the ceiling area above them. It ran throughout the ceiling and at several points was connected to short segments that hung straight down towards the store below.

"What's that doing up there?" Dave didn't really want to say much at this point but his curiosity about the pipe got the better of him. He appreciated Sean's advice but felt a bit embarrassed by the overhauling lesson he had just received from a much older man who didn't possess anywhere near his physical strength.

"Just what are you guys staring at?" Captain Henderson was mildly annoyed at the halt in the work. He wanted to get this ceiling down and get the men back to the firehouse to finish lunch and to move on to the administrative duties he had to accomplish this afternoon.

The Captain's disposition changed as soon as he looked up at the pipe. He knew right away that it was a remnant from the gas lit era of the city. It had probably been disconnected and capped decades ago and the short extensions that ran through the tin ceiling marked the spots where the old gas lighting fixtures had once been located. Henderson knew his stuff. An entire chapter of his book covered the construction details of old buildings and pointed out that some of them might still have antiquated gas lines in place. True to his volatile nature he instantly transformed from the role of pissed off supervisor to that of a well-informed teacher and proceeded to explain to the men exactly what they were looking at.

Dave listened to the Captain but he struggled with the concept of gas lighting. Like most people living in 21st century New York his only experience with gas was limited to seeing the small blue flames that shot from the burners of a kitchen stove. The whole notion of using an explosive vapor to light up a room seemed absurd or, as he would likely put it, totally fucked up. But Jim had no problem with the idea. He had never read the captain's book but he could perceive all the details. The small pieces of pipe that hung down from the tin looked different from the sections that were hidden away above the ceiling. Those segments would have been attached to the chandeliers and were covered in a decorative finish since they were visible from the room below. He could picture the intricate glass globes that contained the small twinkling flames and the tiny valves on the brass lighting fixtures that controlled the flow of the gas. Jim could hear the gentile hiss of the gas as those valves were turned on and envision the store basking in the warm glow of soft yellow light. But he snapped himself out of those visions by throwing himself into the physical task of pulling down the rest of the ceiling. He worked rapidly and aggressively and used his tool to attack his train of thought as much as the ceiling itself. Sean stood off to the side and watched Jim's intense activity.

Each of the men held his own thoughts after they completed their work and walked back to the truck. Dave thought about his sandwich. He had burned off an inordinate number of calories and desperately needed to replenish them. Scanlon had worked up quite a sweat and longed for the comfort of dry underwear. Captain Henderson pictured the enormous pile of paperwork that awaited him back on his desk. Sean contemplated the image of Jim quietly pounding away at the ceiling inside the store. He sensed that he had been wrestling with something lately. Maybe he was just nervous about the upcoming wedding. Perhaps it was deeper than that. Whatever it was he was certainly not going to ask.

Jim walked away from the job trying not to think at all. Lately the images had been coming more frequently. Coal bins, gas pipes, vivid dreams of unfamiliar neighborhoods, maybe the long hours and exhaustion of the past several days had put his imagination on overdrive. He sat in silence on the ride back to the firehouse and passively watched as the taxis and the pedestrians flowed by. And for at least one brief panicky moment he wondered if he was starting to lose his grip on reality.

Chapter 6

There was no one moment when Jim finally decided to speak to someone about the thoughts that had been plaguing him. It was just a subtle feeling that the path he had been on for so long was getting tiresome and wearing him down. The confusions, the dreams, and the sense of alienation had been a part of him since childhood. And the weight of it all was taking a toll. He tried to maintain a cautious sense of optimism about his future. Jim liked his job, and though he certainly harbored his share of pre-marriage nerves, he was happy to have Laura in his life. But he needed some kind of relief valve to release all of those muddled thoughts and to move into his future with a feeling of confidence. Perhaps more than anything he was looking to be reassured that he was just like everyone else and that all of the recent images he had been experiencing were just passing fantasies, thoughts that other people also entertained but were able to dismiss much easier than he could.

The day after the store fire Jim was at home, trying to relax and consider what his options might be. He was stretched out on his favorite couch which sat right next to the large picture window in the front of his apartment. It was the middle of the afternoon and he basked in the sun that filtered through the shades just staring out at the street and relishing the quiet and privacy of the room. He began to focus on a single squirrel that scooted quickly through a narrow patch of the dried grass that sat next to the concrete sidewalk. He watched the nervous intensity of the creature as it abruptly moved and then suddenly stopped to dig for some hidden snack. It nibbled vigorously on the tidbit and then instantly sprang out of view. And for a few seconds Jim had no doubts or fears or worries about the future, just a calm sense of being in the moment as he observed that tiny slice of life.

He tended to spend a lot of time in this position either reading, watching television, or just looking at the ceiling and letting his mind turn to mush. As he thought about the possibility of actually confiding in someone, he determined that there were certain ground rules he would have to insist on. First, the person he would choose to speak to had to be someone who didn't know him at all. That way he could rapidly and painlessly escape from any embarrassment and not have his life disrupted in any way if he decided that the whole thing was a waste of time. He also felt that it would be easier if that person happened to be a woman. He had spent years in a tough, male dominated job and had developed the thick skin that world demanded. The only "counseling" he had ever received from men was limited to the haranguing of a few priests who basically lectured him on what things in life he was forbidden to do. And he had reacted to that by whole heartily jumping right into those banned activities. But past girlfriends, female coworkers, even some of the nuns in school had shown him a softer side. If he was going to go through with this, he would definitely prefer a gentler approach.

So where to turn? This was virgin territory for Jim. People from his background and line of work didn't usually seek out this kind of help. His family had not been into verbalizing problems. You just kept quiet and went on with your life and eventually worked out things on your own. And you didn't discuss any uncomfortable topics. His mother had certainly set the example for that. Jim had never known anyone who had been in any kind of therapy. He envisioned it as a place where you would lie on a couch in a quiet office that had walls painted in comforting shades of light blue while a bearded, sensitive looking guy who looked like Robin Williams would nod his head and carefully jot down notes.

The fire department's counseling unit suddenly popped into his head. Jim knew that sometimes men, like Sean, had been ordered to go there. But there were many who chose to go on their own. In the past they had treated some guys with drinking problems, and they did help a lot of people through the devastation of 9/11. Jim hadn't been affected by either of those issues and Sean never spoke much of his counseling experience. Still, it seemed like they would be familiar with aspects of his world even if his struggles were not the kind of thing they normally dealt with. Besides, the idea of counseling seemed a lot less severe than therapy. If he went there he wouldn't be in "therapy" he would be "counseled" which sounded like getting some good advice as opposed to having every aspect of his past picked apart and analyzed. In his view therapy was for losers who spent decades pouring out their guts and obsessively discussing all the failures in their lives. Counseling on the other hand just might provide the short, quick kick in the ass he needed to move on in his life.

Jim's work calendar sat on a coffee table next to the couch. Each of the individual months in it were overrun with the same confusing jumble of highlighted dates as the one he kept on his firehouse locker. But most of the significant department phone numbers were clearly printed in bold on the back cover, including the number of the counseling unit. He stared at that number with the same focus he had when he watched the squirrel.

Suddenly, without any further thought, he was dialing the number on his cell phone. He listened as the phone rang, once, twice, three times. It felt like he was standing at the open door of an airplane with a parachute on his back.

"Good afternoon, counseling unit," a man's voice spoke just as Jim was about to hang up. He sounded young and competent and friendly, his words pronounced clearly and without a shred of any accent. Normally he'd expect a high volume, "Ladda 57, Firefighta Jones" in a heavy dose of New York jargon when he called the firehouse.

"Er, counseling unit?" Jim was at the door but not quite yet out of the airplane.

"Yes, this is the counseling unit, may I help you?"

For a moment Jim remained silent.

"Hello, are you there?"

"I, ah, I was wondering if you work by appointment?"

"Sure, we have a few people available. In fact, you can come down today if you want."

"No, today's out," he'd rather watch the squirrel. For that matter he'd rather do anything else. Jim wasn't quite ready to jump right into this. He rightly figured that the person he was speaking to knew he was dealing with yet another reluctant blue-collar guy that he'd have to lure in to talk about his feelings.

"Ok, how does next week look for you?"

Jim glanced at his calendar. Lunch with Laura on Wednesday but other than that a lot of empty days.

"Is next Tuesday open?" It would be nice to get it out of the way before he saw her.

"Sure, morning or afternoon?"

"Morning" Jim responded. If he was going to do this better to get it over early and not have to sit around all day waiting for it to happen.

"Alright, I'll put you down for ten that morning if that works for you. What's your name?"

"Jim." He was out of the plane and falling fast. If this guy asks for my last name or assigned unit, I'll hang up the fucking phone, he thought to himself.

"Ok Jim, my name's Steve, we'll see you on Tuesday."

When he hung up the phone Jim felt a sense of relief. He also thought that he had just put himself on the official list of fire department crazies. Thank God they hadn't asked for his last name.

Jim was up early when Tuesday morning arrived. He hadn't mentioned anything about his counseling plans to Laura. This felt like something he had to handle on his own. But he did feel a level of guilt as he headed out for his appointment in lower Manhattan. Laura was a lot more open about things than he was. If she was going to do something like this, he had no doubt that she would speak to him about it. And he knew this wasn't the only thing he kept to himself.

He was in the car a few minutes after nine just as the commuter traffic was winding down. The trip down on the FDR was a change from his normal cross-town route to Ladder 57 and as he drove south he relished the view of the East River as it flowed past him on the left glittering brightly in the morning sunlight. He had scoped out the location of a few firehouses where he might park his car and chose one that was several blocks away from his destination. There was a company located almost next door to the counseling unit but he figured it was better to walk from a distance than to get any suspicious glances from the guy who would be sitting at the house watch desk of that unit.

Jim worked his way through the streets of SoHo and when he arrived at the chosen firehouse, pulled right into one of the open parking spots. When he stepped out of the car he could see the house watchman looking at him through the open bay doors with that "what do you think you're doing" look on his face. But as soon as he saw Jim walking toward him with the box of dough-nuts in his hand he immediately understood that this was just another firefighter looking for a place to dump his car for a while.

"How you doing?" the guy greeted him. He was young and had the bulked-up look of a serious weight lifter but despite the steaming cup of coffee he held in his hand he carried himself with a worn out look that probably stemmed from the night tour he had just finished.

"Good. I'm going to see a friend in the neighborhood. Do you mind if I leave my car here for a couple of hours?"

"Sure, no problem brother. You can keep it there all day if you want," Jim could see that he was distracted by the pastries as he opened up the box, the jelly doughnuts in particular, and he wondered just how many of them would actually make it to the kitchen.

"Thanks so much, see you a little later."

"No problem, thanks for bringing the doughnuts!" As Laura had once teased him, the fastest way to a fireman's heart is often through his stomach.

Jim had some time to kill so he started on a slow walk through the neighborhood. The old loft buildings that lined the streets were clad in the same carefully preserved cast iron facades that had adorned them for a century or more. They still reflected the architectural grandeur of a previous era but now they were occupied by the artists and affluent residents who had replaced the commercial occupants of the distant past. Jim had studied the construction of these buildings and the procedures on how to fight a fire in one of them. He was familiar with their past but he made a conscious effort not to think about history as he walked. It seemed like there had always been moments in his life when his sense of the past was *too* precise, if that was at all possible. He didn't want to go there right now and instead he concentrated on the bustle of the traffic and people around him to force such thoughts out of his head.

When he arrived at the address of the counseling unit, he was surprised to see that it was one of the old loft buildings. Somehow in his mind he had imagined that it would be located in a more modern high-rise kind of place. Jim entered the front door and saw a small "Counseling Unit" sign with an arrow that pointed toward a long set of stairs on his right. Apparently, the unit was on the second floor and he paused for a moment to gaze up the stairway. It was long and steep and at the very top there was a large window that looked like it hadn't been opened in fifty years. One of the windowpanes was missing and had been replaced by a small piece of ply board. A couple of yellow bulbs illuminated the dirty grey walls of the staircase but most of the light came from the very top where a blinding glare beckoned from the old window. The stairwell kind of looked like a long passageway that would lead to heaven, or to doom, Jim wasn't sure which.

The old wooden steps creaked beneath his feet as he started walking up the stairs, each thread covered by a piece of ancient linoleum that had been worn down to a dark muddled finish. Jim could feel the dust on his hand as he slid it along the wooden railing. How do they expect guys to feel better coming to an old wreck like this? The whole place looked run down and depressing. Maybe they gave it a grim appearance on purpose so that you automatically felt a lot better just leaving the place.

When Jim got up to the second floor he saw a sign for the counseling unit posted on the frosted glass of a large wooden door. He hesitated at the door for a moment and then with a sudden twist of the battered brass doorknob he was inside the room.

A tall, blond guy was standing behind a desk pouring water into a coffee machine.

"Good morning!" he said as he turned towards Jim with the coffee pot in his hands.

"Are you here for the ten o'clock?" he asked as if he was catching a bus or train and not there to face an uncomfortable experience.

"Ah, yeah, the ten o'clock" Jim responded, somewhat relieved that he hadn't addressed him by name or asked him to start filling out some forms. He wanted this to be as anonymous as possible and it looked like this guy was cool with that.

"Excellent! How are you doing today?" Jim figured that this must be Steve, his energetic words were pronounced with that same uplifting and welcoming voice he heard on the phone. Steve looked at Jim with an intense bright smile on his face as if just seeing him standing there was the greatest thing he had experienced in over a month. He was dressed in a clean white dress shirt with the counseling unit logo on the pocket. Jim thought Steve could pass for a hard driving motivational speaker or a die-hard Mormon who was having an especially good day.

"Would you like some coffee?" he offered, pointing to the pot.

"No, thanks," Jim responded. He wondered for a moment if he should have also brought a box of doughnuts for the counseling unit. Nah, they may be a part of the fire department, but they weren't really *in* the department and probably had their own way of doing things.

"Ok! Have a seat and someone will call you in a few minutes". So, Jim thought, Steve is not one of the counselors, just the guy who handles the reception and, apparently, the coffee. Kind of like the counseling unit's version of a probie. That meant there was still hope of speaking to the sensitive, nun-like female he thought he'd be more comfortable with.

Jim scanned the office as he headed toward the waiting area. The interior of the place, just like the rest of the building, was not what he had expected. It was clear that at some point the office had been extensively renovated but it still managed to hold on to the decrepit flavor of the rest of the structure. The industrial green walls looked like they were painted sometime before the city's last fiscal crisis. And that was a *long* time ago. There were light brown stains on some of the white ceiling tiles that showed the location of previous water leaks. A steam radiator sat over in a corner all covered in flaking silver paint. It was one of the old, ornate types that looked like it had been cranking out heat since the fire department gave up its last horse and wagon.

He hadn't pictured any of this when he spoke to Steve on the phone. Where were the artfully hung paintings and the comforting blue walls? How about the plush carpet and the gentle, bearded guy who would look like Robin Williams and welcome him to some reassuring moments of sharing?

There were just a few guys sitting in the waiting area when Jim got there. A couple of them had their heads buried in the sports pages of the *Daily News*. Another was staring off into some distant space oblivious to all that was around him. Jim was about to sit down when he noticed that, tucked away in the last row, there sat the unmistakable face of Timmy Rollins. Shit! Over ten thousand people on this job and I have to run into someone I know? Jim debated whether he should just sit down and pretend that he hadn't seen him or if it would be better to go over and say hello. He decided that it was best to walk over and talk to him rather than face the embarrassment of having Timmy suddenly discover that he was there. He had actually prepared himself for this exact scenario as he was driving in this morning. Whether he was responding to a fire or headed toward some other traumatic experience, "Mr. Thoroughly" liked to feel that he had taken every conceivable step to control the situation. It was an approach that had helped make him a good firefighter but held him back in many other aspects of his life.

"Timmy! How you doing, buddy?" Jim mentally rehearsed his line over and over in his head as he looked down at Timmy. I'm having some trouble sleeping, I'm having some trouble sleeping was his mantra. Certainly, that would provide a legitimate, noninvasive explanation as to why he happened to be here in the waiting area with the rest of the crazies. It seemed like an understandable issue that could naturally be caused by the long work hours and unorthodox schedule. He had toyed with the idea of saying he was there for the smoke cessation program the counseling unit offered but it was common knowledge among his coworkers that he was not a smoker.

"Hey Jim, long time no see," Timmy looked up from his seat and responded in a whisper. He looked worn out and defeated, like he had been quietly and patiently waiting in that solitary chair for an entire week. Timmy Rollins was assigned to Ladder 57 but had not actually worked there for a few months. The counseling unit set up an administrative job for him in headquarters while he ironed out some issues in his life. Timmy had fit in well at the firehouse. He was tough and funny, and the guys enjoyed sparring with him in the kitchen. But over time things seemed to turn and it started to show in the way he carried himself. Timmy was normally a self-assured wiseass, but he slowly transformed into someone who looked troubled and withdrawn. The Timmy who looked up at Jim now had an unshaven face and sad eyes that stood in sharp contrast to the happy go lucky guy he knew from the firehouse. He liked his beer, but the guys knew that the most likely source of the problem stemmed not from booze, but from his on again, off again relationship with his wife. Events in their stormy home on Staten Island had taken a toll on both of them.

"So, what's going on with you?" Jim immediately regretted asking Timmy. He realized that, like himself, there was a lot Timmy would just prefer to keep to himself and, having met his somewhat volatile wife, he didn't want to make it seem like he was prying or trying to put him on the spot. He should have made some inane comment about the Yankees or the Mets, or any damn topic that they could safely discuss while they both waited to see a counselor and pretended that life was normal.

But instead, Jim's question opened up a floodgate.

"I'm totally shot. I hate that job in headquarters, it's boring and the commute is a fucking nightmare and I haven't seen my kids for five days" streamed out of Timmy's mouth.

"She's talking about divorce and wants the kids. She's already got a lawyer and I'm living with my sister and I'm already paying the mortgage and she's talking about alimony and I'm not even allowed to work any overtime right now!"

His words gushed out in desperation and as Jim listened he felt truly sorry for the pain he was witnessing. He also felt a sense of relief. As he continued to listen to his tormented monologue Jim knew that Timmy was not going to bring up the elephant in the room and ask the most obvious question. Like, "so, what the fuck is your problem and what brings you here?" Which was a good thing because Jim really had no clear idea of how to answer that question, even to himself.

Jim sat down on the chair next to Timmy. He now felt a sense of kinship toward him rather than just viewing him as a potential source of embarrassment. For a few minutes they left their troubled worlds outside the old waiting room and shared some fond memories of hysterical moments in the firehouse kitchen. Steve suddenly appeared in front of them and politely interrupted their conversation.

"Ok, you want to come with me please?" he said, with that ingratiating smile still beaming on his face.

Not really but I'm here so I might as well go through with it, Jim thought as he stood up and shook Timmy's hand.

"See you back at the firehouse."

But even as he spoke the words he knew it was unlikely that anyone was going to see much of Timmy in the near future. Steve led him down the hallway and beckoned him through the open door of a small office. When he entered there was a woman sitting at a desk who immediately rose from her seat and extended her hand out to him.

"Hi Jim. Please have a seat." She was middle aged, slightly plump, and wearing a brightly colored dress that stood out from the walls of her office which were also done in the same industrial green of the waiting area. Jim could see through the lenses of her wire rimmed glasses that she had kind eyes that seemed to be saying "I know you're scared and probably fucked up but that's ok and I'm glad you're here," or at least that's what he thought he saw.

"Jim, I'm Carol Fitzpatrick and I'm one of the counselors here."

Fitzpatrick, Jim thought, there's about a thousand of them on this job. Her father was probably a firefighter and after she graduated from City College with her degree in psychology this was a logical step for her. Second generation offspring of firemen often didn't fall far from the tree.

"So, Jim, how are you doing today?" she cheerfully asked.

Carol, Jim, Steve, looks like they're on a first name basis only here and that's a good thing. Jim had a brief fantasy of calling Captain Henderson "Julius" back in the firehouse. The barker would probably bite his head off.

"Ok, thanks for seeing me," Jim responded as he sat down on the plush seat next to her desk. It was considerably more comfortable than the plastic chair in the waiting area.

He felt relaxed with this woman. She seemed nice and unthreatening. And the gentle nature of this entire place was a pleasant change of pace from the aggressive, male world of the firehouse. There were times when that felt like a prison. He noted a framed poster hanging on the wall that spelled out "God grant me the serenity to accept the things I cannot change, the courage to change the things I can, and the wisdom to know the difference". There was a stack of pamphlets sitting on her desk and from his angle Jim could make out the title, "Learning to be Your Own Best Friend" on the cover. After all the debate about even coming down here was this just going to be an exercise in cookbook therapy?

That was one of the things that had turned him off to organized religion which Jim felt was full of routines that lacked any real meaning or relevance to his life. He thought of the priest who had presided at his father's funeral and how he droned on and on with platitudes about eternity and love but made absolutely no effort to really learn anything about his father. Vietnam had been the most influential experience of his dad's life and over the years he had helped out many friends and neighbors. But there was no mention of any of that and it was as if the priest was cranking out yet another generic ceremony. The only good thing was that his mother had seemed comforted by it all. He put those thoughts aside as he sat looking at Carol and wondered if Sean had maybe sat in this same seat years ago when the job had ordered him to the counseling unit and if he had brought his can of "Coke" with him.

"So, what can I do for you today?" Carol's question interrupted Jim's train of thought.

He didn't know quite how to handle this and struggled for the right words. She was no doubt accustomed to hearing about broken marriages or drinking problems or even issues in dealing with the relentless exposure to the death and devastation that were constants in this line of work. But how do you tell someone that you dream about people you have feelings for but don't even know and neighborhoods you've never been to yet are somehow vaguely familiar? Jim felt like he possessed firsthand knowledge of things that haven't even existed in 100 years. And he wanted to finally have the relief of sharing these fantasies with *someone* if only for the reassurance that that's all they were, like characters in a movie everyone in the audience could relate to even though they weren't real. But from the look of the poster on the wall and the pamphlets on the desk this looked like a place to help people with "normal" problems, people like Timmy, and not to explain the vague, ethereal issue he was wrestling with.

"I've been feeling run down and a bit confused about things lately," Jim tentatively started. Not only was that true but it also gave him free access to his escape clause of not sleeping well.

"Have you had a lot of fires recently?"

"No, nothing unusual," it had nothing to do with the number of fires. He knew he could handle that. It was the things he had "seen" at those fires.

"Anything going on at home, health or family problems?"

"No. My mother is fine, my dad died years ago. I just had my annual department medical and everything looked good."

"You eating ok? Exercising?"

"Yeah, I'm eating fine and working out a few times a week." Jim thought of the massive shrimp parmesan hero they recently had at lunch. He couldn't imagine *any* firefighter losing his appetite. That would be one really screwed up guy. He pictured running through Astoria Park and how he could sense the history that sat beneath the powerful currents of water in the East River.

"Any changes coming up that might be causing you some anxiety?"

"Well, I'm getting married in a few months," Jim could see Carol's eyes light up right through her wire rimmed glasses as soon as he mentioned this, like she had suddenly uncovered the "Ah Ha!" moment of discovery.

"So, how do you feel about that?"

Jim knew exactly how he felt about that. He also knew that wasn't at all why he had come here. It wasn't about Laura or any doubts he had about her. In fact, she had proven to be a great addition to his life. Any doubts he harbored about marriage stemmed from inside himself, not from Laura.

"Actually, it's not a problem." He wanted to cut that topic off right there and keep Carol from pursuing something that was beside the point. But what, exactly, was the point? And just how much did he want to confide in this woman? He looked at Carol and realized that this was a nice woman who really wanted to help him. For a moment he wished that he had a difficulty that could actually be identified and attacked like a difficult ex-wife or a drinking problem, the kinds of things that the other guys in the waiting area were probably dealing with. And in that same moment he realized that this had been a mistake, that for all her good intentions Carol was not the answer.

"I've been having a lot of trouble sleeping." There, I said it. A moment of relief. Jim felt like he had bailed himself out for now. He maintained his privacy and kept all of his strange obsessions within. But that sense of relief was quickly overwhelmed by a sense of loss, a feeling that even here in this gentle atmosphere with decent, well-intended people like Carol and Steve he could not share the things he experienced. Perhaps, he thought, he was beyond all help.

Carol proceeded to examine the sleeping issue. She thoroughly explored all of the usual physical factors that might contribute to the problem. The erratic work hours were always suspect along with the stress of the job. Jim seemed like he was keeping himself in good shape, but she touched on the effects of caffeine and recommended that he consider using melatonin to get back to more restful sleep patterns. But as she spoke, Carol sensed that Jim was harboring some deep, yet to be defined issues that went beyond the tangible influences she was addressing. And that would require some subtle digging to get to.

Jim pretended to listen to her with interest. But he was becoming increasingly antsy as he sat there in his well-padded chair. He had thrown Carol a bone to distract her and couldn't wait to get out of the office, to get out of Manhattan altogether for that matter and return to the solace and comfort of his Queens apartment. This won't work. It was a mistake.

"Tell you what Jim. There could be a lot of reasons for sleeping issues. When we work out our problems it's kind of like peeling an onion, very often there are a number of layers to get through" Carol suggested, hoping to leave the door open to possibly start the digging she knew he would be adverse to.

"We've made a nice start today just getting to know each other. Here's my card, give me a call to set up a time to meet again. My schedule is pretty much open and I'm available for you."

She stood up to shake his hand and presented both the card and a "Learning to be Your Own Best Friend" pamphlet to Jim. Her handshake was warm and soft and as he looked again through those wire rimmed glasses, he could see the depth of sincerity in her eyes.

"Thanks, I really appreciate your help" Jim responded. Although the entire experience had proven to be a disappointment, he genuinely valued her efforts.

Jim could see that Timmy was gone from the waiting area as he was making his way out of the office. Maybe he's in one of the rooms spilling out his marital troubles to one of the other counselors. He nodded to Steve at the front desk who immediately responded with that same bright smile and an energetic thumbs up sign and then made his way down the long grey stairway back to the street. He walked down the steps much quicker than he had going up.

Jim paused on the sidewalk and looked at the business card in his hand. It read *Carol Fitzpatrick, FDNY Counseling Unit* in neat black lettering and had the red and blue department logo carefully centered under her phone number. What a nice lady, he thought.

He tossed the card and the pamphlet into the trash can that he passed on the corner.

Chapter 7

Jim woke up early on Wednesday morning. He was looking forward to the day in part because it would allow him to move away from the disappointment of yesterday's counseling experience. But mostly he was excited about meeting Laura in the city. The game plan was to hook up in midtown where they would do some clothes shopping, go out for lunch, and then just meander around Manhattan. For once he wouldn't be just sitting uncomfortably in some fashionable boutique and watching as Laura tried on various outfits. He had shared that experience with her in the past and usually found that after the fourth or fifth dress his mind would wander and his response to Laura's "How does this one look?" would become somewhat mechanical. In his mind the mauves and the cerulean and the fuchsias would all start to blend together into one continuous mix. But he was always patient with the whole process since he realized that Laura's work world demanded that she maintain the proper look, unlike his job which granted a certain amount of status to worn out "salty" looking garb. And he also got a kick out of seeing the pleasure she took in the process.

This morning Laura would be playing the vital role of fashion evaluator and Jim would be doing the modeling. He hadn't purchased a new suit in years and with the wedding coming up soon, Laura was going to guide him through the trauma of shopping. It wasn't like he was opposed to stylish dress. He could appreciate the sharp lines of a suit if Leonardo DiCaprio or Johnny Depp was wearing it. But sartorial splendor had no relevance to his daily life. Sweatshirts comprised a large portion of his wardrobe. And he could whip out the occasional sports coat when necessary, which was usually for some event the Whitacre's invited him to. Comfort was the key word in Jim's apparel and normally he'd rather stick toothpicks in his eyes than go clothes shopping. But today he found himself excited about the prospect of the new suit. He envisioned sliding his arms into the softly lined sleeves of some worsted marvel, buttoning it up, and then staring into one of those full-length mirrors that let you see yourself from all different angles. It would be kind of like slipping into a new identity and, given the identity he'd been struggling with lately, that wouldn't be such a bad idea.

Since they were going to be moving around to a number of different locations in the city Jim decided to take the subway rather than drive. He always drove to the firehouse, and it had been a long time since he had actually gotten on a train. Before he became a firefighter, though, he had commuted every day on the subway to Manhattan just like thousands of other New Yorkers. And his memories of those trips were not pleasant ones. He had mastered the skill of gracefully scooting into an unimaginably crowded car without stepping on anyone and learned to avoid eye contact with fellow passengers even as he shared closer physical intimacy with them than he did with some of his previous girlfriends. And he developed the ability to maintain a grip on any pole or handle that would keep him and four or five other people from falling when the train suddenly bucked. Jim remembered the underground subway tunnel as a dark, uninviting realm

104

that nobody ever visited, a space of mesmerizing blackness that raced by the car windows as the train sped through, punctuated by the occasional dingy yellow light bulb and an endless array of vertical, dust covered I-beams.

So, it was a pleasant surprise when he arrived at the elevated train station that sat a few blocks from his apartment and saw that there were very few people waiting on the platform. Rush hour was over, and it looked like it wasn't going to be a battle just to get into one of the train cars. He enjoyed the fresh morning air from his lofty perch and watched the traffic moving below as he waited for the train. Jim had forgotten about the unique vista of the city you experienced when you traveled on the elevated train tracks. Unlike the darkened underground subway caverns, you could casually observe the streets and buildings as they glided by and appreciate a view of urban spaces that were normally hidden. One could see piles of long forgotten debris that had been left on roofs decades ago and pass by dusty apartment windows that sat just a few feet away from the speeding trains, the privacy of their interiors guarded by a few flimsy shades. Jim often wondered how on earth people managed to actually live in those buildings with the constant noise and vibration that issued from the end-less barrage of passing trains.

Like anything else they were constantly exposed to, regular subway riders quickly took such views for granted. They no longer saw them, or really cared for that matter, once they became mesmerized by the steady grind of commuting. Jim knew that the train would pass through several elevated stations in Queens before it dove into the tunnel that led to Manhattan, and he got excited to once again relish the scenery the ride had to offer. When the train arrived he got on and quickly positioned himself right by the front window of the first subway car. That was the spot he had most enjoyed when he was a boy. From there he would watch the tracks as they rolled beneath him and enjoy a sense of the speed and direction of the train as it screeched through the curves. It was as if he was driving the train himself and flying past the buildings as they rushed past in a blur.

Jim remained at that front window as the train moved through Astoria and cut a path through blocks of the small apartment houses and large commercial buildings that lie below. He looked at the tar covered roofs as they roared past with a perspective he hadn't possessed as a child. Back then they were just large dark surfaces that covered the buildings. Now, after years on the job, he viewed those roofs as places he would be working on if the building was burning. As the other passengers read their newspapers or just stared off into the distance, Jim envisioned himself carefully maneuvering to a spot directly above a roaring blaze in one of the top floor apartments and cutting holes in the roof to vent the smoke and flames that would push out furiously from below. He could hear the loud roar of the power saw as he cut those openings and could smell the scent of the tar that would be kicked up onto his boots. He imagined the sound of shattering glass as he smashed the skylights and the tinkling of the glass shards as they bounced down the stairwells. One of the things that appealed to Jim in his line of work was the hands on, almost sensual, interaction with physical experiences. He liked the feel of holding a tool in his hands and using it to force a door open, demolish a window, or pull down a ceiling. Smoke, water, melted tar, charred wood, these were all part of his collective work memory. And in a way he was probably not even aware of, those experiences provided a focus for him, an opportunity to concentrate on the moment and avoid any thoughts that might be troubling him.

As the train worked its way through the Long Island City section of Queens, the low-lying buildings were suddenly replaced with a view of the high rises that had sprung up in recent years. The neighborhood had grimy industrial roots but had been gentrified from the spillover of midtown residents. It was as if the borough of Manhattan had put on too much weight and its love handles rolled over the East River out to the adjacent borough. The result was an incongruous mix of old buildings and tall modern apartment houses that shared an incredible view of midtown but had few of the delicacies that Manhattan had to offer.

At this point the train was engulfed by the tunnel that led under the river and Jim lost his view of daylight and all the outside scenery. He sat down and slowly rocked with the movement of the train and tried without success to actually hear the conductor's voice on the intercom when he announced the upcoming stops. He did hear the loud "ding-dong" chime as the doors opened at those stops and wondered why one sound could be so clear and the others so carefully disguised. Little wonder that tourists often found the subways so confusing.

As the train rattled through the dark, he regarded the few passengers who were sharing the car with him. There were two really attractive women sitting nearby, both of whom were careful not to meet his gaze. One was model thin, a classic beauty with long blond hair who had no doubt spent much of her adult life fending off the advances of many men. Jim figured that the spandex outfit of the voluptuous woman who sat near her probably attracted catcalls from construction workers, and firefighters for that matter, in her jaunts around the city. Although he was pleased to be with Laura, Jim never lost his appreciation for viewing attractive women. "First you check your emails then you check your females," Sean always said.

There were a few men in suits who he analyzed from a fashion perspective and a guy wearing a stained sweatshirt who looked like he might be a painter on his way to some job. And, way over on the last seat, a woman who looked and smelled like a homeless person. Kind of the usual cast of New York characters and, accustomed as he was to driving by himself into the city, Jim was fascinated by it all and wondered if any of them viewed life as he did or if they just fit in without questioning anything.

He got off at the stop for 5th Avenue and 59th Street and worked his way up to the street. Jim never quite got over the shock of the sudden transition from his sleepy Queens neighborhood to the intense ebb and flow of Manhattan. And now emerging from the subway the change seemed even more extreme than when he drove onto the city. The lines of traffic and masses of moving people were overwhelming and exciting at the same time. He was supposed to meet Laura on 59th Street, but with the crowds of people, it seemed like trying to hook up with someone on a busy night in Disneyland. But there, off in the distance and surrounded by pedestrians, he immediately picked her out as she was moving in a direction away from him. Jim could identify her by her walk alone. Even if she had been wearing some kind of disguise, he could instantly recognize her by the crisp, determined way she moved. She suddenly turned in his direction and, without his even calling out for her, she was able to quickly spot him in the crowd as if there was some kind of radar emanating between them.

Jim could smell her familiar sweet scent as he hugged her.

"So, are you ready for today?" Laura asked.

"I've got my credit card all warmed up and I'm all ready to go," he responded.

She was fashionably dressed in a dark, well-tailored pants suit matched with the perfectly selected accoutrements. It seemed like ninety nine percent of the women in Manhattan wore dark clothing. Black was the official uniform of the borough and served both as a fashion statement and a decoy that instantly took ten pounds off of everyone's profile. As usual Jim was informally attired in chino pants, a long sleeve dress shirt and, in his only concession to the fact that he was going suit shopping, a pair of shiny black dress shoes in place of his beloved sneakers. To the casual observer the two of them looked more like a successful businesswoman meeting with a contractor for a plumbing estimate than a couple who were soon to be married.

They started walking down 5th Avenue towards a men's shop on 48th Street. The sidewalks were full of pedestrians who glanced anxiously at their watches and cell phones as they squeezed in lunch, shopping, and other chores before they were due back in the office. They carried brief cases and shoulder bags and enormous containers of coffee, all moving in rapid New York fashion. In contrast Jim and Laura walked slowly and casually glanced into the store windows. They passed Rockefeller Center, a place that Jim always associated with being very cold regardless of what the temperature happened to be. He had memories of his parents taking him there as a small child and shivering in the plaza while he stared in awe at the size of the Christmas tree. When Jim and Laura gazed up at the grey spires of St Patrick's Cathedral, he remembered what it looked like inside. He pictured the colors in the enormous stained-glass windows and the tall marble arches that soared up to the ceiling like they were pathways to heaven. Little wonder that people went there to find solace and meaning. Lately he certainly could have used some of that solace.

Laura seemed very alive and excited as she took in the sights. Jim could see that she was really enjoying being away from work and savoring the simple pleasure of their walk. He wondered if on some level she was not as determined to follow her career path as he originally thought. And that was a reassuring thought because if she was pondering her own confusions in life, she could no doubt be receptive to some of the things he was wrestling with.

Those thoughts were put on hold once they arrived at the men's shop. As he stood on the sidewalk and looked at the store Jim could instantly see that this was no off the rack, Macy's kind of place. Brandon's Men's Atrium had occupied this space for the past eighty years and the old, gilded sign above the entranceway had not changed in that time except for the occasional touch up of the classic gold lettering. Two large black iron pilasters stood like sentinels on both sides of a large wooden doorway and gave the impression that one didn't just walk into the place. It was more like you were to be ushered inside by some formal Englishman with a tape measure hanging from his shoulders who would size you up and determine your worthiness to enter. The large display windows held a number of mannequins sporting impeccable suits, perfectly knotted ties, and tailored shirts, all without a wrinkle in sight. They stood in confident poses with soulless eyes that looked off into the distance as if the mere mortals who admired the clothing displays from the sidewalk were not worth acknowledging. Jim instantly felt underdressed, like he had shown up for the junior prom in basketball shorts.

They entered and were immediately met with the scent of fresh carpet. As a firefighter Jim had learned to look for linoleum or masonry flooring whenever he fought a fire inside a store. Those were the paths that were most often used by customers and called for a resilient type of floor covering. And more importantly when the shit hit the fan you could quickly determine how to get out of the place just by feeling for those surfaces with your boot. For the most part the carpeted areas were located by the merchandise on the side aisles which weren't subjected to the same constant pounding of foot traffic. However, Brandon's Atrium was completely carpeted in a plush, wall to wall overlay that embraced their feet as they sunk into its soft mauve fiber. Jim looked down at his shiny black dress shoes and thought about how good it would feel to run on such a well-padded surface and just how bad the static electricity shock would be if he touched one of the metal racks.

They stood for just a brief moment before a salesman approached.

"Good morning and welcome to Brandon's! I'm Carlo, how may I be of assistance?"

Carlo was middle aged and thin and had an endearing white smile that beamed from his closely shaved face. He was wearing a dark blue outfit that had been so carefully tailored it looked like he hadn't dressed that morning but dipped into some kind of molten suit juice. His tie and pocket handkerchief matched in a shade of violet that perfectly fit the suit. Jim wondered if he bled violet if he happened to nick himself when he shaved.

"Hi! We're here to do some suit shopping," Laura responded. She and Carlo immediately recognized each other as fellow fashionistas. Their dark suits were almost the same color and each outfit reeked of style and taste. Carlo was a slightly built man, and it was almost as if the two of them could just swap suits and no one would notice the difference.

"And just what might you be interested in?" Carlo asked. He noted Jim's informal attire and looked at him like he had just stepped on a dog turd.

"Ah, something in a 42 regular," Jim quickly responded as if to say, "let's just get this over with," his original excitement diminished by the fact that he felt a bit alienated by the ambiance of the place.

"We're getting married in a few months so maybe something classy and formal?" Laura said to Carlo.

"Excellent! Why don't you follow me?" And they did, as Laura walked next to Carlo and charmed him in that type of pleasant, engaging conversation she had refined in her business dealings and was so good at improvising in a negotiation.

Jim quietly followed a few steps behind them and watched with a sense of relief and appreciation as Laura artfully steered Carlo away from the racks of the $1,400 Italian masterpieces he initially led them to. That was Laura, always looking out for him and willing to compromise her style to fit his needs. She was one of the few people in his life that he really trusted. Jim briefly thought about Carol in the counseling unit and how her eyes lit up when he mentioned that he was soon getting married. How wrong she was. But it wasn't her fault. It was those *other* things that troubled and confused him, things he chose not to share with anyone out of fear or embarrassment.

By the time he tried on the fourth suit, Jim was getting a bit worn out by the whole process. Finally, though, the fifth one seemed to be the magic number. Carlo and Laura managed to pick out a classic, pin stripped coat that fit all the parameters. It cost more than Jim would normally choose to spend, but even he had to admit that he looked really sharp as he viewed himself from all of the angles in the mirror. Laura liked it and even Carlo with his taste for high octane garb was impressed. Jim felt that it fit just fine but this was an establishment that would not even consider allowing a customer to leave with one of their suits unless they had carefully addressed any tailoring deficiencies however slight they might be. That would be like a new Porsche leaving the dealer with dirt on its windows. Jim stepped away from the mirror and Carlo proceeded to make a series of chalk marks on the precise spots that had to be let out or taken in. He tightened up for a moment when Carlo stretched the tape measure from the cuff up to his crouch and thought about all of the homophobic comments the guys at the firehouse would make if they could observe this moment.

"I think you look great. When I get a chance, I'm going to

pick up a tie for you that would go great with this suit," Jim was glad to hear from Laura as they were leaving the store. That meant one less thing he would have to shop for. To him a suit could at least keep you warm. A tie was just another functionless thing that restricted you and he couldn't imagine spending a lot of time looking for one. He also knew that any tie Laura purchased would absolutely be an excellent choice, and obscenely expensive.

Carlo flashed his warm smile again as they were leaving, content with the knowledge that he had serviced a satisfied customer and at the same time rescued a fashion challenged man from a lifetime of pedestrian style. As Jim and Laura walked toward the exit, their feet made absolutely no sound as they stepped over the thick carpet. The fresh air back out on the sidewalk provided an abrupt and pleasant change from the stuffy, carpet scented interior of the store. Jim had a brief image of his childhood in Brooklyn and how refreshing it felt to escape out to the street from the stifling apartments he grew up in.

It was a nice day, and rather than eating lunch nearby they decided to take advantage of their time together and just meander around the city. They headed uptown at a leisurely pace just enjoying each other's presence and sharing that kind of silent connection known only by people who were totally at ease with each other.

"So, what did you do yesterday?" Laura inquired as they walked.

"Oh, nothing special. Worked out, got some bills paid."

Jim tensed up knowing that he was holding his counseling visit secretly within himself, and this from a woman who shared so much with him. Someone he was going to be married to for goodness sakes. He could feel the perspiration forming under his armpits as he strained to keep up an indifferent appearance. But there was no denying the chasm that existed between them when it came to this topic.

"Well, I had a tough day at the office. You remember that guy I work with, Richard? I told you about him."

"Yeah, I remember you don't like him," Jim was relieved to be drawn back into a conversation that took his mind off of the counseling experience.

"He's been a real jerk lately. You should have seen his performance at the meeting."

Jim could see that whatever had happened at that meeting was clearly still upsetting to Laura and although he wanted to hear what she had to say about it he found himself momentarily distracted. Just a few paces away he spotted a young woman who was walking briskly on the sidewalk in front of them. She had a very attractive figure, but it was something else that caught his eye. The long dark hair that flowed down beneath the straw hat she was wearing bounced with each rapid step she took. Those bobbing curls evoked something in Jim. He had an eye for good looking women like the ones he had seen on the subway, but this was different. Her hair was a vague reminder of something though he had no idea of what. A connection, a closeness, but one he just could not explain.

"So in the middle of our meeting, I'm giving the results of an analysis I've been working on for weeks and he just interrupts me and starts giving everyone his opinion. I swear, he wouldn't have done it if it was one of the men giving the presentation."

Laura's words interrupted Jim's focus on the woman's hair. He looked at her and could see that she was still very pissed off about the incident with Richard. But here he was, once again experiencing one of those very brief but very persistent moments that had always shadowed him. He wanted so badly to tell her about it. But tell her what? How could he explain something that was so much a part of himself yet was totally undefinable? He felt like he was bursting at the seams with all of the thoughts hidden inside him.

"Anyway, I stayed calm, looked right at him, and finished my talk. I think they liked what I had given them, and I know that I wasn't the only person in that conference room who thought that Richard was a jerk."

Bursting at the seams, bursting at the seams, the words bounced inside Jim's head as he listened to Laura and they continued their walk. Before long they arrived at the corner of 59th Street and 5th Avenue and were right on the fringes of Central Park which sat like a large green oasis in the middle of all the Manhattan high rise buildings. They paused for a while to listen to an elderly Chinese man who was sitting by the park entrance and playing some kind of exotic looking stringed instrument. He produced a gentle, soothing sound and slowly rocked his body back and forth as he performed. Jim found it all very relaxing and he threw a dollar into the glass jar that sat at the man's feet who immediately bowed his head and offered a grateful smile.

When they left the park entrance and headed down 59th Street, Jim picked up the scent of the horses before he actually spotted them. As he looked down the block there were a number of white carriages all lined up at the curb. They were hitched to black and white horses who passively stood by as their drivers beckoned to pedestrians hoping to recruit some fares. The carriage's canvas roofs were folded down and Jim could see that the padded seats in the back of the cabs were just the right size for two people to fit comfortably together. Here, right in the middle of a bustling city, was a throwback, a low tech, slow speed vehicle that was geared to a leisurely jaunt around the park rather than rushing to the next urgent appointment, vital meeting, or unappealing work assignment. Although he had grown up in the city, he had never been in one of these cabs and had kind of dismissed them as something a tourist from Indiana would put on a list of things to cram in over the course of a frantic four-day visit to the city along with the Statue of Liberty, the Empire State Building, and the Circle Line cruise around Manhattan. Like many native New Yorkers there were a lot of local attractions that Jim had not actually experienced in years or had totally ignored.

"How about I take you and your lady for a ride?" the driver of the first cab said to Jim as he walked past but he just smiled at the man and waved him away.

"Come on, neither of us has ever done this! It'll be my treat," Laura offered. As usual she was always the more committed one. Jim eyed the snug looking cab seats and decided, what the hell. He really did want to do this but, as with a lot of things, it took a nudge from Laura to get him to actually do anything.

Jim had never ridden a horse. His equestrian background was limited to a childhood experience of sitting on a brightly painted plastic steed as it spun around a carousel with organ music blaring in the background. Still, as he stood and observed the horse, he felt a connection to the animal. He would have liked to reach out and pet it but figured that was something most passengers would not do and might be upsetting to the cab driver. He looked at its enormous nostrils and noted the fine eyelashes over its eyes and observed how the ears would suddenly shift position in response to any sudden noise. Jim felt the enormous power in this creature but at the same time he could sense its gentle nature. It stirred up a fleeting memory deep in his mind, an awareness of something that he could not quite define and he quickly dismissed the thought.

Jim felt totally relaxed as he settled down on the plush seat next to Laura. The greenery and quiet of the park was an immediate and refreshing transition from the noise and congestion of the city streets that lie just beyond the park walls. As they rode on at a leisurely pace the only sound they heard was the steady clopping of the horse's hoofs on the pavement, a timeless sound that added to their enjoyment. The only interruption came from the blast of a horn from a yellow taxi as it sped through the park. That startled Jim more than the horse. And they got some dirty looks from a cyclist who apparently felt that the carriage had passed by him too closely. But overall, it was a peaceful affair that entirely absorbed Jim. As he sat there with Laura at his side, he enjoyed the lush trees and intricate stone underpasses that were scattered throughout the park. He looked at the spokes of the wagon wheels that spun rapidly beneath him and watched as the horses' haunches slowly moved with each step he took. There was a certain comfort and familiarity to the experience which was strange given that his background was totally devoid of wagons or horses. But for the moment he was tranquil, living in the moment, and thoroughly enjoying Laura's presence. When she said, "screw Richard, this is really great," he knew that she too was really into it and had put all of her work frustrations on hold.

Their time in the park energized both of them and when they left, they started walking along 59th Street towards the West Side. The street served as a clear dividing line that cut right through the city and separated the green sanctuary on their right from the sun blocking high rise buildings on their left. Before long they arrived at Columbus Circle which marked the western border of the park.

"So where do you want to eat?" Laura inquired.

"I don't know, why don't we just walk for a while and see what we come up with?"

For once Jim wasn't stuck on just locating the nearest diner or Italian restaurant. The carriage experience had freed up his usual reluctance to try something new, a development he realized was again largely due to Laura's influence.

Maybe it stemmed from the overall pleasantries of the carriage ride or perhaps from the simple ease that he felt sitting next to Laura in that cab. But for once Jim was untroubled by his vague sense of familiarity with things that were not normally a part of his life. It didn't matter at the moment that the wagon and horse had stirred some semblance of a confusing memory. On some level he could write it all off to images of the westerns he had seen on television or watched at a movie theatre. But deep inside, he also knew that those cinematic episodes could not explain all of the other images he had been dealing with for so long.

There was no one moment when he finally decided to speak openly with her. As they walked away from the park it was more like a gradual determination to finally broach the topic when they sat down for lunch. They were heading up Central Park West when he arrived at that catharsis. The effort of holding it all in had finally worn away his resolve and overwhelmed his need to suppress it all.

"What kind of food would you like for lunch?" Laura asked.

"I don't know. I'm up for anything so I'll leave it up to you," food was the last thing on his mind at the moment.

"Someone at work mentioned a Brazilian restaurant that's not far from here," she replied.

"Yeah, that sounds great," Jim had absolutely no idea what constituted Brazilian food. All he could picture was a soccer team that hadn't done too well in recent years.

As they headed up Central Park West Jim started to feel nervous, almost like he was going to a job interview or about to be called up to the principal's office. He reasoned that this was a woman who really cared for him and would try to understand what he wanted to talk about. But he knew that what he was about to talk about made absolutely no sense and could prove to be embarrassing. He glanced over at the inviting trees and greenery of the park which calmed him down and reminded him of the great time they had just shared there.

"It should be just down the next block," Laura's words brought him back from his musings.

They turned on the side street and spotted the dark green awning for Fogo de Chao. When they entered, they were met by a smiling young hostess who led them to a table in the rear of the restaurant. It was very quiet, in fact there was only one other occupied table and that was all the way at the front where an elderly couple sat reading their menus. It was lunchtime and Jim wondered if the lack of customers reflected the quality of the food or, for that matter, if they did in fact have Brazilian chiefs. It seemed that so many of the "Italian" restaurants he frequented had tasty food that was actually prepared by a largely Hispanic kitchen staff. But he liked the feeling of the place. There was a soft light glowing from the green lamp that hung over the table and the wall right next to them had the kind of old exposed brick that he missed in the head-to- toe sheetrock ambiance of his Astoria apartment.

Neither Laura nor Jim generally liked to drink at lunch. They were both busy, productive people and caffeine was more their choice of stimulant to get them through the afternoon. But today seemed like a special day with the suit purchase and the carriage ride so they indulged, a glass of wine for Laura and an Antarctica Cerveja for Jim. That was a Brazilian beer with a high alcohol content which gave him a quick buzz from his empty stomach, but also relaxed him. When the menus came Jim saw that the various dishes were listed by their Brazilian names but, in a concession to any culinary challenged patrons, the place had thoughtfully described each dish in plain English. Laura settled on Fraldinha, which Jim learned was sirloin, and he chose a thing called Robalo Grelhado which sounded like it should have been the name of a soccer star but was actually a sea bass dish. He had seen enough steak and sausage at the firehouse recently and this was definitely not a "lets order some more buffalo wings and Budweiser," kind of place.

As he sipped his beer Jim decided to break the ice.

"I was in the city yesterday,"

"Really? Where'd you go?" Laura asked.

"Downtown in the SoHo area."

"What were you doing there?" Laura knew enough about the area that Ladder 57 covered to realize it couldn't have had anything to do with work.

"I decided to go and speak to a job counselor."

"Are you actually thinking about changing careers? I thought you liked what you did," Laura responded, somewhat surprised at what she was hearing. But when firefighters used the word "job" it was just another way of referring to the department as in "my cousin is coming on the job" or "the job is getting to be a pain in the ass." Naturally in Laura's world a job counselor meant something entirely different.

"Are you thinking about transferring out to Queens? That would save you a lot of commuting," Laura was taken aback and tried to figure out exactly what Jim was saying.

"No, it wasn't an employment thing, more of like a different kind of counselor," Jim cautiously responded. He knew that he was starting to thread on some precarious ground and took another gulp of his beer.

"What do you mean, a different kind of counselor?" Laura groped more anxiously for an explanation.

"The fire department has people who are supposed to help, they're sort of like mind counselors,"

"You mean like a shrink?"

Jim delayed for a moment before he responded. Once Laura used the shrink word that seemed to make it official. He *had* gone and visited a shrink, or therapist, or analyst, or whatever the hell you wanted to call it, something he thought he could have never envisioned himself doing and he felt exposed and embarrassed.

"Yeah, kind of a shrink," he reluctantly answered.

"Jim, what's the matter?" Laura asked and he could see the sudden alarm in her face. But at the same time there was something deeper in the way she responded. Her words were spoken with a genuine level of concern for him and that was certainly reassuring. Maybe she would understand. Maybe it was possible in some way to explain all of it to her.

Laura's confusion was quickly replaced by a deep sense of distress. She knew that Jim was very nervous about the upcoming marriage. She wondered if she had pushed too far in this and if Jim was the proverbial square peg she had hoped to fit into a round hole. And just what other things had Jim done or thought about and chosen not to share with her?

"Jim, if you really don't want to get married, please tell me now before we go any further with this," she said.

"No, that's not it at all. In fact, that's the only thing that the counselor seemed interested in talking about."

"Then what is it? Please, talk to me," Laura pleaded.

Jim wondered where the hell he was going to start. The dreams? His childhood memories? The more recent episodes? They were all different but at the same time fit a consistent pattern.

"I have these moments." he cautiously began.

"Yeah? What kind of moments?"

"You know, sort of confusing moments."

"Confusing in what way?" Laura had no idea what he meant.

"Sometimes I feel disconnected, like I'm somewhere else. Not all the time but when it happens it's upsetting."

"Well, I think we all feel that way sometimes. You've been working a lot lately and it sounds like most of the guys you work with are good people but the truth is you don't really have all that much in common with them. You've never been a really good fit for the fire department. Maybe all the hours in the firehouse are catching up with you."

Laura's words make sense. But Jim knew he hadn't really made himself clear.

"How long have you been feeling this way?" she asked.

"Always."

"Always?"

"Yeah, as long as I can remember."

"Do you ever feel that way when you're with me?"

"No, never." Jim meant that, though he knew there were moments when he thought her father seemed to be on another planet.

"What kinds of things were upsetting you?"

This took some thought. Should he start in grade school? When the teacher asked the class to draw a picture of their "happy home" all of the other kids created sunny images of little houses with smoke puffing from the chimneys and cheerful stick figures romping about on grass lawns. He had been embarrassed to show what he came up with: a drawing of what certainly looked like the interior of a 19th century tenement kitchen although he had never actually seen one. How about the bouncing dark curls on the woman he spotted on their walk from the store? That was sure to go over big with Laura, his fascination with a woman he knew nothing about but who just happened to be walking in front of them. Or should he tell her about the experiences at work? Recently some pretty vivid ones had popped up.

"Well, for example I was in the basement of the firehouse a couple of days ago…"

Jim started to tell her about the coal bin and how he could even smell the coal that wasn't really there and that led to talking about the old gas lighting fixture in the store fire. He even mentioned the carriage ride they had just been on and how he knew nothing about horses and everything about them at the same time. He had opened the floodgate and held back nothing and as Laura sat in silence listening to him, he thought of Timmy sitting in the waiting area of the counseling unit and how he had unloaded a litany of his pent-up issues.

When he had finished talking Jim felt relieved. He was resigned to the fact that he had opened up his mind to Laura. He had laid it all out on the table and in unspoken words had communicated to her "Accept this or reject this. But this is me. Do what you want with it".

Laura was uncertain of how to respond or even of what to make of the things Jim had just described. She could not really understand what he had experienced but there was no doubting the pain and resignation that she saw in his face.

"Jim, you've always had a very active imagination. That's one of the things I like about you. You're not just a guy who fights fires, you're always curious about how things work or where they come from. Maybe that's all this is. You read a lot of history books and love watching movies, maybe you don't give yourself enough credit for the creative mind you have."

Laura's words were reassuring but even as she spoke them, she wondered just how much else she didn't know about this man she cared so much for.

"How about if we take a few days off and get out of the city for a while? Sounds like you could use a break," she offered.

"No, that's not going to work. You know you've got a lot of

important stuff coming up on your job in the next few weeks."

"Well maybe it's time for you to think long term. I know you don't like to do that, but do you really see yourself staying in your job forever? And you have such mixed feelings about the city. Aren't you curious about what it would be like to live somewhere else? Like Colorado for instance. We can always just pick up and start a life somewhere elsewhere."

That was pure Laura talking, always the one to be making the plans or at least staying open to other possibilities in life. Jim knew he was somewhat deficient in those areas. He seemed to take life as it came from week to week rather than step back and actually choose a direction. It also reinforced something he liked about her. She was willing to break away from the life that had been laid out for her: her job, New York, perhaps even the expectations of her family, or more precisely, the things her father valued.

And, yes, he did like Colorado. He had been out there a few years ago on a skiing trip. It was a wide-open state, a place where you could see the snow covered Rockies from Interstate 25 even though you were miles away. The sky was limitless there, a free and unrestricted space that stretched off into the distance and was so different from the confining forests of the East Coast and the congested streets of the city. It seemed like a place that would provide a physical and mental release where any troubling thoughts would just drift away over the rolling plains.

"Maybe we can talk some more about this another time. The lunch was great," Jim had shot his load for now and wanted to move away from the topic.

"Sure Jim. You know you can talk to me about anything," Laura responded knowing full well that he was reverting right back to his normal, noncommittal mode.

After lunch Jim and Laura walked down the side street

together. The traffic noise was an abrupt change from the quiet of the restaurant and the dinner talk had put both into a pensive mood. Jim's initial sense of relief was replaced by a feeling of exhaustion, kind of like the way he felt after a long run in Astoria Park. Laura was confused. She was used to attacking a problem head on. Competing in sports, studying in college, analyzing financial statements, these were all tasks that had called for logical choices and concrete steps to achieve success. The things that Jim spoke of required a different kind of approach if she was to truly understand or to be of any help to him.

Laura had an early meeting scheduled at work the next morning and Jim was facing a dental appointment in Queens at 9 AM. They had planned on heading back and spending the night at their own apartments and then getting together later in the week. This had seemed to be the most practical arrangement and now had the additional advantage of giving both of them some time on their own to digest all they had discussed. Jim knew that nothing had really been resolved but felt like a lot had been accomplished. He had opened up to her and felt closer than ever. When they parted, he could smell the scent in her hair as they hugged. He held her tightly and buried his face in her essence knowing that today she had served as more than his confidant. She was also a safe refuge from a confusing world.

Jim watched Laura as she walked toward the bus stop to catch the crosstown line back to the East Side and then he headed towards the subway entrance for his trip to Queens. But on a sudden whim he turned around abruptly and decided to walk back toward Central Park. He wanted to clear out his head a bit and enjoy one last look at the green space he had so much enjoyed. As he walked along the low stone wall that ran along the edge of the park he glanced over at the lush woods and stone paths that twisted through the meadows. Jim continued walking north until the continuous line of modern buildings on his left was suddenly interrupted by the sight of the old Dakota Apartments. He paused and looked at the building which had sat in splendid grandeur on the corner of 72nd Street and Central Park West for well over a century. Jim always liked this structure and how it contrasted with the predictable architecture of the surrounding neighborhood. He stood in the street and admired the building's steep gables and intriguing dormers. The place looked like it belonged in a fairy tale, a throwback to an era when its terracotta niches and cast-iron balconies towered over the park in castle-like elegance.

For a split second his view was suddenly interrupted by another image. It came and went so fast it was as if he had just imagined it. But there was no denying its presence. In that moment he had not seen the building as it now existed but how it once was. And in that view the Dakota was not just another apartment house in a crowded neighborhood but a structure standing by itself surrounded by open, undeveloped land that contained no other buildings at all. It was a fleeting image but so much was crammed into it. Across the street in Central Park, men in bowlers and women in long dresses skated on a frozen pond. Horse drawn omnibuses plodded along Central Park West making their way north through the wooded scenery. The building was the same but everything around it was different.

The view came and went in a heartbeat, but the brief image left Jim shaken and weak at the knees. He grabbed onto the corner lamppost to steady himself. The cool metal surface of the pole was a reassuring presence that grounded him and secured his presence back onto a crowded, 21st century-street. But, as always, he was groping for answers. Jim had seen old photographs of the Dakota in some of his history books. And years ago, he read an illustrated novel that contained a picture of that exact scene of the people in the park skating on the ice with the Dakota standing off in the distance. Laura was right, he did have a very active imagination. Perhaps all of these "memories" were nothing more than tiny fragments of books, TV shows, and movies he had seen. Maybe that's all it was. But the more he thought of it the more it seemed like too simple an explanation for the thoughts that had been stewing inside him for so long.

He started walking toward the subway entrance for his trip back home. Colorado was looking better and better.

Chapter 8

Laura was in good spirits when she phoned Jim the next morning. Her meeting had gone well and for once her old nemesis Richard had not pissed her off. He was suffering from a bad cold and spent the entire conference quietly sipping a cup of tea without saying a word. She was able to get her points across without his usual misogynistic interruptions.

"Dash really good Laura," Jim was having difficulty pronouncing the words. His lips and cheeks were still numb from the Novocain the dentist had injected when he repaired a filling.

"I enjoyed our time in the city yesterday," Laura said.

"Yeah, ish was great," He couldn't feel his tongue at all and wondered how he was going to eat lunch without biting it off.

"The restaurant was nice too, I hadn't eaten Brazilian food in a long time," she responded.

"Yeah, I'll have to tell Sean about that Antarctica Cerveja brew. Ish was really tasty and had a bit of a kick," He wasn't about to tell her about his side trip to the Dakota.

"Well, have a good tour tonight, Jim. I'll give you a call tomorrow."

Jim hung up the phone and started to get ready for the day. As usual he'd be leaving for work shortly after four, so he had several hours to kill. He had a hard time getting into his original plan of doing some laundry and then going for a run so instead he just plopped down on his couch to read the paper and look outside the window. There was no squirrel in sight today, just a few cats stalking through the neighborhood which probably accounted for the lack of squirrels.

When he finished his newspaper Jim reached for a book from the coffee table next to the couch. It was a thick, 450-page fire department procedural manual that he had been reading on and off for the past year. He had toyed with the idea of studying for a promotional exam for some time, but the text didn't exactly make for stimulating reading and he had a hard time getting into a serious study routine. Another commitment he'd rather not jump into. The book was an in-depth guide to firefighting, but it was presented in a dense, technical style. Sean, seldom much of a literary critic, liked to say that it had been written with a chisel which just about summed up its appeal. Within fifteen minutes Jim had refreshed some firefighting information in his mind and then promptly fallen into a deep sleep.

By the time he woke up it was too late to attack the laundry duty, but he did get in a nice run in the park which again gave him an opportunity to watch the currents of the East River flow past. It felt good to work up a sweat and to have the feeling back in his mouth. Right on schedule he headed out for the city a bit later in the afternoon. As always the familiar routine of preparing for work and commuting to midtown added some much needed structure to his life.

When Jim arrived at the firehouse, he entered the kitchen and saw Sean sitting in his usual chair chuckling over something he was reading in the Op Ed pages of the *New York Times*. That in itself was unusual since Sean was not a fan of the liberal bent of the paper so Jim figured that he must have found it lying on a subway seat on his ride to work.

"All the news that's fit to print," Sean stated in a strong tone of sarcasm as he scanned the newspaper.

"You know these guys once fired one of their editors because he had the audacity to disagree with one of their political opinions?" he added. That fact, plus the stuff he was reading in the editorial columns, fit so nicely with Sean's "it's all such bullshit" philosophy of life.

"How you been Sean?" Jim pretty much stayed out of politics.

"Good, what have you been up to?"

"I was in the city with Laura yesterday. Walked around a bit and went to a Brazilian restaurant up in the West Side," He didn't really want to talk about the suit, or the wedding for that matter.

"Brazilian?" Sean could identify with Italian, Greek, maybe even Indian. But Brazilian? It was as if Jim had said he had eaten lunch on the far side of the moon.

"Yeah. I had this new beer you might want to try. Tasty but strong. Just a few will knock you right on your ass."

"Ok, I'll have to check it out," Sean said, feigning interest. He was a man driven by his own routines and his beer preference was sacrosanct.

"Who's working tonight?" Jim inquired.

"The usual suspects. You, me, Shakespeare, one of the probies, and some guy on overtime."

"Is the barker in?"

"Yeah, let's hope he's in one of his good moods," Sean responded.

"Well, we'll see what the night has in store for us." Jim had been around long enough to know that there was no way to predict how a tour was going to go. There were nights when they barely left the firehouse and others when they went to three or more fires and got their butts kicked.

He headed up the stairs to his locker and checked the calendar that hung inside the metal door for anything that might be coming up. Not that he expected any surprises. Jim lived a relatively simple life, and it wasn't like he was going to be invited to the mayor's office next Thursday or accept the winning check from the lottery drawing on Friday. And that thought reminded him of his father who used to purchase a lottery ticket religiously every week, something he referred to as "Irish financial planning". Jim still missed his dad and smiled as he thought of him.

When he glanced to his right Jim could see Tyrone getting dressed at his locker. He called out to him and Tyrone responded with a shy wave. Jim understood that Tyrone was still in the process of finding his comfort level in the firehouse, something that he himself was still working on even after having been there for seven years. Faiella was sitting on a stool in front of his locker. His head was bowed down and it almost looked as if he was praying. On closer inspection Jim saw that he was deeply involved in a phone conversation, as always doing his Shakespeare thing. Over in the corner the guy who was working overtime had grabbed an available locker and threw in a duffel bag that contained a towel along with spare socks and underwear. This guy comes prepared, Jim thought and he wondered if he would need all that stuff tonight. When Jim reached into his locker to grab some work clothes he was met with a strong scent of smoke and body odor. He really had to attack that laundry tomorrow. That thought was interrupted by the loud "Roll call in the kitchen!" announcement on the house intercom.

When Jim arrived in the kitchen, he noted that the barker seemed somewhat distracted this evening. Maybe he was facing a desk load of paperwork or perhaps he was just in one of his moods. Either way his presence added a level of stress to the room. The Captain looked at each of his men like he was already pissed off at them. Rumor had it that he was in a bad marriage that should have run its course long ago. All the men sat at the long kitchen table regarding the Captain. All except Tyrone who stood ramrod straight with a nervous look on his face. The guy working overtime sat impassively and wondered if the additional money he was going to earn from this tour was going to be worth all the nonsense he might be subjected to. Shakespeare cast quick furtive glances down at his cell phone as if he were expecting some kind of vital text message. And Sean sat quietly with a slight smile on his face, Coke can hidden at his side. He had seen his share of pain in the ass officers over the years and he wasn't about to have his evening ruined by any of them.

Henderson assigned Jim to the forcible entry position which would involve working with Tyrone to break open any locked doors they might encounter at a fire.

"You and me Tyrone, let's do some damage tonight," Jim said to Tyrone who responded with a nod of his head and the slightest hint of a smile.

Tyrone was not only a shy person, he was also somewhat intimidated by the volatile nature and loud presence of Captain Henderson. As a new probie feeling his way through an uncomfortable work environment he just couldn't get himself to refer to him as "the barker" as the other guys did. But he was relieved to know that he would be teamed up with Jim tonight. Jim would not only teach him things he would also provide a reassuring presence if the Captain started barking as he most certainly would.

The early evening turned out to be quite slow. Just a few runs for a water leak and an auto accident followed by a couple of false alarms. They got through their mealtime routine accompanied with the usual high volume mealtime banter and then each man found his own activity. Tyrone mopped the floors, Sean watched television in the small house watch area, and Faiella made some more phone calls. Jim took advantage of the time by throwing his load of backed up laundry into the washing machine in the basement. There was no thought of coal bins tonight, just a quiet, productive evening in the firehouse that allowed him to catch up on some chores.

Around nine o'clock he headed upstairs to relieve Sean at the house watch desk. Jim was assigned the 9 to 12 watch which meant he was responsible to monitor the phone calls and acknowledge receipt of any runs assigned by the dispatcher from nine until midnight. At that point he'd hopefully be relieved by Faiella though he suspected that he'd probably have to go hunting for him in the darkness of the bunkroom.

"Keep it quiet, I've got to finish my movie without any bullshit interruptions," Sean said as Jim sat down in the battered swivel chair at the house watch desk.

"No problem. What are you watching?"

"*Saving Private Ryan*. That's the last time this country had any balls."

"Ok, I'll see you in the morning."

"Yeah, right," both Sean and Jim knew that it was nearly impossible for Ladder 57 to get through the night without any runs.

As promised Jim did keep it quiet for the duration of his watch. Not a run came in and he spent the time reading a novel he'd been slowly working his way through for the past several weeks. He knew that he should have spent at least a little time with his firefighting procedural manual and he had even set up his collection of yellow highlighters but he just couldn't get himself to open the thing up. He looked at the dense volume as it sat on the desk in a nearly brand new three ring binder. Once again he had failed to stick to what was supposed to be a six week study regiment. But then again, he thought, that was just another of the many commitments he liked to avoid. His mind drifted off to being with Laura in the Brazilian restaurant and that led to seeing the Dakota Apartments, but his train of thought was interrupted by Faiella's sudden appearance. He was somewhat surprised that Faiella actually showed up to relieve him several minutes before midnight.

"Ok, I've got it" he informed Jim. He was holding a folder that was thick with pages of handwritten notes. Corrections, Jim figured.

"How's the writing going?" Jim inquired.

"Fine," Having been ridiculed in the past for his creative efforts Faiella wasn't about to share much about his novel. Certainly not with any firefighters. Perhaps with his fellow students in the creative writing class he was taking at NYU but even there he felt a lot of them were just pompous imposters and not real writers.

"Alright, I'll see you later," Jim responded as he headed back toward the kitchen thinking that he really didn't care about Shakespeare's damn book, he was just being polite. When he got there he opened the refrigerator to hunt for some ice cream but was disappointed to discover just a partially empty half gallon of Breyer's vanilla in the freezer. That was very bland crap compared to the high-octane Ben and Jerry's flavors he favored, so he sat down instead and decided to see what was worth watching on the television. He flicked with the remote for some time and slowly worked his way through 100 cable channels. A hundred channels and not a thing to watch, just a few movies he'd already seen and an ancient black and white episode of *The Honeymooners*. He watched for a few minutes as Ralph Kramden bellowed at his friend Norton about a lost bowling trophy and, in that pre-Me-Too era, threatened to send his wife Alice to the moon.

After spending some time in the kitchen Jim decided to head

up to the bunk room. Maybe they'd be lucky enough to have a slow night and he'd actually wake up with enough energy to do things tomorrow. If a job happened to come in, he had found that even one hour of sleep would help keep him going. He entered the dark bunk room and navigated his way toward his bed. That was a challenge in itself. He could see almost nothing and his eyes struggled to adapt to the sudden change of light from the brightness of the fluorescent hallway to the black cavern of the bunkroom where dark shades covered the glass panes in the old windows. The glass itself was painted in a dark green color that filtered out any remnant of urban light. There were guys who thought nothing of bursting into the room in the middle of the night and using a bright flashlight to locate an available bunk. Sometimes it would be the house watchman looking to wake up his relief. Occasionally it would be one or two off duty firefighters who would stumble their inebriated way through the room feeling the effects of a night of heavy drinking. That kind of behavior always pissed Jim off. He preferred to quietly locate his bed and if at all possible, not disturb anyone.

When Jim got to his bunk he took off his shoes and slid under the sheets with his clothes on. That would allow him to respond immediately if a run came in without having to face the challenge of dressing in the middle of a sleep induced haze. One time he'd actually seen a guy try to put his pants on over his head for a late night response but he was uncertain if that was the result of a suddenly interrupted dream or a gut full of beer. He pulled the heavy quilt up to his chin to warm up. As always the massive, ultrahigh BTU window air conditioner was blasting away not far from his bed. The bunkroom was always cold regardless of the season. In the winter frigid blasts of air worked their way through the thin panes of the large windows which still retained their 1950's climate efficiency. The summer was no different, still very dark and icy cold, more like a place to hibernate than sleep. Still, there was a sense of comfort and reassurance to the room. It was a retreat from the brightly lit, noisy environment of the rest of the firehouse.

As Jim lay awake in the bunk his mind drifted toward memories of other rooms he had slept in. He thought of being in Laura's bed and how her long hair would spread out over the pillow and surround her head in a fine blond halo, almost as if she was floating underwater. And the scent, that vague wisp of cologne that was embedded in the sheets and seemed to follow her everywhere. That fragrance would forever be a reminder of her. He pictured how the light would filter through the blinds on her bedroom window and silently move across the ceiling as it reflected the movement of traffic on the streets below. And that led him to think of his childhood bedroom. He recalled sleeping directly over a noisy bus stop and a Puerto Rican restaurant, and he thought of hot summer nights when the room would be filled with echoes of Spanish music and the aroma of arroz con gandules. What a contrast from the Upper East Side apartment house that Laura lived in with its doorman and efficient elevators and numerous tenants, most of whom had no idea who their fellow residents were.

Jim was surrounded by the usual bunkroom echoes as his mind roamed. He could hear the steady sound of Sean's soft raspy breathing as he slept way off in the corner in a bed that had traditionally been reserved for the senior man. And three beds away the guy working overtime, he was pretty sure he said his name was Bob, was blasting away with occasional explosions of thunderous snoring. His booming racket would suddenly cease for a moment and offer a promise of restoring some peace to the room only to continue again in a symphony of annoying disharmony. Tyrone was lying asleep and totally silent in the bunk next to Jim. This guy's an introvert even when he's asleep, Jim thought. Despite all the background noise his recollections about places and scents slowly drifted away and around 12:30 he fell into a deep sleep.

Seven blocks south of the firehouse, a ten-year-old boy was also sleeping. His tiny room was right next to his parents' bedroom on the top floor of an old tenement building which had somehow escaped the urban development and renewal efforts that transformed much of the West Side. The place was run down and poorly maintained, but the rent was cheap and it offered an attractive alternative for residents who didn't have a lot of options. In fact people were lining up to have an opportunity to rent a spot in one of the few places in Manhattan that was still affordable. To meet the market demand the landlord had subdivided many of the apartments with illegal alterations which increased the number of living units and at the same time inflated his rental income. Smoke detectors were an afterthought. Some had been installed years ago but time had worn out most of them and those that were left were merely plastic appendages that hung uselessly next to the peeling paint on the ceilings. It was a sad looking place but the family had made the most of it. Both parents worked at low paying jobs that wouldn't have appealed to most people, but they used the income they managed to scrounge up to make a decent home for their boy, a home that was very different from their native Guatemala but one that held much more promise for the family.

At the exact same time that Jim drifted off into sleep in the firehouse a few tiny sparks began flashing in an electrical outlet behind a side table in the boy's room. The frayed wires had been poorly installed long ago by an unlicensed electrician who failed to ground the outlet and for years it had quietly functioned, giving no evidence of its inherent flaws. Over that time an accumulation of dust slowly built up inside the outlet and no one had noted the slight electrical odor that arose when the wires heated up. The damage was gradual but significant and on this particular night the forces of fate, heat, and physics finally lined up in a perfectly timed sequence of events.

There was a tiny scrap of paper lying on the table next to the bed. The boy enjoyed drawing pictures with the pencils his mom had purchased and he had finished this one for her just before he went to sleep. It sat there for hours until the slight breeze that filtered through his window provided just enough force to move it off the table and land it right on top of the plug for the lamp cord. There it rested, precariously balanced next to the wall, until just the right amount of heat finally managed to melt away minute sections of wire insulation inside the outlet. That accelerated the sparking which in turn ignited the scrap of paper and within seconds the small flame reached the bottom of the curtains that the boy's mother had hung from the window to hide the unattractive air shaft that sat on the other side.

The fire was already rolling up the wall and across the ceiling when he suddenly woke up, but it took a moment for the shock of what he saw to take effect. He struggled for air as the biting smoke was drawn into his hyperventilating lungs and with a final burst of fear driven adrenaline, he was able to roll out of bed, his body automatically reacting to escape the threat and his mind desperately driven to find his parents. All of his thoughts ceased the moment he managed to stand up. He was just tall enough to reach the level of intense heat that had already risen in the small room and it took just one quick inhalation for his airway to constrict and put him into a merciful state of unconsciousness. Then it was only a matter of a few seconds for the flames to ignite his Batman pajamas and begin to roast and char his flesh.

Down in the street an entourage of young people were

walking past the building and they couldn't have been more different from the family who lived in the small apartment above them. These were suburban kids from comfortable homes in New Jersey who had flocked into town to live out their dream of being a part of the New York City club scene. They had just left The Underground, a small subterranean bar in the West Side where the quality of the music, the size of the crowd, and the availability of drugs had all been equally disappointing. As they worked their way towards their next night spot one of them happened to look up towards the roof of the tenement.

"My God, look at all that smoke!" he commented.

"An oil burner must have kicked in," suggested one of the others.

"Oil burner my ass, that's a fire!"

"A fire?"

They were all looking up now, their evening escapade suddenly interrupted by an actual physical threat, the flames as real and uncontrolled as the powerful currents in the nearby Hudson and the strong gusts of wind that blew in from the west.

Cheryl, the most practical and least intoxicated member of the group immediately reached for her cell phone.

"9/11, what is your emergency?" came the dispatcher's calm, professional voice as he handled the call from a console in a secure communications bunker that was incongruously located smack in the middle of Central Park.

"There's a lot of smoke it's a fire a building is burning!" Cheryl nervously rambled to the dispatcher, her voice affected by the third sloe gin fizz she had consumed as well as her disturbance at what she was seeing.

"Ok, just slow down a second, where exactly are you located?" the dispatcher inquired as he tried to calm her down.

"I think we're on West 37th Street, no, 38th maybe?" There

was a pause and the dispatcher could hear the group in the background engaging in a heated discussion of where exactly they were.

"It's got to be 37th Street" one of the guys said.

"No! The cars are heading east so this *has* to be an even numbered street" Cheryl insisted, still the most rational member of the group despite the growing anxiety she was feeling as she watched the volume of dark smoke expand above her.

"Nah, we're still down in Chelsea so we're in the 20's" her friend insisted. He was by far the most inebriated of the clique.

As soon as he managed to ascertain a correct building address the dispatcher sprang into action. He initiated a series of alarm assignments that simultaneously caused computers to start quietly beeping at the house watch desks in five different firehouses. The beeping sounds were immediately followed by much louder chimes that echoed throughout the fire stations. The noise was not loud enough to wake the sounder sleepers but those in a light doze were immediately awakened in a Pavlovian response developed from years of interrupted nights when their peaceful interludes had been abruptly shattered. The electronic tones were followed by the amplified voices of the house watchmen on the building intercoms who forcefully informed the men that they had received a phone alarm for a structural fire. That was certain to catch their attention. A phone alarm in the middle of the night was more often than not going to be something serious and not just another water leak or false alarm.

Jim was in the middle of intense REM's when the run came in. He was normally a light sleeper, but it took the shock of Faiella's voice and the sudden glare of the bright fluorescents that instantly lit up the bunk room to snap him out of a deep dream state. For a split second he laid immobile on the bunk gathering bits of sudden consciousness. A brief fragment of the dream

140

remained for a moment, something about a woman, and then it was gone.

"First due! Phone alarm!" Faiella echoed again through the intercom, this time louder and with more emphasis and now everyone's adrenaline started pumping.

Jim had no memory of sliding down the pole from the bunk room. He was just present in the moment now, standing next to the rig and mechanically stepping into his bunker pants which were tucked into his boots just as he had done hundreds of times in the past in a mindless routine. He tossed the strap of his radio over his shoulder, slid his hood over his head, and buckled his black turnout coat up to his chin. Within a minute all the men had boarded the truck and Faiella was speeding down the street.

By this time a number of people had followed up the club kid's initial notification with phone calls of their own as the fire continued to grow. People in the street watched in a rapt state of fascination and terror as flames began to push out of a top floor window. Residents of adjoining buildings woke up and slammed their windows shut to block out the billowing smoke which was expanding and darkening by the second and filling the street with its acrid scent. The sleeping neighborhood was abruptly transformed from a quiet row of grey urban buildings into a sudden display of natural destruction that roared out of the tenement and lit up the night sky.

Faiella had driven just half a block when the dispatcher's voice came over the radio.

"Ladder 57, we're getting numerous phone calls, reports of people trapped."

On hearing this Captain Henderson banged on the glass partition that separated the front cab section of the rig from the firefighters seated in the back and yelled "We're going to work!"

Not that they needed to be told since the men already sensed that they were heading toward something significant. By now all were alert and in combat mode. The crew cab was suddenly filled by the sounds of air masks being turned on as each man reached back awkwardly in his seat to open up the valve of his air tank. Vibrating noises echoed in the cab as the emergency alert devices that were attached to each mask were activated. They were designed to produce a loud piercing alarm if a fire-fighter remained motionless for a few seconds and could prove to be a lifesaver if one of them became trapped or overcome by the smoke. But they were not thinking about injuries right now, nor were they particularly concerned with the danger that was an essential element of their work. They were primed to execute the tasks they had been trained to do and each in his own way was mentally preparing for the unknowns of what appeared to be a tough job that was only seconds away. As the new probie Tyrone did not have anywhere near the level of the other men's experience. His heart was beating rapidly and when he glanced over and saw the stressed look on Sean's usually relaxed face he tensed up even further. All of the questions and doubts he had about this line of work and this peculiar organization he had joined bounded through his head. And, deep inside of him, sat the unanswered question of whether or not he would really be able to perform adequately.

Captain Henderson made full use of the truck's air horn as they sped through the night, hitting the switch at every intersection and issuing an ear-splitting blast as they passed by the newspaper delivery vans, taxis, and private garbage trucks that roamed the dark streets. As he observed the barker from his seat in the rear, Jim had a brief thought of how well paired the captain was with that horn and how each in their own way were so unpredictably explosive. That insight was immediately replaced by a report that suddenly erupted from the speaker of the apparatus radio.

"Engine 2 to Manhattan 10-75!" was all he heard, the signal for a working fire. It wasn't so much what was said but the shaky tenor of the voice that grabbed his attention. One of the local engine companies had just arrived at the scene of the fire and the officer, a young and newly promoted lieutenant, had given the radio signal to the dispatcher, probably for the first time in his career. And it showed in his message which was high pitched, breathless, and excited almost as if he really wanted to say, "holy shit, we have a fire!" but instead managed to hold off in a nervous display of professionalism.

They could see it as soon as the rig turned into the block. Fire was pushing out of a window on the top floor of a tenement about half-way down the block on the left hand side of the street. A couple of people on the sidewalk were waving at them and frantically pointing toward the building as they arrived. Not that they needed any direction at that point as the inferno grew and lit up the top of the tenement fed by the stiff breeze that whipped over the open expanse of the Hudson. Jim was actually relieved to see the flames pouring out of the building. At least there would be no problem locating the fire and clearly it was venting itself. What he found most frightening were those jobs where you couldn't find the location of the blaze. The ones that produced enormous amounts of smoke and levels of heat that grew and grew and drove you ever closer to the floor as you crawled around blindly trying to find it, all the while desperately hoping that you hadn't already passed it by and have it suddenly light up behind you.

Faiella had no problem putting the truck in the right spot. The young engine officer who arrived first at the scene had done a good job. Although he sounded kind of shaky on the radio he turned out to be a pretty solid firefighter. He had placed his rig right next to a hydrant and allowed enough room for Ladder 57 to pass by and set up right in front of the building, exactly where it had to be. Sean mentally prepared himself for what would be a long climb up that ladder to get to the roof of the building. It would be a difficult assent but one he had done hundreds of times in his career. Once he got there, he could rev up the saw and start cutting holes to vent fire and smoke from below. And the sooner that happened the better.

The men all vaulted off the rig as soon as it stopped, and Captain Henderson headed straight for the front door and entered the lobby. It would take Jim and Tyrone a few seconds to grab their tools and follow him in.

"Don't forget to bring the can," Jim said to Tyrone referring to the heavy fire extinguisher he was assigned to carry in addition to his six-foot hook. Tyrone looked at him for an instant with a confused look on his face. Why on earth would they need the minuscule 2 ½ gallons of water it contained when they were facing such an overwhelming amount of fire?

"Just bring it!" Jim repeated when he saw his hesitation. He knew that it might provide just enough water to drive flames away from the apartment door they were likely to have to force open or to knock down just enough fire to allow a quick search of one of the rooms. But even as he noted the confusion in Tyrone's eyes Jim spotted something else. It was the look of fear. Pure and simple. Tyrone had never been a first due firefighter at a job of this magnitude. Jim recognized the look since at one time he had also experienced the sudden bewilderment of being in a position where you actually have to *do* the job you thought you wanted to do, to face the danger and fight off the stress and perform your duty.

Although he had responded to many nighttime fires in the past, Jim still regarded the view of fire lapping out of a window as a very odd sight. This was especially true in the dark when the flames sought a path into the night air and pushed out in a hushed but powerful rage. That's when the street would be illuminated in a mesmerizing glow and for a brief moment there was a certain beauty in its danger. How strange it was to see a building suddenly transformed from an ordinary place that just blended in with the long line of grey structures next to it into a roaring beacon of startling energy, all accomplished amid a background of eerie silence.

Jim was not alone in his observations. The night people standing by in the street were also looking and pointing and commenting breathlessly as they watched a disaster unfold. The club kids and the cops, the night shift guy who had been making his way to the subway, the homeless man still pathetically grasping his empty bottle of cheap wine and the neighbor who was walking back from the 24-hour drug store with medicine for his two year old, all were captivated by the show. Together they watched as the silent dancing flames produced a disturbing but spectacular display in the middle of a sleepy New York night.

The silence was finally interrupted when the second window broke. The intensity and pressure of the fire, enhanced by the wind coming off the Hudson, finally developed enough energy to burst the glass out of the old window frame. Flames exploded out and reached up to the cornice at the roof level where they sought new fuel to consume. The fire was a different animal now, even more powerful but just as indifferent to the building and the neighborhood and the people who watched it. The sound of shattered windowpanes echoed through the street followed by the tinkling noise of the glass shards that fell through the metal fire escapes onto the sidewalks below. Firefighters kept their heads down hoping to avoid the sharp edges of the fallen glass and the street watchers who had drawn too close quickly moved back to safer positions.

The noise and rapid-fire development drew an excited groan from the people in the street who had been watching the fire in a state of rapt fascination. Now they were immediately snapped out of that trance and instead observed it with a sense of horror as the reality of the situation became apparent. This wasn't just a show. Somebody lived here and at this very second, they were being ripped from the quiet intimacy of their sleep to a fearful encounter with an overwhelming force that would hurt and damage and kill.

Tyrone also stared at the fire as he swung his mask over his shoulders.

"Ok, let's go," Jim said to him as they gathered their tools and headed toward the front entrance. He tried to sound calm and reassuring to Tyrone. They were facing a difficult challenge, but he needed him to relax enough to perform the work they would have to do together.

It was difficult to keep up with the captain. Henderson was naturally aggressive at a fire, particularly as the first ladder company officer at the scene. He was already through the front door and into the lobby while Jim and Tyrone were still struggling into their masks and grabbing their tools off the rig. While they were making their way towards the building Jim noticed a young man standing nearby taking photos with his cell phone. It was one of the club kids who was looking to bring a memento of his New York adventure back to his suburban home. They brushed past him and headed toward the front door.

Jim entered the doorway with Tyrone following right behind. He noted that the captain had already chocked the door in the open position and made a mental note to mention that to Tyrone after the fire. It was a small detail but well worth reinforcing since it would secure a quick way out of the building, and even more significantly, keep the door from closing on the hose line and cutting off the vital flow of water in the middle of the firefight.

"Pace yourself Tyrone, we're gonna have to take a door," Jim said as soon as they entered the lobby. He knew they had a long, tiring climb up the stairs and once they got there their work was just beginning.

They started walking up the staircase which seemed to wind endlessly above them despite the fact that the building was only five stories high. With the heavy tools they carried and the restrictive bunker gear they wore, even three flights could be taxing. Jim had never been in this building before, but all tenement stairs were essentially the same. Their boots resounded loudly as they stepped on the old marble threads, each one worn to a dirty white surface produced by decades of tenants tramping up and down the building. They worked their way around the tight turns on the half landings as the noise of men coming up behind them echoed off the masonry walls. Metal tools clanged against the railing, and they could hear the connecting butts of the hose knocking on the steps below them as the engine guys dragged their line and negotiated it through the tight confines of the stair. Men yelled out to each other in the midst of the commotion trying their best to coordinate their efforts. The high-pitched messages that screeched out of each man's fire ground radio added to the assault of piercing sounds.

It was noisy, it was frantic, and to Tyrone it was all confusing. So much was happening at once it was difficult for him to see a plan or clear course of action in all the activity.

"Should we leave?" a frightened woman asked him as she nervously peeked out from the doorway of her second-floor apartment.

"No, stay inside for now. Keep your doors and windows shut, we'll let you know if you have to get outside" Jim responded to her. Tyrone was glad he did because he really wasn't sure what to tell her.

As he continued to work his way up Jim pictured what awaited them. He had been through all of this before and didn't even have to think about what to do. There would no doubt be a locked door to force open just to get inside the apartment. That was going to involve some real effort since the hydraulically powered forcible entry tool they normally used was out of service. That meant old fashioned grunt work with him holding the steel Halligan tool in position while Tyrone pounded away at it with the blunt side of his axe. He hadn't forced a door with Tyrone before and hoped that he would be accurate enough with his axe blows to get the job done and not accidentally hit him with a mistimed swing of the tool. But the image of watching Tyrone and Dave sweeping the sidewalk in front of the firehouse popped into his head and put him at ease. Jim recalled the controlled, efficient way that Tyrone had used his broom to gather the debris. Dave was a much more powerful guy but he would be a lot more difficult to control.

Jim was actually quite at ease in the middle of all the disruption. He knew this work and on a very basic level enjoyed the adrenaline rush and excitement of firefighting. It was an environment he was acclimated to. And, in a similar way, he had a comfortable familiarity with the tenement stair he was climbing. It seemed like he had spent much of his life walking up stairways just like this- seven years in the fire department and a couple of decades growing up in Brooklyn apartment buildings. The marble steps and metal staircases were the same wherever you were in the city and the one he was in now seemed pretty well maintained despite the age of the building. There was no illegible spray-painted graffiti plastered on the walls and it didn't have the tart scent of urine that plagued some of the other stairways he had experienced in the more run down sections of the city.

As a new probie Tyrone could not feel any sense of comfort as he walked up the steps. This was all new to him. But in the middle of all his confusion something was resolved in his mind. It was no active decision or conscious attempt at calming his nerves. It was more of a gradual realization that he was with two men who really seemed to know what they were doing. Tyrone was uncomfortable with Captain Henderson and on some level feared him. But the man had been around forever and, as intimidating as he could be, he was almost like a father figure to the men, a protector as well as a rigid disciplinarian. And Jim not only seemed competent, but he had also always treated him fairly.

It came down to trust. Trusting the person you worked for and the men who worked alongside you. That was what allowed them to perform as they did in the middle of all this chaos. He wanted to be part of that, someone who could be relied on just as he relied so much on guidance from these men. And despite his fear and uncertainty he was determined to try his best, to put all his doubts aside and do what was required of him, to be part of that team that looked out for each other and accomplished things as a group that none could do on their own. It was that "brotherhood" word they were always talking about that had nothing to do with race or personality or wherever the hell you came from but surfaced just at moments like this in this loud, crowded stairway in a burning building that he had rushed into while the rest of the world watched from the street. He could not know it at the time but years later he would look back and realize that this night was the first time he really became a member of the New York City Fire Department. Tyrone picked up his pace and continued up the stairway determined to keep up with Jim and reach the Captain who was probably already waiting for them at the door to the apartment.

The smoke was banking down and became thicker as they

worked their way to the upper floors. When they arrived at the top floor both Jim and Tyrone's legs were trembling from the effort of the climb. They could see Captain Henderson already kneeling at the door to the apartment.

"Mask up! Take the door!" the Captain demanded.

The barker was one of the few men who could still be readily heard while wearing his mask face piece. His powerful, gravelly voice easily worked its way through the plastic shield that covered his face. As usual the Captain was ready, and he was intense. He was anxious to get through that door and into the apartment as quickly as possible to perform a quick search and rescue anyone trapped inside.

Jim and Tyrone put on their face pieces and the sound of the three air masks reverberated in the tight hallway as they squatted in front of the apartment door. The barker's breathing was slow and steady, Jim's was rapid from the effort of climbing up the stairs, and Tyrone's was racing with nerves and exhaustion. Tyrone happened to glance at the Captain's helmet as he positioned himself next to Jim to start forcing the door. It was quite old and displayed the extent of the barker's firefighting resume. The helmet was flat black in color and sections of the leather shell had frayed and dried out from years of use. The guys often joked that the captain's lungs must look like his helmet after all the smoke and beatings he had taken. Tyrone could barely make out the red "57" numerals on the darkened front piece of the helmet. That front piece had originally been immaculately white when Henderson was first promoted to the rank of captain. That was fifteen years ago and since then, it had been stained to the same dark finish as the rest of the helmet from hundreds of times of doing exactly what they were doing right now. Tyrone's helmet still had that brand new, shining black, I'm right out of probie school look. As Sean would put it, both Tyrone and his helmet were yet to get their cherry popped.

Jim knelt right in front of the door and positioned the end of his Halligan tool into the crack of the door jamb. The tight confines of the tenement hallway got even nosier as the engine guys crowded in and flaked out their limp, dry hose line. Then they too knelt down and anxiously awaited the message from the engine chauffeur that water was on the way. They were also waiting for Jim to force the door open. All eyes were focused on him now for his was the final task that had to be accomplished before anything else could proceed.

Jim examined the secured door that sat in front of him. It was painted dark brown and covered with a dented metal surface that suggested many years of wear. Black smoke was pushing out from the gaps between the door and the wooden jamb that surrounded it. He hoped it wouldn't be one of those New York City apartment doors with three or four locks on it. It often seemed like people were very anxious to move into the city and then did everything possible to keep it out of their homes once they got there.

"Here comes your water" the engine chauffeur's voice crackled over the radio and the hose line abruptly shifted as it filled, the sudden rush straightening the bends in the line and stiffening the hose which moved and squirmed like an aroused snake. Jim could hear the brief rush of noise that escaped from the nozzle when the man holding it cracked it open to bleed the air from the hose line. All was now ready for the attack on the fire. And all were waiting for him to finish his task.

He positioned the end of the Halligan right next to what appeared to be the main door lock. Tyrone's solid axe swings reverberated with an overwhelming metallic clanging sound that bounced off the old plaster walls as Jim watched the tool slowly work its way through the jamb. In seconds the door had opened a few inches but still wouldn't give. Fuck! There appeared to be a bar or sliding bolt on the door, and he was still unable to get it open. Jim tightened up knowing that right now it all hinged on him. The engine was waiting and the barker was breathing down his neck, anxious to get in and get started. Though the Captain said nothing he could just imagine him thinking "get this fucking door open and get it open now!"

But Mr. Thoroughly had seen this act before. Jim had an innate ability to concentrate on things and turn off distractions. Like checking the tools at the start of the tour or watching the currents that flowed through the rivers or contemplating on the squirrels that romped near his apartment. It was a skill that allowed him to hide from unpleasant thoughts and uncomfortable situations, to withdraw into himself to that safe place where he could hide from the confusion and alienation he had so often experienced in life.

Jim paused for a moment to size up the door and he quickly determined which locking device was causing the most difficulty. Once he repositioned his tool it took just a few hard hits from Tyrone's axe to drive it off. After that he was able to push his weight against the Halligan and finally pry the door open. He noted that the Captain had grabbed the doorknob with his gloved hand just as the door was about to give. Another good move he'd have to point out to Tyrone after the job. The last thing you wanted when you forced entry was to lose control of the door and allow the sudden blast of heat or fire to drive you right out of the hallway. He had once experienced that at another job and he never forgot the feeling of diving headfirst down a stairwell to escape the flames that had blown out from the doorway and rolled over his head.

It had taken no more than two minutes to force the door, but it seemed much longer.

"It's a railroad flat. Hanley try to make the front room, Hillman you stay near me!" Captain Henderson quickly instructed Jim and Tyrone just as they started crawling through the open doorway.

The Captain had said much in those few words. The rooms in the old tenement were laid out in railroad fashion. They were entering what would be the kitchen in the rear of the apartment and the other rooms would line up next to each other, like a string of railroad cars, as they moved toward the front of the building. That's where the fire was roaring and where the bedrooms would be located. And, given the time of night, it was vitally important to search those bedrooms as quickly as possible. Henderson wanted the probie near him as he checked the first bedroom and he instructed Jim, the experienced guy, to make a push on his own toward the front of the apartment to search the second one.

Henderson crawled into the cloud of thick black smoke that filled the apartment with Tyrone following right behind him. Jim watched as the Captain turned to the right and rapidly made his way across the floor. Considering Henderson's age and size, he was somewhat surprised to see how well he could move as he crawled forward on his hands and knees. But he was observing the captain in his element, moving through an environment with the ease of a man who had been there many times in the past. The Captain would pay for his efforts tomorrow when his arthritic knee would act up again but right now he felt no pain, only the instinct to get to the first bedroom as quickly as possible. Tyrone noted that Henderson was sweeping his arm across the floor as he moved and it suddenly occurred to him that he was searching for bodies since there was the distinct possibility that whoever had slept in that place may have passed out in the kitchen as they made their way toward the door. Tyrone started to do the same thing. He was beginning the process of learning to function as a firefighter rather than thinking like an overwhelmed new guy who was just blindly following someone else in the smoke.

Jim knew that he would have to be careful with his search. He was moving closer toward the front of the building, closer to the fire and further away from the safe escape path of the apartment door. He could hear the engine moving into the kitchen to position the hose line. But the line had not yet opened up and he could make out the yellow glow of the fire as it pulsed with violent energy from the very top of the black smoke down at the end of the hallway. As he crawled forward, he made sure to keep his right hand on the wall next to him. If that fire suddenly flared up, if a sudden burst of wind hit the building in the wrong direction, if the engine abruptly lost water pressure in the line, if any of several possibilities occurred, he was on his own and he could follow the security of that wall back to the doorway.

He crawled deeper and deeper down the hallway. The further he went the hotter it got and he hugged the floor as much as possible to avoid the intense heat that was rapidly building above him. In the dense smoke he could barely make out the figures of Henderson and Tyrone who were moving inside a room on his left. That would be the first bedroom. There had to be a bathroom here somewhere as well as that other bedroom he was seeking. Jim continued to move. The engine would start water in a minute, then that fire would be knocked down. Then he'd be safe. He was right on the edge now, the next little room that he passed on his left had to be the bathroom. Just a few more feet. And he found it. An open door, a small room, looked like it might have a window. Fire was rolling across the bedroom ceiling and lapping out of the top of the bedroom door right above Jim's prone body. He could feel the heat radiating down right through the hood that covered his ears.

He had reached his limit. The fire was about to flash over in the small room, and he started to back off and slowly work his way back down the hallway. Back to the location of the hose line where the engine guys were positioning themselves for an attack on the fire. Jim reached for the hallway wall and used it to guide his way back to the kitchen. He was moving blindly now. Smoke had banked down to the floor. There was no visibility at all and it was impossible even to see his hand in front of his face. He could hear his rapidly increasing breaths reverberate inside the face piece of his mask and wondered how much longer his air supply would last. As he crawled forward, he stumbled into the guy who was holding the nozzle. Now he was safe. He had given it his best shot. Performing an aggressive search before any water was on the fire was always a nerve-racking experience and he had just been confronted with an overwhelming amount of heat and fire.

The engine pushed their line down the hallway and opened up the nozzle on the fire which was now pushing forcefully out of the small bedroom Jim had just left. As the water whipped across the ceiling the bright yellow flames were immediately transformed into a steamy white oblivion and the nozzle man then advanced the hose toward the front parlor.

Jim moved in right behind the engine intent on getting back into that bedroom to complete his search. He still couldn't see anything. The thick blackness had been replaced by blinding white smoke and steam that had been produced by the blast of water. As he crawled in, the walls of the small room shielded him from the intense heat of the flames which were still ripping through the front parlor and blowing out the windows. Jim crawled over things as he moved in. Blankets, stuffed animals? Might be a child's room. He worked his way toward the window. If he could break it open it would relieve the smoke and allow him to see a little better.

He used his tool to shatter the windowpanes, starting with the top ones and working his way down. He could hear the shards of glass echoing as they fell down the air shaft. Smoke instantly began to push out but there was still not much visibility in the room. While he was taking out the window he upset a small side table and things spilled onto the floor. Pieces of paper. And pencils, lots of pencils rolled all around.

When he reached out to his right Jim felt the small bed that was lying right next to him. He immediately swept his hand over the top of it and was relieved to find that no one was in it. He then checked beneath the bed with the same result.

"Ladder 57 to Battalion, we've got two 10-45's!" the Captain's voice suddenly vibrated out of the radio that was strapped under Jim's coat. His voice sounded urgent and a bit nervous which was unusual for Henderson. He and Tyrone had just located two victims in the first bedroom.

"Battalion to Ladder 57, two 10-45's, message received. I'm sending up a unit to assist in getting them out" the chief in the street replied.

"Bobby, transmit a second alarm, tell them we have two 10-45's" the chief immediately radioed to his aide. They were going to need more help. The fire was still ripping and now they also had a couple of victims to remove from the building and try to resuscitate.

The dispatcher immediately went to work assigning additional units to the scene. The announcement of the second alarm toned out in every firehouse in the city. Firefighters way out in Queens and Staten Island stirred in their beds or perked up in the kitchen and listened, trying to envision what was happening at that moment in Manhattan.

Jim could hear the sound of breaking glass as men smashed

out the rest of the windows in the apartment. The smoke was beginning to vent and very gradually he could start to make out some of the features of the room he stood in. He could tell from the shuffling of boots on the floor near the first bedroom that the unit assigned to help Henderson and Tyrone remove the two victims had arrived. Jim wanted to assist with that but figured he'd first complete his search of the bedroom now that he could actually see more clearly. He felt his way around the room, past shelves, under chairs, and back again toward the bed. Nobody there, always a good feeling and sense of relief when you knew that the search was negative. As the white fog lifted, he experienced that always strange perspective of suddenly being able to see things in the room with such clarity, features that just minutes ago were hidden by the smoke and could only be perceived by a blind sense of touch.

He was walking back out towards the hallway when he stepped on something. It felt soft and spongy under his boot. Jim initially took it for a rolled up blanket or maybe a stuffed animal. He was still thinking about getting to the other bedroom to help get the two 10-45's down to the street so they could be treated by EMS as quickly as possible. Then he glanced down for a moment and saw what he was standing on.

The pajama was yellow and had Batman figures printed on it. The kind of thing a young boy might like to sleep in. But he wasn't exactly looking at a boy. Just a leg. A leg wearing this thin piece of yellow clothing which happened to be covered by a thick blanket that shielded it from the fire. The rest of the figure was only a charred mass. It looked nothing at all like a person.

Jim was both shocked and revolted by what he saw. How had he missed this? He must have crawled right over the body when he first entered the room, when it was full of smoke, when he could see nothing, when there was still a chance that he could have found the boy and not just accidentally stumble over him. Logic said that the boy had died before Jim had ever gotten near the bedroom, before Ladder 57 even arrived at the scene. But he wasn't feeling logic right now, just experiencing a sense of regret. Regret that this boy was dead and defaced in such a horrible manner. Regret that he had stepped on him, felt his soft flesh move under his boot. He had unknowingly treated him like he was a piece of furniture rather than a human being with all the dignity a human body deserved whether it was alive or dead.

"Captain, we have a 10-45!" he yelled out to Henderson loudly, urgently. The air had cleared, and he had removed his face piece. He could hear his voice echo through the steamy hallway where droplets of water were still dripping down onto the flooded wooden floor. Jim hadn't begun to overcome the shock of finding the body much less the queasy feeling of having stepped on it.

"Yeah, I know. We've got two of them. They're already being taken downstairs," the Captain replied.

"No this is another one. I'm in the small bedroom."

Jim stared at the boy's remains as he waited for Henderson. He half expected to be yelled at, like "how the hell did you miss this and what took you so long?" A sense of guilt still mixed with his feeling of shock at seeing a life ended so suddenly and horribly. Although he had seen dead people at other fires, he never quite got over the strange, sudden transition of mortality. How a living, breathing, thinking person could be instantly transformed into a piece of inanimate flesh that felt and saw nothing and was no different than the stained sofas and charred tables and the rest of the debris fire left in its wake.

The Captain entered the room followed by Tyrone. Both glanced down at the boy's body and then looked right at Jim.

"We did the best we could," was Henderson's brief message to Jim. It was an effort at consoling him, of letting him know that shit happens regardless of your efforts. His age and experience had fostered that philosophy, a conviction that he and Sean both embraced. The Captain had seen this before. There were six or seven people walking around in the city right now, living and breathing, working and experiencing their lives because of his aggressive efforts at previous fires. He had the medals to show for that. But he had also seen many others who hadn't made it, like this boy, and maybe even his parents who right now were lying on the sidewalk, EMT's feverishly working on their limp bodies trying to preserve the tenuous life force they still clung to.

"I'll give the 10-45 to the battalion, grab your tools and we'll head downstairs" the Captain said.

"Don't move it, the marshals will want to see all the evidence," he mentioned as he was making his way back to the hallway. Henderson was referring to the boy's body which the fire investigators would view along with the charred remains of the apartment as they did their investigation and performed a detached calculus of what had started the fire.

Jim remained in the bedroom after Henderson left. "It". That was the word he had used. A cold, impersonal verification of the fact that this was no longer a person but a charred piece of flesh. He looked down at the body lying at his feet and thought about the boy who had existed in it. What were his last moments like? Was he panicked as he died, choking on the smoke and desperately trying to escape the fierce pain of the flames that engulfed him? He wondered what happened to the spirit of this boy, that unique essence that perhaps made him a Mets fan or a kid who liked riding a bike and playing ball. He no doubt loved his parents and frantically reached out for them in the final seconds of his life. And what happened now? Did a "heaven" exist or did his energy pass on to a plant or an animal or even some other person in a new existence?

Tyrone lingered inside the bedroom for a moment. When Jim saw the look on his face he realized that the probie had suddenly grown as a firefighter. Tonight, Tyrone had a firsthand experience of the harsh realities of this job, a quantum leap from the theoretical knowledge that people died in this line of work to a firsthand smack in the face by the distinct concept of mortality.

Jim remained in the room after Tyrone left. He just stood there for a moment and looked out into the air shaft through the remnant of the broken window. There was nothing to see but the weathered brick wall that sat on the other side, a view that hadn't changed in over a century. What had changed was the people. The ones who come and go, the countless tenants who called this home and then were just gone. Like this boy and soon perhaps his parents. And all of their efforts, the struggle just to earn a living and to eat and to love and survive, all of it was eventually forgotten as the city moved on in its unremitting, indifferent stream of existence. He felt like he had seen more than just another death tonight. He had delved into the very soul of the city, a timeless undercurrent that stretched way back through history issuing a ceaseless groan of whipped horses, broken people, and desperate lives. There were good things in that history but there was also pain, like the pain he witnessed tonight.

Jim gathered his tools and headed back down to the street. The other guys would be waiting.

When they got back to the firehouse the men went through their regular post fire routine of putting fresh air cylinders on the masks, cleaning the tools, and taking some time to shower. After he had cleaned up Jim returned to the bunkroom and laid down on his bed. He didn't sleep but just stared up at the ceiling and thought about the job and the boy. He could tell from the tiny glimmer of daylight that peeked through the window shades that it was getting near to the end of the tour. His relief would be in soon and he decided to head down to the kitchen.

The kitchen table was crowded with firefighters. Each seat was taken as the guys coming in for the day tour mingled with those who had worked during the night. Someone had brought in an enormous bag of bagels and the men were covering them with thick slabs of cream cheese and munching them down. The leftovers sat on the table, still warm in the paper bag they came in. The room was charged with loud caffeine laced conversations that reverberated off of the tile walls. The talk was all about the job, which was the lead story on the morning news shows, each of which had reporters standing in the street in front of the building with grave expressions on their faces. All three family members had died. An investigation was underway to determine the cause of the fire and to locate the building owner. A number of fire violations had been uncovered in the place. A short, fifteen second interview with Captain Henderson was being shown over and over. He photographed well in his ancient helmet and soot covered face and he knew how to say something without revealing anything relevant at all. One award winning station had an exclusive interview with an electrical contractor who claimed to have turned down a job in the building because of what he considered to be unacceptable conditions.

Jim poured himself a coffee and found a place to sit at the table. As usual Dave had come in early and fried up some eggs. He put a plate together for Jim and placed it in front of him. But he had no appetite. He just stared at the Rorschach designs of the greasy egg yolks which sat, congealed and unappetizing on the plastic dish.

The crowd at the table soon thinned out and just Dave, Tyrone, Sean, and Jim were there.

"Fuck! First due at a second alarm and I miss the job!" Dave said, upset that he hadn't been working and missed all the action.

There were 10-45's, it was on the news, and the guys were all talking about it. And he wasn't there.

"Did you have to force a door? Was the barker snapping at everybody?" he inquired of Tyrone who was sitting right next to him nursing his own cup of coffee and who he envied for having had the opportunity to catch the job.

On hearing Dave's questions Tyrone looked up and made brief eye contact with Jim who was sitting across from him at the table. And in that instant, they shared an unspoken message. Dave just didn't get it. Tyrone did. He had seen the elephant, witnessed firsthand the realities of firefighting. It was exciting work, it could even be fun, but it was a job that was always a hair away from terrible events and horrible sights. Tyrone had taken a step tonight that Dave was yet to make and until he did the work would still seem like one big adventure.

"Yeah, we forced a door. It went pretty well, Jim did most of the work," he calmly replied to Dave.

Sean was sitting at his usual seat paging through the sports section of the *Daily News* while the conversation went on. He didn't have much at all to say about the fire. To some extent it had already been filed away with the hundreds of previous incidents in his long career. He was more concerned with how fatigued he would feel around four in the afternoon when the exhaustion from a missed night's sleep would hit him like a brick wall. They were not scheduled for any fire prevention activities this afternoon so maybe he could manage to get up to the bunkroom at some point and catch some shut eye. He looked over towards Jim who was sitting quietly and staring down into the depths of his coffee cup. Something was troubling his friend. He could tell from the look on his face. In his years in the department, he had seen that look before. It had not always turned out well.

Chapter 9

Jim left the firehouse shortly after nine. The coffee had perked up his body but not his spirit. He noticed on his cell phone that Laura had called. Twice. She had no doubt heard about the fire on the morning news and wanted to talk to him about it. He considered that for a moment and decided to hold off on calling back. He didn't feel like talking about how he had stepped on that boy's body. And he certainly wasn't looking to share his thoughts on how the fate of that poor family flowed into the historical maelstrom of New York City tragedies. Active imagination? Maybe. Hopefully no more than that. But after their conversation in the Brazilian restaurant he felt just about talked out on that particular subject for now.

He got into his car and started driving uptown intending to follow his usual route back to Queens. Toward home. To his quiet apartment with the comfortable couch next to the large window that looked out onto the sidewalk. But as he drove, he realized that wasn't really what he wanted. He was longing to be out of this city, to escape the streets and all the noise. He wanted to be in a place where there was room and space, and after last night, a place where nothing bad was happening. Instead of turning right when he got to 57th Street he suddenly turned left and got onto the parkway that headed north up the west side of Manhattan. For several minutes he really wasn't sure where he was going but his memories of the scenery up in Westchester County seemed very appealing.

Once he reached the northern part of the city and spotted the bright white sails of the boats that skimmed across the Hudson he came up with a destination. It was a nice warm day. There was a steady breeze coming from the west and he hadn't actually dragged his boat into the water for several weeks. The job, the overtime tours, the shopping, all the requirements of life, were also the very things that kept him from the quiet, personal moments he savored. The more he thought about the boat the more enthused he became, and he drove on with a determination that energized him and allowed him to ignore his fatigue.

The congested background of urban apartment buildings was soon replaced by a view of private houses, each one separated from the other by a short driveway paved in fresh blacktop. The shrubs and trees created an appealing green contrast from the grey hue of the city he had just left. He knew the route without thinking and had been on this same journey many times in the past when he accompanied Laura on trips to her parent's house. When he got to the northern part of Westchester County the scenery changed again. Here the homes were much larger and they sprawled out gracefully over large plots carved out of old farmland. Jim could feel his mind and body relax as he gazed out at the lush, forested hills that rolled past.

By the time he reached the narrow path that led down an incline toward the Hudson River, Jim was no longer thinking about the night tour. This part of the trip was always an enjoyable moment for him. He followed the curves of the road and waited for a first glance of the broad river which would suddenly appear behind the final bend in the lane. After the repetitive view of rolling hills and thick woods the Hudson would explode into view, a vast open space of light and moving water that sat in the morning sun, drawing you in and overwhelming you at the same time. He had seen that same view many times but somehow it never lost its splendor. It spread out beyond the edge of a marina, the waves shimmering in the sunlight, the water flowing slowly and powerfully with the tide.

He turned into a small gateway and parked his car. When he stepped out, he could feel the morning sun on his face and smell the moist breeze that rolled across the water. The width of the river was deceptive from where he stood. As he squinted in the sunlight he could just make out the hills that stood nearly a mile away on the opposite shore. Way out in the middle of the channel, a tugboat was slowly making its way south towing a barge. The Hudson was always a bit intimidating at first sight. Its size and its strength and the fact that he would be sharing it with such large commercial vessels seemed kind of overwhelming. It was only when he was actually on the water, moving with the wind and steering a path through the waves that he felt at ease, like he was a part of the river rather than a mere shoreline spectator.

Jim had to change into the swimming trunks he always kept in the trunk of his car so he headed toward a sign with "The Hudson Club" neatly painted on it in carefully scripted gold lettering. It sat in front of a large building right next to the water. The Hudson Club served as both a restaurant and a sailing club for the well-connected boat owners who docked at the marina. As usual he sensed the distinctly expensive ambiance of the building as soon as he entered. The interior was the complete antithesis of the plastic lobster, fake lighthouse ambiance of the fast-food fish and chips place he sometimes frequented in Queens. All of the tables were covered in fresh linen, offered beautiful views of the river, and were resplendent with shining silverware and candelabra. A crisp clean laundry scent mixed in with the aroma of fresh cut flowers that sat on each table. Lace curtains covered the windows and the morning sun reflected on pale blue walls that displayed original paintings, all neatly framed and maritime themed. Jim couldn't help comparing the laced elegance of those windows with the sad open gap he had been looking through just a few hours ago in the boy's bedroom. All that remained of that widow was a charred opening into a brick shaft way.

As he moved further into the restaurant he could hear the loud creak of the floor beams beneath his feet, the old bones of the building still announcing their presence despite the modern décor of the place. The Hudson Club was a late 19th century structure with a long history. One wall was covered with photographs of club members enjoying themselves at social functions that had been held over the years. Some went way back in time and showed happy faces of well-dressed people looking out from decades ago, all of them now long gone and remaining in the club merely as faded black and white images. Jim looked at one photo in particular from the 1920's and half expected to see Jack Nicholson staring back at him. He had watched *The Shinning* six or seven times.

Jim occasionally ate here with the Whitacres (dined was the much more appropriate word) and the food was exquisite. But he never really felt comfortable with the experience. Cash and credit cards were no good here. Laura's father paid an obscenely expensive yearly fee as a member of the club and was billed for all the meals. Jim wasn't even allowed to leave a tip and that left him feeling indebted which didn't sit well with his overall resistance to any sort of commitment.

The restaurant didn't open until noon, and it had that strangely quiet feel of a place that would soon be filled with a backdrop of animated conversations, tinkling silverware, and chiming glasses as club members filed in to eat and drink and desperately cling to their social networks. Jim spotted one woman in the bar area who was cleaning up and preparing for the day's activities. She gave Jim a suspicious, "you don't seem to be a member look" as he walked toward her. He responded with his best "good morning and how have you been smile" and proceeded directly to the men's room to change. He washed his hands, threw water on his face and looked at himself in the mirror. The cool water felt refreshing but the bags under his eyes reflected the night he had experienced. He turned to dry his hands but this was not a paper towel kind of place. Instead there was a pile of neatly folded washcloths sitting in a basket on the sink counter. Jim grabbed one and buried his face in it savoring the soft press of its clean fluff.

As soon as he got back outside the building Jim walked down toward the water. He listened to the familiar background sound of the marina as the wind blew bits of rigging against the boat masts and created a symphony of softly clanging metal. The *Dhow Jones* was tied up at the pier in all of its 36 feet of fiberglass splendor with numerous ropes rolled into neat circles and a tightly wound mainsail covered by a blue tarpaulin. Jim looked at it for a moment and considered the fact that replacing just one fitting in its intricate rigging would probably cost more than he had paid for his entire tiny, secondhand sailboat.

The tide was out and Jim could smell the river, a mixed scent of mud and fish and moist weeds. He spotted Billy, the club maintenance guy, walking down by the dock. He was carrying a toolbox and wearing a paint smeared sweatshirt and old ratty jeans that didn't fit in at all with the tone of the restaurant he had just left. Guillermo Cruz, "Billy" to all his friends, was universally loved by everyone in the Hudson Club. Not a single person failed to appreciate his friendly nature or his innate ability to fix almost anything. Whether it was for a repair on one of their expensive boats or something in their homes Billy, and his toolbox, were always welcome. But none of the club members could have imagined living anywhere near the Puerto Rican neighborhood he came from in the Bronx. Their liberal sentiments were limited to voting for the correct candidate in any election and sending the occasional check to the most appropriate charity, activities which fulfilled their self-identities but still allowed them the ability to escape to the refuge of their exclusive communities.

Billy traveled to work on the train from the Bronx where he lived with his wife and two daughters. He was hired a number of years ago when he was helping his cousin paint the house of the club president who immediately noted his skills and offered him a job. Billy was a "throw out the blueprints" kind of guy who could size up a construction project the way some of the club members could read a stock portfolio. He had an ability to quickly estimate the cost and materials needed for a job and, beyond that, he was a quick read on people. Billy knew who was to be trusted and who was full of crap.

"Hey, Billy!" Jim called out to him.

"Jim, how you doing?" he responded. He knew that Jim had a connection with the Whitacres because he was dating Laura. Billy liked Jim. He knew that he was a firefighter and related to him as a fellow blue-collar guy who also wore ragged tee shirts and old swim trunks that contrasted so sharply from the Top-Sider apparel of the club members. Once in a long while he had seen him with the Whitacres on that big boat they owned. Billy had also been on the boat once when Mr. Whitacre hired him to varnish the fine teak wood fittings. He had paid well.

But Jim was never really comfortable on the *Dhow Jones*. He thought it was too big, too slow, and too removed from the kind of experience he enjoyed in his old 14-foot boat. Jim liked being

168

close to the waves, feeling the splash of the water, and sensing the swift movement as he perched in the small hull, leaning and shifting as the boat skimmed through the river. All of those sensations seemed quite muted in the comfort of Connie's 36-foot monster. There was a major difference too in their approach to sailing. Connie drove his boat like he drove his business, and occasionally his family- aggressively, competitively, always with a goal in mind. To Jim sailing was something else, an escape, certainly not a competition but a means of leaving any upsetting thoughts on land. Once he immersed himself in the sense of wind and water all his other thoughts were put on hold. He knew that's why he had come here today.

"You taking your boat out?" Billy asked.

"Yeah, just going to mess around with it for a while," Jim responded.

"Hang on, I'll help you drag it into the water," that was pure Billy, always willing to help.

"Thanks, Billy," Jim was very capable of getting the small boat into the water himself but welcomed the company.

They both walked over to a weed-filled corner of the marina where Jim's boat was covered by an old tarp which still retained small pockets of rainwater. They dragged off the tarp and uncovered the small vessel. The hull was a dull white and had pockets of mildew in some of the corners, the original gleaming fiberglass long faded by years of exposure to the elements. The rolled-up sail was a faded yellow hue, the same color as the boy's Batman pajamas, or what was left of them, a thought Jim forced from his mind.

They pulled the boat onto the sand at the edge of the water where Jim proceeded to attach the wooden rudder, set up the slightly bent aluminum mast, and make all the customary knots and connections needed to rig the boat. The slick nylon rigging lines had a nice feel as he slid them through his hands and he could have made the knots without even looking since he used the same ones in the fire department. It was a familiar task that he always enjoyed, and he found a Zen like comfort in the slow and intricate process of getting ready to sail. It evoked the same calm pace and relaxed concentration that he experienced at work when he checked the tools on the truck. Billy stood by quietly and watched Jim as he worked. They shared the ease of two people who were comfortable with each other and didn't feel the need to say something just to fill the gaps in conversation.

"You should come out with me some time," he said to Billy, breaking up the silence.

"No thanks my man, the only boat I want to be on is the Staten Island Ferry."

This was also part of their routine. Even though it would be a bit crowded with two men in the small cockpit, Jim would always make an offer for Billy to join him and he would always politely refuse. He never pushed the issue because he suspected that Billy was uncomfortable on the water and maybe had never learned to swim. Jim had been detailed to work in a Bronx firehouse for several weeks the previous summer and he knew what kind of water related activities were available for most of the kids on the hot streets. He remembered skinny Spanish kids laughing and yelling as they jumped through the spray of open fire hydrants in their soaked denim shorts, their bare brown skin slick with the cool moisture. They looked like they had a lot of fun. But that world was far from where he now stood.

"Ok Billy, next time," Jim responded, just to keep up their tradition. But today was a day when he really felt a need to be alone on the water.

Once they moved the boat to the edge of the river Jim took over on his own. He leaned in and pushed it forward. He could feel his feet dig into the dry sand with the effort and in an instant the boat was floating and his toes were buried in the cool mud. He continued to push until the water reached the level of his thighs. Then with the help of a sudden lift of his shoulders and one final push from his legs Jim flopped awkwardly into the boat and sat in the small hollow of the deck. The sail instantly began to fill with the breeze. That was always the transformative moment, the instant when the boat would magically transition from a heavy piece of bulky fiberglass into a sleek vessel that could skim through the water and move with a silent grace free of the land and its confining restrictions, subject only to the dimensions of air and fluid that quietly guided it.

As he moved away from the shore Jim could feel the wind whipping across the open water and sense its strength through the halyard he tightly gripped in his left hand. The stiffened sail tilted the entire boat and he made the subtle adjustments required to keep it moving rapidly without flipping it over. Now began the delicate balancing act as he let out the halyard slightly and leaned back to counter the push of the wind and the boat began to rapidly accelerate. He could feel the power of the wind in his left hand while he held onto the comforting wooden tiller with his right and directed the boat on a tack that made him feel like he was flying over the river rather than sliding across its surface.

Now he was free. Free from the land and the streets and their rigidly defined property lines and traffic rules. Free from the strict bureaucracy of a harsh job and an often-confusing life. Here there was nothing but open water and space he could move in at will, space that no one owned or controlled. He was no longer a firefighter or a fiancé or an alienated, conflicted individual. It was just him and the wind and the water, and he could feel those forces through the pressure of the tiller and the tension in the sail almost as if they were a part of his body. In these moments there was no confusion about the present or discomfort with the future, just movement and a sense of the ever-changing passage of the river that became a part of his essence.

Jim continued to race across the water and sailed out till he was almost in the middle of the river. From there the shoreline looked like a hazy, distant mirage and he felt a combination of excitement and discomfort with the fact that he was now completely surrounded by nothing but choppy waves that had been stirred up by the wind. A large navigation buoy floated nearby and leaned over as it was pushed by the tide and the powerful currents that ripped past. It was splattered with sea gull droppings and its base was covered with slick seaweed and clusters of barnacles that accumulated through the years as it performed its solitary task of guiding vessels. He had a brief image of how trivial his boat must look compared to the size and overwhelming power of the Hudson and just how insignificant he was sitting in the vastness of it. All of his thoughts and fears and loves and questions about life, none of them seemed to carry much meaning at all. This river would move on with or without him.

The image of the large tugboat and barge he had spotted earlier from the shore popped into his head and immediately brought him back to the physical reality of his situation. He was in the middle of the channel, where the big boys navigated, and he decided to head back towards the shore, back to where it was safe and where he had a girlfriend and a job and a life. He set a heading towards the Hudson Club which sat way off in the distance and looked like a small white dot on the green shoreline. The sail filled with the strong breeze, and he worked his way back in one steady tack. As the boat picked up speed he glanced behind for a moment and enjoyed the view of the brisk wake that followed. He felt the boat respond to even the slightest movement of the tiller and now felt in control of the river as he sensed the vibration of the water that rushed past the hull. The feeling of movement was magnified as he got closer to the shore. Here the trees and the rocks seemed to zip past as he sailed aggressively, steering into sudden changes of direction and leaning way back as the boat tilted. After twenty minutes he was shot. The physical effort of constantly shifting and moving inside the confines of the tiny cockpit had exhausted him and put him at ease and he casually headed towards the marina.

Billy was there to meet him when Jim gently guided the bow back onto the soft sand that ringed the shoreline, and together they dragged the boat back on land.

"I've got some cold ones for us when you're ready to come up," he said to Jim.

"Sounds good," The thought of a cold beer was especially appealing after his physical exertions out on the water. Jim proceeded to stow away the boat and all of its accessories. He carefully wrapped the sail, untied all the knots and covered it all up again under the tarp. This time the whole process was fatiguing and seemed more like a chore rather than the relaxing routine he experienced when he set it up. It occurred to him when he was walking away that he had never named his boat. "The Laura"? "The Escape"? Maybe "The Misfit" most suited him. But he was too tired to pursue that now and he headed towards the club building where Billy was waiting for him.

He walked up to a patch of grass that sloped down just below one of the restaurant windows where Billy sat, plastic cooler at his side. He flopped down next to him and popped open the beer can Billy handed him. They both sat in silence sipping their drinks and looking out at the river.

"You had any good fires lately?"

This was something Billy always asked. It was part of their

routine.

Jim paused for a moment unsure of just how much he really wanted to share. Billy was no dummy. He read the papers and watched the news and had to know about the job last night and that people had died. He realized that Billy was feeling him out, just subtly checking on whether or not he wanted to talk about it. He didn't, but he appreciated the considerate way he approached the topic. Not everyone was like that. There were some who knew nothing of the world he worked in and viewed it almost as a quaint way of making a living and would ask annoying questions like "do you really slide down a pole?"

"Yeah, we had a second alarm last night and we were there for a couple of hours," was all he said in response to Billy who knew enough to know to just let the topic go. As always he was good at reading people's feelings.

They continued to sit just sipping their beers, watching the river, and enjoying their silent companionship. Billy's wife had prepared arroz con pollo for his lunch. He scooped out a generous portion from a Tupperware container and offered it to Jim on a paper plate. He hadn't eaten anything since the cup of coffee at the firehouse and he was famished. The chicken was tender and tasty and coated with just the right amount of sauce. The lightly salted flavor of the rice nicely complemented the chicken and it all washed down perfectly with gulps of the cold beer. The combination of alcohol and food relaxed Jim and as he licked the remnant of flavor from his fingers he laid back on the grass and enjoyed the view that flowed below them. He looked off in the distance and spotted the large channel buoy he had sailed past just a short while ago. From here it looked like a small green dot floating peacefully in the middle of the river, completely unlike the large, algae coated object that looked so intimidating when he was right next to it. He felt like there was some lesson or insight to be drawn from that observation. Like how time or distance could change one's perspective and leave you wondering which buoy was real. The tiny dot he could see now or the large object floating in the middle of the roiling current? But by now the third beer and the general weariness had fogged his mind and he let the concept go.

When he focused back on the food Jim got a kick out of the fact that he was enjoying such a pleasant gastronomic experience as he sat just a few feet away from a restaurant where the entries *started* at $39.95. And he was really more at ease sitting on the grass next to his friend than he had ever felt when he was inside that restaurant.

"Well my man, this was cool, but I've got to get back to work," Billy said, interrupting Jim's introspection.

"This was great, tell your wife thanks for the food. Next time come out on the boat with me" he responded.

"Sure, as long as you're taking the Staten Island Ferry."

They both laughed and stood up for one last view of the river. And after gazing out on that vast waterway where centuries ago, Henry Hudson had earned a reputation and the Lenape tribe had gathered oysters, they proceeded to gather their empty beer cans.

Jim decided to walk off his slight beer buzz before starting back to the city. He headed past the Hudson Club, through the parking lot, and up the hill until he found a comfortable spot to sit and observe all that lay below. As he sat, he could feel the dirt clinging to his swimming trunks. They were still wet and his butt had an uncomfortable moist feeling from being soaked for far too long. But he also felt relaxed, his body washed by the river, his stomach soothed by the food, and his psyche eased by the alcohol.

He watched as a train sped by, its wheels making a steady clicking noise as it roared past. When it headed off into the distance it looked like a silver snake as it quietly advanced along the tracks that ran right next to the Hudson. There were commuters on that train, people who took it every day like clockwork, chained to the rigid constraints of a strict timetable. He imagined the toll that such a routine would take. Worn down passengers would sit and stare at cell phones or lose themselves in newspapers. They saw the river constantly on their daily trips but after a while it was like they didn't see it at all, just took it for granted and ignored the mighty ebb and flow of the water, the very power that he had just experienced in his boat. And though that view always looked the same he realized that it was ever changing as the tides and currents flowed over the PCB's laced deep in its muddy bottom.

Jim had read books about the history of the Hudson. He recalled that the native tribes had a name for it, something like "Muhheakantuck", he was never sure of the spelling, but he did remember what that name meant: river that flows two ways. He thought about the two directions the river followed, north up to somewhere in the Adirondacks, and south down to New York City. He imagined that if he got into his boat and sailed long enough, he would eventually float past the urban congestion of Manhattan. Past the tenement that had burned last night. What a contrast that was from where he now sat. Two worlds so connected by this same body of water yet each so vastly different. It seemed like when he was in one of those worlds the other wasn't real but just a wisp of distant memory that barely existed. Like his recurrent dreams, like that boy he found in the bedroom. As if none of it really happened. Only it had.

By now his head had cleared. It was time to drive home and he headed toward the restaurant where he hoped to gracefully make his way through the lunchtime crowd and change into some dry clothes in the men's room. He got some strange looks from the well-dressed diners as he entered in his moist swimming trunks and faded tee shirt but following a quick change and a pleasant smile to the hostess as he left, he was back in the car and ready to go.

The trip back went slowly and traffic became more congested the closer he got to Manhattan, a not so subtle reminder that his relaxing escape from the city was coming to an end. He turned on the car radio and patiently worked his way through the stop and go bottlenecks. As he sat in the comfort of the well-padded Toyota seat, he enjoyed the soft feel of his sweatpants which soaked up the trace of the river from his skin. A sense of guilt creeped into his mind when he thought of Laura and remembered that he had not returned her phone calls. Jim knew that he was replaying an old game. Once again, he was hiding some intimate thoughts from her, escaping into his private world when he felt troubled. She would not have done the same. If Laura had a problem at work, if that jerk Richard had once again given her a hard time, he knew she would have shared it with him. Jim's default mode was still essentially to wall himself off, a style that life had taught him was safe and secure. He resolved to call her as soon as he got home.

Jim was sitting on his couch when he dialed her.

"Jim, I've been calling you all day. Are you ok? What was it like at that fire?" She sounded concerned but also slightly pissed at him.

"I'm fine. We had a busy night but this morning I decided to get out on my boat."

"You went sailing? Today? You should have called my father, he would have taken you out on his boat."

It wasn't the sailing, he thought, it was the solitude he had been seeking.

"Yeah, maybe I'll give him a call the next time," Jim said

knowing full well that he would not.

"I read that a family died at that fire. Were you there a long time?"

Jim paused for a moment and thought about the night. He didn't know quite what to say or even where to start. With the look on Tyrone's face when he saw the flames shooting out the front window? What it felt like forcing the apartment door while everyone was looking over his shoulder waiting for him to complete the task?

"I found the boy," the words just quietly popped out of his mouth. Like a scab falling off a wound, like that was the only relevant thing that had happened in the last 24 hours of his life.

"You meant the child that died?"

"Yeah," he didn't want to tell her that he had inadvertently stepped on him or about how he could still feel the flesh of the boy's calf move under his foot almost as if he was still alive and reacting to the pressure of his boot.

"Oh, that's terrible. Do you want to come over?"

"No, I'm kind of tired now but I'll see you tomorrow night after I visit my mother. I told her I'd come see her in the afternoon."

"Ok." Laura paused for a moment. "You sure you're alright tonight?" She wished she could see his face, to get a real take on how he actually felt rather than relying on the vague connection of a phone conversation.

"Yeah, yeah, I'm fine. I'll pick up some Chinese food when I come tomorrow."

"Alright, tell your mother I said hello. I'll call you from the office and I should be home by six. Try to get some sleep."

Jim held the phone to his ear for a moment after they said goodbye to each other. The room was as quiet as the phone, and he looked at the pile of wet clothes he had left on the floor but didn't feel like dealing with them. He was a bit hungry and headed over to the refrigerator to see what he could scrounge up. There were a couple of slices of pizza left over from two days ago. He threw them into the oven and began to search for something to drink. All he found in the cupboard was a single can of soda that had been sitting for months, left over from the time he had made root beer floats for Laura and himself. He grabbed the can and the not quite heated slices and sat on the couch to eat. It didn't matter that the drink was warm and the pizza was cold. After a few bites and one sip of the sweet, tepid drink, he didn't want any more and he just laid down on the couch. When he closed his eyes, it felt like he was still in the boat, still moving through the water and rocking with the waves. In a moment he was asleep, blissfully unaware of the food and the wet laundry and the events of the past day. He would lie on that couch, fully clothed and unmoving, for the next nine hours.

Chapter 10

It was a group of chirping sparrows that were making the racket. There were about six of them loudly peeping away, communicating, arguing, or doing whatever it was that drove their frantic conversation. As Jim slowly opened his eyes he could see them as they sat on branches of the tree that sat just outside the window, tiny grey creatures whose piercing racket belied their minuscule size. They had woken him from a deep slumber into the gradual awareness of a fresh morning. He felt like he was emerging from a dark well as his eyes slowly adapted to the sunlight. He laid on the couch for a few minutes just watching the birds until they all suddenly flew away at the exact same moment as if one of them had blown a whistle and announced it was time to move on.

Jim got up from the couch and walked into the bathroom where he cupped his hands under the faucet and threw cold water on his face. He checked on the time and realized that it was late morning. Time to get moving. Time to get ready to visit his mother in Brooklyn. That was a regular part of his life and the trip always managed to combine a comforting, pleasant experience with a somewhat melancholy view of the past.

He brewed a cup of coffee. That was all he needed for now since he knew that once he got to her house he would dive into a plate of homemade pirogues and soft bread fresh from the Polish bakery, treats that she always had ready in large quantities whenever he visited. His mouth watered as he thought of the food and pictured the setting. Him sitting at the small kitchen table shoveling down the food, her sitting quietly across from him saying little but pleased with his presence and enjoying his satisfaction with the food just as she did when he was a small boy. Like nothing had changed and decades hadn't really passed at all.

The Greenpoint section of Brooklyn where she lived was just a fifteen-minute drive from Astoria but in many ways it was light years away, a world that he had moved on from and a neighborhood that retained mere fringes of his past. His mother was aging, he could see that, and he still visited regularly to check on her and see if anything needed to be done around the house. She always looked forward to those visits and enjoyed listening to him as he told her what was going on in his life. He would speak about the job and some of the things he did with Laura. But there was always much he did not tell her and there were vast areas of his life, and his mind, that he did not share. He often thought how odd it was to be so close to someone and still be complete strangers.

There wasn't much green to be seen in Greenpoint. Jim drove there through the back streets, the quiet forgotten paths of old Brooklyn that did not make it to the Fodor's guide to New York, the ones with the potholes that ran past the industrial wasteland of Newtown Creek and offered stunning views of Manhattan which stood a world away on the other side of the East River. When he reached the sewage plant he turned left and proceeded down a remote street lined with oil tanks and empty warehouses, a place where only the occasional feral dog could be seen walking the sidewalks. Small patches of cobblestones and traces of old trolley tracks peeked out from below the road where the tarred surface had worn out, remnants of a different era. Jim noted that a few hydrants were missing their metal caps and were leaking steady drips of water, a condition that perhaps existed when he was a kid but only now seemed significant given what he had chosen to do for a living.

Jim had grown up on these streets playing endless games of stick ball and tossing around footballs that were covered with layers of duct tape to repair the damage done from incessant contact with the abrasive pavement. He and his friends lived in a remote bubble, oblivious to the drab industrial surroundings, immersed in their games and their occasional squabbles and in the constant rivalry for the affections of neighborhood girls who hung out near the candy store. They all shared the boyish, optimistic view that the world was out there for them just waiting to be conquered, a plump oyster ripe for the picking. Some had achieved that success. A few had been waylaid by dead end jobs, drugs, or by experiencing fatherhood years before they were actually ready for it. One of them had accomplished all three. Jim thought about those old friends as he drove. He remembered that several had Polish last names that were difficult to pronounce and impossible to spell and were bestowed with nicknames that rolled far easier from the tongue, handles like Big Louie, Stash, and the Mole. By now most of them had lost their Greenpoint roots and moved on to comfortable lives out in the green suburbs or entrenched in the crowded splendor of Manhattan. All except Jim, whose regular visits kept him in touch with the neighborhood.

He drove on and passed the building that had once been his grade school. The grey concrete façade and large windows hadn't changed much since he'd gone there though the occupants had. Jim pictured the nuns who used to inhabit the place and remembered how they taught the local kids and tried to guide them into the path of a decent life. He recalled their pale faces shrouded by black veils and their chalk covered fingers. Some of them were very kind and gentle and some were downright intimidating and left you on the edge of your seat anxiously awaiting a severe reprimand. A few blocks away he glanced at an empty storefront that had once housed Nick's Billiards Academy, a local haunt filled with a constant haze of cigarette smoke where he used to spend many Friday nights with his friends. Here he had done postgraduate studies on the delicate art of putting just the right amount of spin on a cue ball while Nick, the proprietor, sat on his stool near the cash register and quietly surveyed his fiefdom of pool tables.

The flavor of the community changed as he got closer to his mother's house. Jim passed through streets where the newly discovered appeal that Brooklyn held for a more modern generation was on clear display. There was a corner café where young couples lounged by sidewalk tables talking and eating and enjoying the more refined tastes they had injected into the neighborhood. That same storefront had once been a tavern, a dim place where longshoremen clad in work boots and layers of sweatshirts sat on bar stools and knocked down quick shots of whiskey while they nursed slow beers and deep grievances. Now the place served quiche and couscous and quinoa along with specialty coffees at prices that would have evoked an uproar from the previous patrons and encouraged angry phone calls to union bosses.

Jim arrived at his mother's street and slowly backed the car into a spot near her house. It was a tight block where parking spaces were always at a premium and many cars went days without being moved at all. The street had unspoken agreement with the local police precinct that no summonses would be issued for the alternate side of the street parking rules since many of those spots were taken by cops who drove in from their homes in the suburbs. The houses that lined the block were all attached row frame buildings that were largely indistinguishable from each other apart from the varying color of the asphalt shingles that covered them. And those colors were mostly limited to drab hues of grey or brown. The one real distinctive feature of each building could be seen in the variety of the stoops that sat in front of them. Some of the older ones were made of wood and were covered with layers of peeling paint but others were more recently constructed and displayed a genuine effort at architectural appeal with their intricate rails and stone steps. Regardless of their age or appearance they all served the same function. They were not just appendages to the buildings or portals to the second-floor doorways. These stoops served as the official urban gathering places where neighbors could sit and discuss life and talk about what their kids were up to and how much money they had saved in their latest shopping trip to Costco.

As Jim was walking towards his mother's house, he spotted her next-door neighbor sitting on the front steps of his home, a spot he occupied for many hours each day.

"Hi Mr. Morelli!" Jim said as he waved.

"Why hi Jimmy, how have you been?"

"Doing good Mr. Morelli. How's life treating you?"

Robert Morelli had lived here for as long as his mother had, which was a long time, houses didn't turn over very frequently on this block. He was a retired man in his mid-70's who stood watch each day from his front stoop ever ready to engage in what usually turned out to be a much longer conversation than anyone really cared for. But he always had been a kind presence in Jim's life, and he watched as he grew up next door. On some level he still perceived Jim as being that kid who rode his bike around the neighborhood and played on the local Pop Warner football team. In one of their conversations Jim discovered that he even remembered which position he had played on that team which left him wondering whether Mr. Morelli had an incredibly accurate memory or if nothing had really changed in his life for the past decade. It did seem as if many of the people on this street were stuck in some kind of a time warp and the only significant memories were of things that had occurred long ago. Still, the older residents were the heart and soul of the neighborhood. They had been here long before the influx of young transplants arrived and jacked up the housing prices. And they would remain here long after those same interlopers escaped back to the suburbs from which they sprang, driven out by the next crime wave and downturn in the economy.

"Tell your mom I got those flower seeds she wanted," he said to Jim.

Mr. Morelli loved to plant things but the "Italian garden" in his backyard was virtually nonexistent since most of it was paved over in concrete. So his mother let him go to town with the fresh patches of soil in her own yard, an arrangement that worked out well for both of them. He got to do his beloved gardening, she was able to watch as the flowers bloomed through the seasons.

"I will, Mr. Morelli. You take care now," Jim smiled and then hustled up the steps of his mother's front stoop. He wanted to avoid being sucked into one of his well-intended but often long-winded conversations.

He unlocked the front door with a key that hung from a chain which also held the keys to his apartment, the Toyota, the entrance to the firehouse, and Laura's place. Jim often thought that the level of complication of one's life could be measured by the weight of their keychain. And his was getting a bit heavy. He entered the tiny vestibule, opened the interior door, and looked up the staircase that led to the top floor. Jim had been going up and down this stair for years and there was a certain comfort in its familiarity. The dark, chocolate brown color of the railing and newel posts had stayed the same for all of those years. That seemed to be the main color theme for most of the buildings on the street as if some aggressive paint salesman had blown through the neighborhood around 1975 and made a real killing. When it came time for a fresh new coat the older, longtime residents would often choose the exact same color and layer after layer of the deep brown hue would build up until they sold the place to some young couple who would hire a guy to scrape through decades of the somewhat depressing shade and replace it with a bright, modern tint.

Jim started waking up the stairway. There was no need for any burglar alarms in many of these buildings, the creaking noise of the old wooden steps alone created enough noise to warn of any intruders. It was a familiar sound, a sound that he associated with home and belonging and the taste of boiled potato pirogues and sour cream. The appetizing scents grew stronger the further he went. When he was about halfway up, his mother appeared at the top of the stairs.

"Hi Jimmy!"

"Hi Ma!"

"You hungry?"

"Yeah, starved," probably the wrong choice of words he thought. She's likely to once again pile too much on his plate and load him down with the usual care package of rich, high calorie leftovers when he leaves.

He gave her a hug and entered the apartment. She almost seemed to be a bit shorter every time he saw her. He knew he wasn't getting any bigger, so he figured it was just another sign of her aging. And that made him glad that he had once again taken the time to see her.

"How's Laura?' she asked. That was usually her opening line. She liked Laura and was glad that she was with Jim, that he had found someone who provided a focal point in his life. It had always seemed like he was searching for something, even when he was a little boy, distracted by a longing for a certain unknown but never quite finding it. It showed in the things he did and the way he carried himself, constantly holding himself back in a subtle way, an outsider wandering his way through the world with an ambiguous longing for things he could never reach. She recalled watching him in Little League propped on the end of the dugout all by himself just staring off toward the outfield and remembered him sitting at the kitchen table gazing out the window and struggling to complete his schoolwork. Where was he at those moments, what could he have been thinking? Whatever it was, he had always kept it to himself. Laura was kind and gracious, but it was much more than Laura's personality that his mom liked. She offered a grounding in Jim's life, a clear future and a connection that would finally provide a place for him in a world that he seemed to have such a hard time fitting into.

"She's fine ma," he responded, and she was, but, as always, there was much that Jim chose not to tell her about.

"I got out on my boat yesterday" he said to her, guiding the conversation onto a comfortable topic.

"That's nice dear," his mom responded, sounding pleased with that image. But she had grown up in the neighborhood, now seldom left it, and the very concept of being out on a boat was beyond her perception. It was as if Jim had told her he had gone hiking on the polar ice cap.

They both entered the kitchen and Jim took a seat at the table while his mother proceeded to dish out his meal. She always put a great deal of effort into cooking for him whenever he visited. Even though he was a grown man, on some level she hadn't quite accepted the fact that he was capable of maintaining a proper level of nourishment for himself and it was vitally important to load him up with calories until the next time he came. Jim looked around the kitchen as he sat. It was a small room that somehow managed to contain the stove, refrigerator, table, and washing machine without feeling especially cramped. Those appliances had been there for as long as he could remember and each continued to function despite being years beyond the warranty period. Almost as if the machines sensed the pace of the neighborhood and continued to stubbornly plod on while the outside world moved and changed and grew without them. He looked out the window as he waited, toward the strip of small yards that ran behind all of the attached buildings on the block, an unbroken run of sheds and stunted trees and patches of concrete. There were clothes lines strung behind all the houses, some hung with bright white sheets and linens that swayed in the breeze. It was a serene view and a timeless one, a vision that hadn't changed for decades. You could have looked out of that rear window in 1950 or 1890 and viewed the exact same scene.

"How's it taste?" she asked Jim as he dove into the food.

"Great, ma," he responded, as he chewed on a mouth full of rich fats and carbohydrates. Screw the nutritionists and their Mediterranean diets, Jim thought, there's something to be said for solid, ethnic food. That's how his parents had eaten, how most of his friend's parents had eaten, and some of them were now in their seventies.

Jim continued to eat as they both sat at the table, quietly content with each other's company. In the past they had a distant and sometimes contentious relationship, but his mom had gradually mellowed as she aged and they slowly managed to settle into a comfortable mode of interacting with each other. Comfortable, but certainly not open. She had never met any of the previous women in his life, in part because none of them had really been all that significant to Jim, but largely because he chose to guard that aspect of his life from her. In fact, for many years she had no idea at all what he had been doing and on some level was afraid to find out. If she could be really honest with herself, which was probably never going to happen, she would have to admit that she really didn't know this man who was her son.

"So, when do you go back to the firehouse?" she asked.

"Not until tomorrow morning."

"That's nice, so you're off tonight?"

"Yeah, I'll get to relax tonight," he responded. He wasn't about to tell her that when he left, he would be heading over to Laura's apartment where he was going to spend the night with her in a place that was a brief drive away but seemed to exist on the other side of the planet.

Jim glanced at his mother as he ate and considered this woman who had raised him. She was like many of the longtime residents in the neighborhood. Good, solid, decent people who lived clean, simple existences. They were religious people who went to church and paid their taxes and didn't ask too much of life. Their blue-collar neighborhood contrasted so much from the Hudson Club realm of the Whitacres, a world that Jim's relationship with Laura had given him an opportunity to experience. He had one foot in each of those worlds but felt like an outsider in both. The new one seemed too decadent, the old one too limited.

When Laura's family invited his mother up to their home for dinner, she would sit quietly at their table smiling and nodding as Connie spoke of his work and Janice engaged her in polite small talk while Laura made sure she was comfortable. She liked the family and was really impressed by their home and their lifestyle. She even enjoyed the ride up there and savored the country scenery that offered such a fresh change from the streets of Brooklyn. But on some level Jim always sensed that she was relieved to be home when he would drive her back to Greenpoint, back to the basic life she was comfortable living in. He often wondered if it was comfort or fear that kept her there.

"Ma, let me do the dishes."

"No, you relax, I'll take care of it." His mother had her own way of doing things.

"Maybe you can look through those letters while I'm doing this," Those "letters" were always the same, come-ons for insurance policies or warrant extensions that had to be acted on within 30 days or you would miss out on a once in a lifetime opportunity at savings. They came in serious looking envelopes with formal headings as if they had been sent out from some eminent government agency. Jim always threw them in the trash, but he understood her concerns. She had grown up in a world that emphasized security above all else and she didn't want to fail to address something that might be vitally important.

Jim walked around the apartment while his mother worked at the sink. The place was a kind of museum of his life. He stepped into his old bedroom and looked around. Nothing much had changed, it was like he had walked away from it at the age of fifteen and came back as a twenty seven year old man to find it all undisturbed. A football trophy sat on top of the dresser right next to a plastic ship model he had built as a teenager. He remembered the scent of the plastic cement and how it used to stick to his fingers as he would assemble the tiny plastic parts, each of them precisely labeled in the complex instructional diagram that came with the set. As a kid Jim had spent many hours immersed in the project, concentrating with the same relaxed enthusiasm he would later feel when he checked the tools at work or prepared his boat for sailing.

The dresser that held the trophy and model was also the same. He didn't even have to open the draws to know the contents. The bottom ones still held the numerous sweaters he had received over the years as birthday gifts or Christmas presents.

They were woolen, a fabric he was uncomfortable wearing, and when he had moved out he left them there despite his mother's pleading to take them. They were too nice to throw out but too itchy to wear on most days, so they just sat there waiting for his next ski trip to Vermont where their warm bulk could be put to good use. Jim slid out the top draw of the dresser and saw that it still held an old collection of NFL football cards, the players posing heroically in colorful jerseys, all of them long retired, some of them now festering in various states of dementia.

As Jim walked back toward the kitchen he passed through his mother's bedroom. He glanced at his parent's wedding photo which, as always, sat on a prominent place on her dresser. There they were, smiling at the camera, she in a white dress, he in his army uniform just five weeks away from being shipped out to Vietnam, both looking impossibly young and oblivious to what life had in store for them. His father appeared strong and confident, and Jim wondered if that precise moment marked the high point of his life, that time before the immediate horrors of war and the slow toll of Agent Orange would take effect and change him forever. He could not know for sure because his father had always held back, suffering without complaint, and choosing to keep any nightmares to himself. There had been much Jim wanted to know but there was much that had been left unsaid.

When His mother finished up with the dishes, they both sat down in the quiet of the living room.

"So, what are you and Laura up to?" she asked as the two of them lounged on the sofa.

It was a simple question, but his mom had a way of saying a lot without speaking much at all. She was looking forward to Jim's wedding, and though she dared not to mention it, held out hopes for maybe even seeing a grandchild someday. She threw the words out in an attempt to feel him out, to get a sense if this time there might be any possibility of seeing some crack in the shell that her son maintained around himself.

Jim gazed at a colorful needlepoint that hung from the wall in a plain white frame. It had been done by hand, by his mother or grandmother he couldn't remember which, and was the only attempt at artistic decoration in the room. He thought for a moment of those paintings in the Whitacre's house that nobody seemed to look at but were perpetually lit by those tiny lamps. He could hear a dog barking away in a nearby backyard and from downstairs he picked up the distinctive sound of the metal lid on the mailbox shutting as the mailman dropped in the day's delivery. The everyday sounds of this house, the sounds of life that everyone hears but no one pays any attention to. A newspaper and a copy of *Reader's Digest* sat on the coffee table both brightly illuminated by the sunlight that flowed through the rear window.

What exactly did he want to tell her? What did she really want to hear? He loved Laura but could he say that marriage frightened him that he had thoughts of moving to a state that was thousands of miles away that he fantasized and dreamt about things that didn't exist?

"Well, she took me to a nice restaurant near Central Park the other day and we're thinking about maybe taking a little trip somewhere when things slow down for her at work."

"That's really nice dear, where are you thinking about going?" She was disappointed that they would only have their usual guarded conversation but was careful not to show it.

"I don't know. We like Block Island, but maybe somewhere up in Vermont."

"Well, be sure to send me a postcard wherever you go," Jim always did, it was her way of traveling vicariously and exploring the world without leaving the comfort of her home though he usually struggled to find sufficient words to write on the small cards other than "having a nice time and the weather's great."

They sat together for the next hour, and she spoke to him about what his aunt and uncle were doing and about cousins he hadn't seen for years and probably wouldn't recognize if they happened to walk into the room. She asked about work and Jim told her that he had caught a few jobs recently but that things were going well. After a while the conversation lagged, and Jim offered to work on the clogged drain and leaking faucet in the kitchen sink. He took on the task with relish since it not only filled the time but also gave him a fulfilling sense of being helpful to her. Jim was always glad for an opportunity to tackle some job when he visited. He knew he wasn't great at expressing much to his mother and it provided a comfortable way of showing that he did in fact care.

The repairs went smoothly as he worked away and the room grew brighter as the sun began to lower and stream through the small kitchen window. His mother sat in the adjoining living room reading the paper, and by the time Jim finished his work it was late afternoon, time to move on.

"Well ma, I'm going to get going. You want me to take down the garbage when I leave?"

"Yes, thank you Jimmy. Let me get some food you can take with you," she said and proceeded back to the kitchen where she placed a generous portion of the lasagna she had made into a plastic container.

Jim guided himself against the brown banister as he headed down the stairs, garbage bag in one hand, the food carefully balanced in the other.

"Bye ma. I'll be back soon," he said when he got down to the lobby. He could see her small figure standing in the shadows of the tight hallway at the top of the staircase.

"Be careful Jimmy!" she responded.

"Don't worry ma I'm always careful!"

Funny, he thought, she had never said that before. His visits usually ended with a brief wave and a "see you soon" with the thought that life would go on and not much would happen and in a short while he'd be back again to check on her and they would have their conversations and he would eat her rich, homemade food. Was she getting more worried in general as she got older? Had she read about that fire in her newspaper? But he could not know his mother's thoughts, did not realize that even as she waved, she was praying for him, praying to God or fate or whatever it was that ran the universe to continue to favor her son and allow him to experience the good things that awaited him in life.

As Jim headed down to the street Mr. Morelli was no longer to be seen. He's probably inside, he thought, checking out his mail, sifting through the bills and credit card offers and the hearing aid advertisements, hoping to find a letter or a postcard from one of his kids, the predictable routine a welcome interruption to his daily activity of observing life from the front stoop of his house. Jim took one last look at his mother's house before walking back to the car, a final glance at the grey shingles and the curtained windows outside his old bedroom. Much of it hadn't changed since he'd grown up on this quiet street. But now, it almost seemed like a part of someone else's past.

He drove on to Manhattan, to the bustle of the Upper East Side, where everything was in constant motion and change seemed to be a way of life, on to his present, adult world. Here he would enter a modern high rise apartment building, greet Adeem in the lobby, listen to the background of elevator music as he rose up fifteen stories, and enter an apartment where he and Laura would share heated moments of intimacy and warm containers of Chinese takeout.

Chapter 11

Jim woke up alone in Laura's bed the next morning. She had gotten up very early and moved about the apartment as silently as possible so as not to disturb him. When she left, she made sure to close the metal entrance door ever so gently behind her. It barely made a quiet click as it closed. She heard the sudden bang of another door echo through the end of the long hallway as another resident left his apartment. Laura moved briskly toward the elevator, handbag hanging from her shoulder, her steps muffled by the brilliant orange Nikes she wore on her feet. The soft, pillow-like running shoes would be replaced by the more fashionable and much less comfortable high heels she carried in her bag once she arrived at work.

Today she had yet another vitally important meeting to attend but a part of her wondered how so many of them could be considered so essential and why this one had to be held at such an ungodly hour. Sometimes it seemed like they were running a small country instead of a business. But she put all those thoughts on hold. She wanted to come across as a serious player when the meeting started.

Jim thought he had heard her leaving. He vaguely remembered a soft feminine presence but was unsure if it was Laura he was recalling or some woman he had been dreaming about. He rolled onto his side in the bed. There was an empty pillow and some ruffled sheets where Laura had been lying. And that rabbit. It had been around forever. Mr. Softee was his name and he had accompanied Laura through high school and college and now resided with her on East 80th Street. The old stuffed animal had seen better days but despite the many repairs to his torn seams he stared back at Jim with the same ludicrous smile that was always planted on his face. Jim could still pick up Laura's scent on the sheets, almost sensing the warmth from her body still buried in the heavy blanket. A piece of her blond hair sat on the pillow, a tiny memento of her presence.

Jim had managed to park his Toyota in a spot that was good for the next two days and wasn't due back at the firehouse until the evening. That allowed him the opportunity to lounge around the apartment by himself for much of the day. That was always a somewhat disorienting experience. The place seemed very quiet and empty with Laura gone. He surveyed the apartment from his position in the bed. It was about the same size as his place in Queens but a lot neater. He could see through an open closet door where her shoes were carefully arranged and neatly pressed suits hung from wooden hangers, all of them covered by plastic bags from the local dry cleaner. Her books were precisely stacked on a wall shelf that he had built for her, all perfectly aligned like a squad of soldiers, their titles a reflection of her life: Business Law, Principles of Investment, several Scott Turow novels, and an old beaten-up copy of *To Kill a Mockingbird*. Laura's laptop and a coffee cup filled with pens and pencils sat on a table near the window that overlooked the street. It all seemed strangely inert, like the items were on hold and just awaiting her return when they would again spring back to life and resume their roles as Laura's garments and possessions.

Jim would be living here in a few months. When they would be married. When this place would become "home". That would be an adjustment. He would miss the quiet of his Queens neighborhood and the convenience of parking his car right outside his door and the large window where he liked to watch the birds and the squirrels. And living in Manhattan would be strange. That had always been an "over there" kind of place where he would go to work or visit a friend or see the Rangers play and then return to the laid back familiarity of Queens or Brooklyn. But the truth was that Jim had never really viewed the Astoria apartment as his home, it was where he would sleep and eat and work out, just another situation in life that he was passing through without a strong commitment. He hoped to eventually feel that Laura's apartment would come to feel like his home but right now that just seemed like a distant possibility.

He got out of bed, headed into the bathroom and stood naked in front of the mirror. Shoulders, biceps, all looking good. Not massive like some of the guys at work, but tight and ready for action. He'd been exercising a lot recently and later he would try to go for a walk in Central Park before leaving for the firehouse. He would have liked a cup of coffee but first he needed a shower. Laura's aroma still clung intimately to his genitals, a scent that evidenced moments of passion from last night, much like the smoky trace that remained in his hair long after a fire and marked what he did for a living. Jim was always amazed at the sudden transition that occurred when he was with Laura, at how the intense physicality of sex would be followed by a totally relaxed state of comfortable exhaustion where he would lie next to her and feel like he could talk about anything, like he *wanted* to talk about anything. A state of mind in which he was not struggling for any sense of meaning or purpose but just living in the moment and feeling at peace with the world. It hadn't been like that with many of his previous women when the moments of pleasure had often been followed by some sense of disappointment and a need to move on by himself, back to the solitude of his own space.

He stepped into the shower and let the warm water flow all over his body. The small space inside the tub felt tight and restrictive and every time he lifted his elbow it brushed up against the wire baskets that hung from the tiles and held Laura's collection of shampoos. He accidentally knocked Laura's pink razor off of its wall bracket twice before he finally decided to set it down on the side of the tub. Even this bathroom was going to take some getting used to. Right now, it was geared for Laura's needs and it held the soaps and bottles and sanitary accoutrements of her life. He recalled getting up very early one morning and blindly feeling his way through the small bathroom without turning on the light so he wouldn't wake her up. He was just about to put his toothbrush in his mouth when he discovered that he had coated it with a generous squeeze from a tube of spermicidal jelly instead of the one that held his mint flavored Colgate toothpaste.

Jim continued to enjoy his leisurely shower and considered the wide array of shampoos that sat in the wire basket. Coconut, strawberry, cherry blossom, some of them enhanced with honey or fortified with oats. They seemed more like a collection of ice cream flavors rather than bottles of cleansing formulas. He selected the strawberry one and stepped under the adjustable shower head. That was something he could definitely get used to. It had a lever that adjusted the pressure and pattern of the water and ranged from a gentle flow to a hard pulsating beat that felt like a brisk massage. Jim often joked to Laura that this showerhead was the perfect girlfriend, it was easy to turn on and willing to cater to your every whim, a joke that she usually dismissed with a disgusted look on her face. It had become one of their routines. They had a number of routines, moments that had developed over time, small, somewhat ridiculous customs that only had meaning to the two of them. As Jim soaked his underarms he thought about those routines. They felt nice and reassuring.

Feeling refreshed by the shower Jim headed to the refrigerator to search out some breakfast. He opened the door and inspected the contents. Fruit, yogurt, leftover Chinese food, and a plastic container full of quinoa. Looks like he'd have to stop by one of the local bagel shops. He was disappointed to see that there was also no coffee left. Add that to the list of things to pick up later. He started rummaging through the kitchen cabinets in search of some kind of hot drink he could make to hold him over. Not even a jar of instant coffee to be had. Just a collection of caffeine-free herbal teas. Ginger peach, aloha pineapple, sweet peppermint, not all that different from the shampoos. Right now, he would have settled for a spoonful of Sanka, but even that was not to be found.

He settled on the peppermint tea and was about to take a sip from the steaming cup when his phone rang. It was Laura.

"*God* you were snoring last night!"

"Please, let's not be so formal. You can call me Jim," he joked in response.

He pictured her sitting in her office downtown. As usual she'd be dressed to kill in a dark business suit that managed to combine elegance with just the right amount of toughness. Jim worked in a rough environment, but from what Laura had told him about her competitive office, it also seemed to require a level of resilience. He had visited her at work, once, been introduced to Karen and Richard and Elizabeth and all the other coworkers until their names kind of blended together. He remembered Richard in particular. Remembered the friendly smile on his face as he shook his hand and said "so you're Jim. How very nice to meet you."

"Hello Richard, very nice to see you also," he had responded though he really wanted to say, "so you're the prick who's always upsetting my girlfriend," it gave him a certain level of satisfaction to know that Richard had no idea that he already knew so much about him and that what he knew about him wasn't very nice. If you could only read my thoughts. But you can't, you jerk.

However, all of Laura's cohorts were actually very gracious when they met Jim. They were friendly and engaging but at the same time most of them also shared a hidden level of curiosity. Who was this guy they had all heard about? How did Laura happen to wind up with someone who seemed to stem from a world that was so different from what most of them were accustomed to? They looked at this man that Laura was going to marry. A firefighter, which was an oddity in itself, but a quiet guy who seemed like a nice person. They could see the intelligence in his eyes. But they also noticed that he was an observer of life, someone who was always watching and evaluating the world around him, but at the same time holding back large parts of himself. He did not quite fit the image of a firefighter that most of them had in their minds. Jim was not six feet three inches and two hundred forty pounds of pure muscle. He was not the gregarious blue-collar guy some of them expected. If he had told Laura's coworkers that he was a poet or a schoolteacher, they would have no doubt believed him. And after their brief introduction most of them understood what Laura saw in Jim.

"How'd the meeting go?" Jim asked Laura as he stood in the kitchen and sipped on his peppermint tea. It didn't have the heft of his usual cup of coffee, but he enjoyed its warmth and refreshing flavor. He was flicking casually through the television remote and settled on CNN where a reporter was going on and on about some political issue.

"Ok, I guess," she responded, sounding not at all that enthusiastic.

"Was there a problem? Richard again?"

"No. It's just that…" she paused, and Jim could hear the wheels turning in her mind.

"I don't know. It seems like they're all the same. They go around the conference table and this one says this and that one says that and when it's all over we wind up pretty much where we began. I wonder sometimes if it's all worth the effort."

"You mean the meetings?"

"No, everything," She sounded lost and confused. This was unusual for Laura. It always seemed like she was the sure one, the one who created a clear path in life. Jim had always felt like he was the messed up one. He was sorry to hear her sounding so upset but on some level, it was also kind of reassuring. He's not the only one questioning it all. Jim thought about their conversation in the Brazilian restaurant. Perhaps she's carrying around her own confusions.

"Well let's talk about this another time," Laura said as she settled herself in a clear effort to return to the pragmatic mindset that her work required.

"Are you going to hang out or go back to your apartment?" she inquired.

"No, I've got the car in a good parking spot. I may head out to the park later," Jim hadn't been in Central Park for some time and the thought of escaping the city seemed appealing, even if it was just for a brief walk.

"Sounds good, there's left over Chinese food for lunch if you want and don't forget your mother's lasagna is in the freezer," Laura thought of Jim's tendency to accumulate piles of frozen food that were never eaten and eventually thrown out.

"I'll have the Chinese and save the lasagna for when we're together," he answered.

"Ok, I've got to run. Give me a call from the firehouse tonight," Laura responded, again with a tone of what Jim figured to be work related distraction.

Jim stared at the phone for a moment after she hung up. She was at the office and not in a position to have a long conversation, but he wished they could have spoken longer, that he could have tried to reassure her just as she had often reassured him in the past. He wanted to dive further into the doubts that she was obviously experiencing, as if exploring her mind might in some way open up insights about himself.

But it was time to get on with the day. Jim put down his cup and walked back to the bedroom to get dressed. The room was silent, just a few faint sounds of traffic moving way down in the street managed to filter through the bedroom window. A ray of sunlight streamed through the window and lit up the particles of dust that floated in the air. He could hear the rush of water moving through a pipe in the wall as someone upstairs flushed a toilet. The apartment was seldom occupied at this hour on a weekday and there was an almost uncomfortable stillness in the room like he was hanging out in a restaurant or museum that had been closed for several hours. The place had definitely lost its soul once Laura left.

With the thought of freshly brewed coffee and a relaxing walk to Central Park in his head Jim took the empty elevator downstairs, exchanged pleasantries with Adeem in the lobby, and then headed out to the street. Within minutes he was standing in a long line at the corner Starbucks where he waited to order a Tall or a Grande. He couldn't remember which size was which and wondered why they wouldn't just make it simple and offer large, medium, and small. It never ceased to amaze him how complex the simple act of purchasing a cup of coffee had become. He was in no rush and waited patiently as he watched the customers in front of him place their orders. Most of them just wanted to get a drink, tip the barista, and move on with their day but a few rattled off an endless array of specific requests as if they were buying a new Porsche and selecting from a long list of available options. Froth, no froth. Almond milk, soy milk. One person asked for a half pump. What exactly was to be pumped into their drink was unclear. When it was Jim's turn, he ordered a small cup of the Organic Yukon Blend just because he liked the name.

"You mean a Tall?" the young barista behind the counter asked rather briskly. He had a strong face and intense dark eyes and Jim thought he looked like an unemployed actor or an aimless graduate student majoring in philosophy, the coffee gig just a temporary detour in his career.

"Ah, yeah, I meant a Tall," Jim responded. But he really did mean a small and he debated whether he should leave a tall or a small tip after he paid for the drink.

After he got his coffee, Jim headed west toward the park. He set a nice leisurely pace and sipped from the paper cup as he took in the sights of the Upper East Side. Trucks, taxis, baby strollers, people staring through the windows of shops, the streets were far more active than his neighborhood in Astoria and an abrupt change from the stillness of Laura's apartment. A fire engine roared past with its lights flashing and siren wailing away, such a familiar New York sight that few pedestrians bothered to notice. Two guys and a woman rode in the back. They all had the worn, almost bored look that came from rolling out the door too many times in too short a period of time. Jim knew the feeling well. It turned the corner and in a few seconds the sound drifted away, and it was like it had never been there.

When he got near 5th Avenue, he could see the impressive

expanse of the Metropolitan Museum of Art spread out on the edge of Central Park. He crossed the street, walked about halfway up the steps in front of the museum and sat down. As he slowly finished the remnant of his Yukon Blend, he thought about the times in the past when he had sat in the exact same spot. That was before he met Laura and it seemed like a different life altogether. Back then Jim would occasionally come into the city just to walk around when his Queens neighborhood felt like it was getting too stale. Most of the time he'd wind up on the museum steps where he enjoyed watching the panorama of cars and tour buses and people as they slowly promenaded in front of the building. It was almost like watching a show. Out of towners sat on the upper level of tour buses and excitedly turned their heads in all different directions to take in the sights. Couples paused and looked up at the large colorful signs that hung like medieval banners from the front of the museum proudly announcing the latest art exhibit. People lined up at the pretzel cart eagerly awaiting their chance to taste the salty flavor of the warm doughy snacks.

Jim wasn't really into art back then. He had first come here just to hang out but after a while it occurred to him that this might be an ideal place to meet women. He tried approaching a few but his efforts usually resulted in awkward conversations with some women who had come all the way from Brooklyn or Queens to stare at an 18th century Vermeer. Flirting with a 21st century guy did not rank high on their list of things to do in the city. It seemed like the classic scene of man meets woman on the delightful streets of New York City was an illusion that only occurred in Hollywood movies.

Jim finished the few drops that remained in the bottom of his coffee cup, got up from the step he'd been sitting on, and started over towards a trash can to throw it out. Someone had left an empty cup on a nearby step and he was about to grab it but he suddenly stopped himself. Though the virus had been under control for a few years it had left an indelible impression on the minds of New Yorkers. Some of the older residents still wore masks on their faces and everyone in the city still carried some remnant of the pandemic nightmare. They all fully appreciated the return to the simple pleasures of eating in a restaurant or going into a theatre but still cringed when someone near them sneezed. Jim decided to leave the cup where it sat.

He left the front of the museum and headed into the park. As always, the instant transition from urban street to tree lined path was a pleasant shock to the system. He walked along a narrow lane that must have been unofficially designated as the place to jog. It was lined with men and women of all ages, many of them dressed in fashionable running outfits in loud yellow and orange colors that contrasted with the green bushes and trees. Jim found a comfortable bench and sat as he watched them bouncing past. Each runner seemed to have their own personal style. Some wore shoes that must have cost hundreds of dollars. Those were the serious runners who wore a determined air on their face and looked like they were training for the Super Bowl. Others had old, beat-up sneakers, tee shirts that looked like they had been worn when they last painted their apartment, and red, puffing expressions that seemed to be saying, "let me just get this over with."

Jim especially enjoyed watching the female runners. Some of them looked like they were in painfully good condition but were entirely too thin. They ran with an intensity, oblivious to all around them, their eyes focused on some distant goal that only they could see. Others had more normal builds, neither fat nor thin. They ran at a much slower pace, some conversing with friends who jogged along next to them. They looked like they were most enjoying the experience. He especially liked watching those who wore tight fitting running pants. The Lululemon crowd, women who looked like they had spray painted the thin material on their bodies, their buttocks moving sensually with every bouncing step.

When he moved on, he spotted one of the Hansom cabs going through the park with a couple sitting in the back seat, the brightly painted wheel spokes spinning rapidly in a red blur as the driver urged on a large white horse. Jim wondered if it was the same wagon that he had taken with Laura the other day. He remembered how comfortable and natural that had felt and how different it was to be moving through the streets in an open carriage while you were surrounded by taxis and cars.

Just beyond the next bend in the path he came upon a pond where some people were renting model sailboats from a concession stand. There were groups of parents standing all along the edges of the water helping their kids with the wireless control units that operated the miniature vessels. A few managed to catch the breeze and scooted rapidly over the calm surface. Most wound up hopelessly stuck next to the concrete wall that surrounded the pond, their young pilots nonetheless thrilled with the experience. As he watched the tiny white sails moving across the water Jim thought of his own boat and pictured how very small it must have looked when he floated in the wide expanse of the Hudson.

Jim walked away from the pond and came upon a very quiet section of the park where thick bushes and lush trees blotted out most of the city. Just the top floors of a nearby high rise could be seen peeking over the top of a large sycamore tree. After a couple on roller blades skated past the only people there were Jim and a woman who was sitting in the grass next to a stroller. Jim watched her as he lounged on one of the wooden benches. She was sitting next to a young boy, and they were both examining some items they had picked up from the ground. It was pretty obvious from her affectionate attention that he was her son. Jim didn't spend much time around kids and wasn't a good judge of their ages, but he figured the boy to be two or three years old. He had collected a small stack of acorns and was closely examining each one as he held them in his fingers. Jim could hear the mother telling her son a story in which the acorns were little people searching for a tree that they could live in.

There was something about the scene that Jim found mesmerizing. Here, in this one moment, the acorns and his mother's story were the only reality for this child. He was not in the middle of a busy congested city. His only sense of space was the small patch of grass he shared with his mother. For him this was an instant of pure fascination free of any regrets or confusions, a timeless moment with no past and no future. He wondered if the boy would remember this experience, if he would look back some day and recall it with fondness when he was grown up and entrenched in a demanding job or burdened by some challenge and think of it as one of the pure moments in his life. Or would it be forgotten, a tiny second in his life lost forever as if it had never even occurred. Jim hoped that wouldn't happen.

It was nearly three thirty and since he planned on walking to the firehouse Jim knew it was time to get going. He could still hear the mother's low, soothing voice behind him as he walked away from the bench. Soon he was on 5th Avenue waiting for a pause in the flow of taxis and buses. He crossed the street and walked on briskly towards Laura's apartment, dodging cars and sidewalks full of pedestrians. When he got to Park Avenue there were four lanes of traffic to negotiate, and he made his way on to a narrow green meridian in the middle of the street. Traffic sped past uncomfortably close to both sides of where he stood and he felt like he was on a tiny island surrounded by raging ocean currents. As he waited for the light to turn green he glanced at the long green strip of the neatly landscaped meridian which ran all the way down to 42nd Street where it came to an abrupt end at a mass of midtown skyscrapers. Jim liked Park Avenue, it was wide and open compared to other streets and its narrow band of trees and flower gardens provided some relief to Manhattan's uninterrupted surface of tar and concrete.

Adeem was unable to greet Jim in his usual friendly manner when he finally arrived at Laura's building. He was involved in an intense conversation with a delivery man.

"I'm telling you sir there is no Mr. Lefkowitz living here!" Adeem said, sounding frustrated and somewhat annoyed, which was certainly out of character for him.

"Yeah, well what does the label say right on that package? 'Mr. Myron Lefkowitz' and the address is *this* building," the delivery guy responded. He was wearing a brown shirt and shorts that were too big for him. His black socks and shoes highlighted the pale skin on his legs. Apparently, they'd been going back and forth about this for some time.

"I can't sign for someone who isn't here. For all I know he might be some guy who lives in Brooklyn. The address on the label is wrong," Jim could see that Adeem was straining to remain persistent but under control.

"Ok let me check with my boss," The delivery guy started dialing his cell phone. He was sweating through his shirt and looked like he had had a long day.

"Very good sir. You check it out but I'm sure you'll find the address is incorrect," Adeem rolled his eyes and nodded to Jim as he passed by.

Jim walked toward the elevator as the search for the alleged Mr. Lefkowitz continued. He genuinely liked Adeem and didn't like seeing him upset. He had worked in the building for several years, but Jim wondered if Adeem ever had the chance to walk through Central Park himself even once over all that time. His guess was that he had not, that he spent a long day smiling and opening a door for people who really didn't know him and then stepped into a crowded subway car for the trip back to his home in the Bronx where he would help his kid with homework or work with his wife on some unpaid bill.

"Oh, they meant to write *one hundred* Eighty Street!" The delivery guy's voice echoed through the lobby just as the elevator door closed. Jim was glad to see it all get resolved.

When he got inside the apartment Jim decided to give Laura a quick call before he left for work. He dialed but got her answering machine.

"Hi, you have reached Laura Whitacre. I am away from my desk at the moment but if you leave a message, I'll get back to you as soon as I can. Thank you."

He didn't want to leave a message or couldn't think of anything he really wanted to say or record on a machine. It wasn't her, it was just noise, a collection of electronic impulses that sounded like her. He grabbed some fresh clothes for work and walked over to the window to look out on the street. Cars and buses were inching their way through the congestion, the ceaseless passage of Manhattan traffic. It seemed like much of life was an endless series of events that just passed through. Time and people and experiences that came and went. Like those cars in the street or the delivery guy in the lobby and the boy in the park. Or that family that died in the fire. All those fleeting moments that arrived and just as suddenly disappeared.

Jim usually looked forward to going to the firehouse. But today was different. He found himself clinging to all the pleasant things he had experienced over the past several hours. The moments with Laura, the time on the steps of the museum, the image of the women running in the park and the pure innocence of the boy collecting the acorns all flashed through his mind. That was what it was all about. That was life and he wished he had time to experience more of it instead of having to return to work.

It was now time to leave, and Jim knew he had to put those sentiments on hold. But as he started his long walk, he couldn't shake the thought that with every step he took he was one step further away from all those memories.

Chapter 12

The man called himself a real estate developer, but one would be hard pressed to find anything he had developed more thoroughly than his own wallet. He normally stayed away from purchasing businesses but the idea for acquiring the place came highly recommended from one of his associates. A hardware store on the West Side, one that had been in business for over sixty years and had an established group of customers in the neighborhood. You take out a loan, hire a few people to run it, then just sit back and rake in the money. Next you take that money and spend it on other properties. Maybe a bit of a financial juggling act but he had been through all of that before. It seemed like a great opportunity, and he'd have to jump on it right away. The owner had passed away and all of his kids were living out on the west coast and none of them had any interest at all in taking over the place. They were chewing at the bit just waiting to sell. In a few weeks the deal was completed, and it looked like he had made another killing.

He was a realist and the proud new owner of the hardware store anticipated there'd be some initial issues to deal with. But he hadn't counted on the amount of work that would be involved. Nor did he realize that the rent was about to be raised to what seemed to be an astronomical level as the building and development bubble continued to transform the West Side from a remote whelm of street walkers into a popular business district. It became difficult to keep part time employees in the store. They'd work for a few days and then move on to better opportunities. The store manager was frustratingly incompetent. He'd purchase too much of one item and then quickly run out of things that customers really needed. Questions about inventory were generally met with a blank stare. And the man suspected that his store manager might be skimming off just enough cash to make it worth his while without making it obvious enough to get caught. Truth was, he'd be doing the same thing if he was in the manager's position. The store began to take up more and more of his time. It became an annoying distraction that kept him from tending to his other deals and gradually drew off increasing amounts of his energy, not to mention his money. He no longer wanted to run this business or go through the ordeal of selling it, most likely at a loss.

The idea came to him suddenly and randomly. One of those brief thoughts that just pop out of the blue with no rhyme or reason and tempt a person with its possibilities. A way out of this albatross of an investment. He tried to force it out of his mind, to find some other way of working things out. But the idea kept returning and alluring him with its simplicity. He began to make subtle inquiries, phone calls to people who in turn made calls to other people. They were never direct conversations. He always communicated through layers of connections and carefully isolated himself as much as possible. If he actually decided to pull the trigger on this there must be no way of tracing it back to him.

Of course, it could be done, it was done all the time he was informed. They called it a "small burn" which sounded kind of harmless, like a tool that wouldn't hurt anyone and almost sounded legal. They would do just enough fire damage to a portion of the stock. Smoke would ruin everything else. Insurance would handle the rest. And it would happen after hours, when the store was closed and nobody was there. His customers and clerks and the incompetent store manager wouldn't be anywhere near the place. It would be just like that series of small fires that had recently broken out in those 99 cent stores in the Bronx.

He thought about it for two days. He was a businessman and knew that not all investments worked out. It was time to cut this one loose. There were pitfalls in any new enterprise and this one had more than its share. He felt a nervous sense of relief when he finally made the call.

But as he dialed the phone, he was unaware of the fact that his hardware store sat in an old building with its own pitfalls. He did not know about the dry rot in the wooden joists that had been holding up the floor for the past century. Nor did he realize that decades of slow water leaks had damaged the very ends of the beams right where they rested on small pockets in the brick side walls. And that was where they supported most of the weight of the floor and the piles of stock and the people who constantly traipsed through the place.

Jim was walking south on 5th Avenue as the man was speaking to his underworld partner. By now he was back into a work mind set and he wondered who would be joining him in the firehouse tonight. Hopefully it wouldn't be that annoying Lopez guy. However the tour went, he'd be back here tomorrow morning to pick up his car. Maybe he'd go back to Starbucks for breakfast. This time he'd ask for a medium sized coffee just to piss off that barista.

When he turned west on 59th Street Jim spotted the Hansom cabs all lined up against the curb, the horses and drivers both looking somewhat bored as they patiently stood by waiting for customers. He stopped for a moment and looked at the third carriage in the line. It looked familiar and he wondered if it was the same one he had shared with Laura. Jim had never actually touched a horse in his life, and he recalled how he wanted to pet the one that pulled them on their ride. As he approached the animal the driver gave him a friendly nod as if he could sense his curiosity. Jim slowly reached out with his arm and began to cautiously stroke the horse's forehead. His hand slid easily over the short, smooth bristles of hair that covered his enormous skull and he was somewhat surprised by the feeling of firm bone that lay just below. The horse stood by impassively and Jim couldn't tell if he was enjoying the attention or was entirely indifferent to his touch. But Jim was most certainly enjoying the moment. For a few brief seconds he was not just a guy on his way to work but someone who was experiencing a close encounter with a creature who had not really been a part of the city for decades. Stroking the horse on this busy urban street was kind of like reaching back into those decades. Back into a time when 59th Street was covered with reeking deposits of manure left by dozens of horses who routinely plodded by accomplishing the work and the transportation of a different era. It took some effort for Jim to finally remove his hand, nod to the driver, and continue on his way.

He was several blocks south on 7th Avenue when he picked up the aroma of fresh bagels. Jim had skipped lunch and was famished, in part because he was too busy enjoying his time in the park but also because he couldn't get into heating up the leftover Chinese food. He found that he had to eat Chinese every couple of months just to remind himself that he really didn't like it. He stepped into the bagel shop and ordered his favorite, poppy covered with cream cheese. Even though bagels were usually a morning thing he decided to buy a dozen for the guys at the firehouse. There were several different kinds sitting in separate baskets behind the counter, all looking plump and inviting. You can have your Lincoln Center and Broadway plays Jim thought, this is what Manhattan was really all about. He considered what kinds he should buy. Certainly not the whole wheat ones, they would most likely be received with comments like "What are these fucking things made out of? Saw dust?" Sean liked the ones with the raisins. Dave, the big probie, loved "everything" bagels which he generally loaded with copious amounts of every cold cut he could retrieve from the refrigerator. Faiella? He had no idea what he liked so he threw in a couple of plain ones. The paper bag felt nice and warm in his hand as he walked out of the store.

It took another twenty minutes of walking before Jim finally arrived at the firehouse. As always, the old building was a familiar and comforting sight when he got there. Despite all of his earlier reluctance to go to work this afternoon it was a place that he liked being in even if spending 24 hours with some of the guys did get quite tedious. The top of the paper bag was beginning to soften from the moisture of the warm bagels inside and he was anxious to get them into the kitchen before the whole thing fell apart. Just as he was entering the open bay door he ran into Captain Lopez who was abruptly leaving the building. He had a large bag full of fire gear slung over his shoulder and was apparently on his way to work a tour in one of the neighboring firehouses. Lopez said nothing and met Jim with a brief nod. Jim was certain that he had no idea what his name was even though they had worked together on several occasions in the past. In an unspoken conversation their brief interchange went something like, "I know you but I can't remember your name" to which Jim mentally responded, "I do remember *your* name and I also recall that you're a real pain in the ass."

Once he got inside Jim saw that both probies were hanging

out at the house watch desk. He waved to them and received a hardy "What's happening Jim!" from Dave who immediately eyed the bag of bagels. Tyrone offered his usual shy but welcoming nod. The two of them looked like they enjoyed each other's company. Only one of them would have been scheduled to man the desk so they were obviously choosing to spend their time together, no doubt sharing the burden of being the lowest men on the firehouse totem pole. Jim felt a certain reassurance that two guys with such different personalities and from such different backgrounds could become friends. Like maybe there's some hope for mankind after all despite all the social and political battles that were always highlighted in the news.

Jim headed toward the kitchen and when he passed the truck, he noted that some of the tools looked a bit dirty. They must have had a job at some point today. Most of the senior men would have been right on top of the two probies with this. He could just picture Sean saying "Guys, asses and elbows on the rig, *now*," but Jim had his own way of doing things. "Mr. Thoroughly" much preferred the hands-on security of checking tools and masks on his own, seniority be damned. The kitchen was empty once he got there. He dropped the bag on the table and noted that Fox News was playing on the TV and the sports section of the *Daily News* was lying open at Sean's normal seat. It looked like Sean was working tonight and Jim was looking forward to seeing him. For all of his staunch political views, Sean was a decent man and an entertaining character who always made the tour more enjoyable.

Jim left the kitchen and headed up the stairs toward his locker. His hand slid along the polished brass handrail that ran on his left, clean white wall tiles covered the wall on his right. There was a scent of disinfectant in the air. He was always struck by the fact that the guys managed to maintain what was essentially a garage in such impeccable condition. Sometimes it seemed like mopping, polishing, and bed making were as much a part of the job as firefighting. When he passed through the second floor he made brief eye contact with Captain Henderson who was sitting in his office and talking on the phone. The barker was deeply involved in what appeared to be a serious and troubling conversation. His wife? His daughter? Maybe some pissed off chief? Jim had no way of knowing but it certainly didn't portend for an easy evening ahead. He broke off eye contact with him as quickly as he had made it and headed up the last flight of stairs to the third floor.

Faiella was sitting by his locker when he got there. As usual he was lost in folders of paperwork and cell phone messages.

"Hey Anthony, I left some fresh bagels in the kitchen if you're hungry." Jim really didn't like calling him Shakespeare like most of the other guys did. It seemed kind of insulting or at least showed their inability to accept the fact that the man happened to have interests that were different from theirs. Faiella was a bit of a misfit in the fire world and Jim could definitely identify with that.

"Yeah, thanks," he responded somewhat distracted by a text message he was composing.

As he stood by his locker observing Faiella Jim realized that for all their time together he really didn't know this man. They had both been assigned to Ladder 57 for years but in many ways, it was like they had never really worked together at all. Part of that was Faiella and part was just circumstance. He was generally the chauffeur and that meant that he rode in the front cab with the officer. Jim was always sitting in the crew compartment in the rear with the guys. Where the conversations and the complaints and the harsh humor would bounce through the tight space over the roar of the rig's motor, where they would nervously await the first view of smoke and fire pushing out of the windows when they were responding to a job. There was a certain comradery that grew out of that space that the guys sitting up front didn't experience. The shared insults and anxious moments and the ongoing evaluation of every woman they passed on the streets all helped to create a deep, unspoken bond among them. And once they arrived at a fire, Faiella usually remained in the street where he was responsible for operating the rig's aerial ladder while the rest of the guys were inside the building, often getting their brains beaten out.

Jim felt like he knew Dave and Tyrone better than he knew Faiella and they had only been in the company for a few months. It was like the guy was in some kind of bubble. He was employed here but existed outside much of the daily flow of the place. A full-time struggling writer but only a part time firefighter.

Jim began rummaging through his locker for some clean tee shirts. He casually searched through his uniforms and when he finally picked out the right ones he dressed very slowly and deliberately. Jim liked to gradually ease himself into the start of a tour, it was his way of mentally preparing for the job. He always arrived at the firehouse early and found that the routine of preparing for work gave him some sense of control in a job and a world that had so many variables. He slid into his "smush downs," an old pair of work shoes that were totally bent out of shape by the heel, the result of the hundreds of times he stepped in and out of them when he switched into his fire boots. They looked like shoes a homeless man would be wearing. He thought about getting a new pair but that would entail scheduling that trip to the supply store he'd been putting off for months. Jim gazed at the calendar that hung from the locker door to see if he could come up with a day to fit it in. He had a hard time coming up with a free day, partly because he really didn't want to put in the effort but mostly because he was very comfortable with his old, beaten-up shoes. It took several years to get them in that condition, and he hated breaking in a new pair. He scanned through the next few weeks on the calendar half expecting to spot something new or significant that might be coming up. But there was just the usual array of obligations and appointments.

"Can I get a signed copy of your book when it comes out?" he said to Faiella, making one final attempt to find something to talk to him about.

"Yeah sure, no problem. What did you say your name was again?" Faiella responded with a smile on his face in a rare display of outright humor.

Jim felt good about making at least some kind of connection with him and went back to tidying up his locker.

It was at this precise moment, one half mile south of the firehouse, that a man entered the front door of the hardware store. The place had been closed for almost an hour, but he had no trouble getting inside. They had provided him with a key which was a good thing because his forcible entry skills were severely lacking. Although he would not have understood the term, many would have referred to him as a kind of a criminal version of a Renaissance man. Drugs were definitely not his thing. Too many of his friends had done some serious time for that. But other than that he was always available to do a little of this and a bit of that. He had a diversified background, but real success always seemed to be just around the corner. He had started out in stolen goods but that proved to be too complicated since that involved being able to actually sell the things he acquired. And that involved dealing with other people which increased the risk of getting caught. It turned out to be information from a fence with a big mouth, along with an incompetent public defender, that got him thirteen months. Still, he chose to struggle on in his profession, an entrepreneur in disorganized crime in a world run by organized crime.

It seemed like a good opportunity when he got the call. Someone who had spoken to someone else. They didn't use résumés in this line of work, just a series of phone calls to people who knew other people. His name had come up, they needed a reliable guy who could keep his mouth shut, someone who had been around and was looking to make some money. Sure, he told them, he could set a fire. He didn't have to burn down a building, just a little damage for an insurance job. Sounded like a quick in and out. And he would be working on his own. He told them he had experience with fire. But he didn't mention that his experience was limited to lighting up a barbeque in the picnic section of Orchard Beach along with hundreds of other Bronx residents who enjoyed the park and the clean sand beach on Long Island Sound.

The man was actually enjoying his time in the store. Unlike his previous breaking and entry escapades here he was actually welcomed into the place and he had locked the front door behind him. This was different from breaking into people's cars and apartments. He had always been extremely on edge in that line of work, anxious to just get in and get the job done as quickly as possible. Here he could take his time, nobody was about to suddenly appear and interrupt his activities. His old burglary days came to mind as he walked up and down the aisles surveying all of the items that were stacked on the shelves. Just look at all this stuff, he thought, and I can grab anything I want. But after spending some time checking out racks of tools, stacks of plumbing fittings, and cans of paint he realized that there was nothing in here he really wanted, nothing he could quickly sell on the streets for a few bucks. He thought about the cash register for a moment but realized that it was probably empty seeing that they were looking to burn the place. Still, he figured it would be a waste to just walk out of here empty handed and he proceeded to stuff his pockets with small screwdrivers and packets of beef jerky. He took one last look at the front door to make sure that there was nobody nearby. Then he went to work.

Jim had just closed the door to his locker. He too was getting ready to start his evening. He nodded to Faiella and walked over to the nearest sliding pole. Officially they were only supposed to be used when responding on a run. But he much preferred sliding any time he wanted to get to a lower floor. It was quicker and easier than using the long flights of stairs. And, as many times as he had done it over the years, he still enjoyed the feeling of gracefully descending down through the two stories in the firehouse. It felt like controlled flying, you could use your grip on the pole to go slowly, speed your way down as rapidly as possible, or even come to a complete stop somewhere in the middle of the high ceiling floors if you felt like you wanted an unusual perspective of the room. He stepped quickly into the small closet that housed the pole, leapt onto the shining brass and sped his way down to the bunk room below and then switched to the next pole for the final slide down to the apparatus floor. The slick metal felt warm and welcoming in his hands as he descended, and he slowed to a gentle stop just as his smush downs met the dark rubber padding that sat at the bottom of each pole.

When Jim entered the kitchen Sean was back in his familiar seat munching on a raisin bagel.

"These fuckin ball players. They make more money in one season than I've earned in my whole life!" he said as he scanned through the sports pages of the newspaper.

"Well you can't throw a ball 98 miles an hour," Jim responded.

"Yeah and some of them probably drive about 98 miles an hour."

"Maybe. How'd your day go?" Jim inquired.

"Ah it was a long tour. That jerk Lopez worked here today."

"Well he's gone now. I just saw him walk out the front door. Henderson's in tonight. I passed him in the office and he looked pissed off about something."

"So what else is new? Shakespeare is driving, maybe the two of them will distract each other in the cab and leave the rest of us in peace," Sean had spent much of his career pretending to be annoyed by things, but the truth was he really enjoyed the constant interplay of personality clashes in the firehouse and sometimes contributed to it. It made the tour more interesting.

Sean walked over to the stove to light up a kettle of water. It was time to switch from the bitter coffee and the other beverage that got him through the day to a nice warm cup of tea for the evening. He stood there waiting for it to boil and watched as the bright blue flames shot from the burner of the large industrial stove.

The guy in the hardware store was also preparing to light something up. Once he had stuffed his pockets with as many free things as he could possibly grab, he proceeded to splash gasoline on the floor from the plastic container he had purchased earlier in the day. I did ok, he thought, I paid $15 dollars for it and they charge $21 for the same container in this store. He was definitely not a big picture kind of guy and that had always led to trouble in his life. He poured what he figured to be just the right amount of gas. It was hard to judge exactly how much was needed. They had told him to do some damage to the place without totally burning it out. His only guide was from the times he had squirted lighter fluid onto the charcoal in the picnic grill at Orchard Beach. What he failed to realize was that gasoline didn't burn by itself. He could have thrown matches into a bucket of the stuff all day and nothing would happen. It was the fumes that burned, suddenly and powerfully with explosive force. And he had generated copious amounts of those fumes within the confines of the closed store.

When he finally dropped the match on the floor it was the shock that first registered more than the burns. A ball of fire flashed in front of him. It singed his eyebrows and burnt his face and then immediately shot along the trail of gas he had just poured on the floor. It moved like it was alive, hungry, and eager to attack anything in its path. It instantly darted straight up a cardboard display case and ignited the paper "For Rent" signs that were stuffed inside it. In an instant, an entire shelf was burning and the flames were reaching up towards the ceiling. For a second, he was totally immobile. Then his startled body automatically reacted to the sudden blast of heat. He stepped backward and nearly tripped over a pile of buckets that sat near his feet. In his panic he dropped the plastic container of gas he had been holding in his left hand. That immediately added to the intensity of the flames. The man was now in full retreat and desperately trying to make his way back to the front door. The fire was burning freely, but thankfully for him the bitter choking smoke that would soon be generated from all the plastic products in the store had not yet overwhelmed the place. He could still see the door about fifteen feet away from him, still make out the day-light that showed through the glass. The sidewalk. His escape. All that mattered.

The jolt of adrenaline got him there in a heartbeat, despite the fire and his burns and the fact that it had all gone to shit. When he reached for the doorknob he was not aware of the fact that the skin on his fingers was no longer a part of him. It had peeled off like a thin pair of gloves. He desperately groped for the latch that would unlock the door but couldn't quite find it. What would normally have been a simple task turned out to be an enormous challenge. His terror grew as he pounded his shoulder into the closed door in an effort to force it open. He grabbed the latch with his damaged fingers and flipped it back and forth in a panic, unlocking and relocking the door two or three times before he finally managed to get it open. When he made it out to the sidewalk he sucked in large breaths of fresh air, a much-needed blast that replaced the choking fumes he had inhaled. And then he ran like hell with no direction in mind other than away from this place, nearly knocking down a woman who happened to be passing by.

Jim was just about to call Laura when the run came in. He figured she'd be back in her apartment by now and he had a few minutes before the start of the tour. There was a lot he wanted to talk about. The guy in the Starbucks, his walk through the park, the Chinese leftovers that still sat in her refrigerator and really should be eaten before it got too old and gross. But mostly he wanted to talk about what she had touched on when she called him from work. She was questioning things and seemed confused and troubled. He wanted to listen and see if he could put her at ease. Beyond that he wanted to hear about whatever conflicts she was experiencing at work or with life in general. It was something he could very much relate to. His own life sometimes seemed like a series of conflicts. And she had always been willing to patiently listen to him when he actually felt like talking about them.

The tones from the house watch computer rang out right after he had dialed the first three digits of her phone number. Fire in a store. They were getting numerous phone calls. Looked like they were going to work. Jim never liked it when jobs came in around the change of tour. He was a guy who liked to be prepared. He liked his routines, the things he always did to exert as much control as possible over the uncertainties of his job. There were too many unknowns when you had to respond to a fire around nine in the morning or six in the afternoon. That's when the work tours officially started and ended, when you may not even be sure of who you're working with. There might be some guys left over from the previous tour. Others may have been relieved by incoming personnel and already left the building. The officers hadn't yet had the opportunity to meet with the guys and conduct their roll calls, either informally in the kitchen like Henderson normally did or the official kind in front of the firehouse that Lopez demanded. That's when they would give out specific assignments for the tour and you would know where you'd be riding on the rig, which mask you'd be using and what tools you would need to carry. And Jim liked to take the time to check all that equipment, make sure they were clean and sitting in the right places and ready to grab as soon as they were needed.

It seemed like a bit of a scramble as they stepped into their boots and fire gear. Captain Henderson quickly yelled out the assignments to the guys as they stepped onto the rig and in seconds, they were out the door, the air horn and siren screaming as they rushed down the street. Jim sat in his spot straining to hear a report from the first unit that would arrive at the scene. He turned up the volume knob on the radio he wore under his fire coat and hoped that someone had charged it up sufficiently at some point during the day. Then he buckled up the remaining snaps on the coat and, surrounded by traffic and horn blasts, he waited.

Laura was just entering her bedroom. She was anxious to get out of her dress, slip into her comfortable grey sweatpants and sip a glass of white wine. It had been a long day. Jim had left the bed unmade. Again. That was not surprising. She knew he'd be gone by the time she got home but still missed him. This was an evening she really would have liked to just hang out and talk. But he'd be back tomorrow by nine thirty or so and she debated going in late to work or maybe even calling in sick.

"10-75, fire in a store, request an extra engine and truck." The words came out quickly and professionally through the speaker on the rig. It was Lopez arriving as the first due engine officer at the fire. The guy was a pain in the ass but at least it sounded like he knew what he was doing. Captain Henderson banged on the glass partition behind him in the front cab but the guys in back were already adjusting the straps of their air masks. Preparing for action. Jim tried to visualize what was going on at the job. They were responding in as the second ladder company and the first truck was probably forcing their way into the store at that very moment. He imagined the sound of the power saws and pictured the iridescent display of sparks that would fly through the air as they ripped into the metal gates that covered the windows.

The fire was largely knocked down by the time they arrived at the scene and the engine company was standing nearby. Their hose line was shut down now, but it looked like they had done some good work. A quick, aggressive attack with their two-and-a-half-inch diameter hose had blasted out several hundred gallons of water and drowned the fire before it was able to spread throughout the store. Jim noted the pissed off expressions on their faces when they took off their mask face pieces. A quick look at their officer explained why. Captain Lopez was right on top of them fully engaged in his usual annoying style of management. It looked like they had extinguished the fire despite his oppressive supervision rather than because of it.

The Ladder 57 guys stood by as Captain Henderson approached the chief in charge to see what he needed to be done. The first ladder company was trimming off shards of glass that stuck out of the edges of the broken picture windows and raking through the piles of burnt stock that had fallen out onto the sidewalk. The sharp, tinkling sound of glass falling on concrete stood out amid the background noise of droning diesel engines and high-pitched radio transmissions. Soggy piles of melted objects were scattered about, things that just minutes ago had been brand new sale items. A biting scent of melted plastic and slight whiffs of smoke still drifted out of the store. As Henderson huddled with the chief Lopez came over to them and mentioned that he had found the front door open when he first arrived at the scene.

For all his injuries and screw ups the arsonist had none the less accomplished his immediate goal. Much of the stock was burnt and useless. The rest of it was definitely smoke damaged. But from a financial perspective the attempt would prove to be a total failure. There would be no insurance pay out. The open door and remnant of gasoline would immediately identify the incident as a torch job. And a quick identification of the arsonist from the woman he had almost knocked down as he ran from the store would lead to his arrest and a trip back to prison. Only this time he'd be returning with some ugly scars on his face. Getting to the owner was another matter insulated as he was by the numerous intermediaries that lie between him and the guy who actually did the work.

"We've got to complete the searches and do some overhauling," the barker informed his crew. "Wozniak, Hillman, go back to the rig and grab some ten-foot hooks, you're going to be pulling down some ceilings."

Jim and Sean entered the store to look around. Faiella remained out on the sidewalk casually chatting with one of the engine guys as if the whole thing was some kind of inconvenience that had interrupted his plans for the evening.

"We'll be out of here in no time" Sean said as the two probies headed back to the truck to grab the tools. "Wozniak's cooking tonight. Let's see what kind of shit he comes up with."

Food was not on Jim's mind at the moment. When the Captain had mentioned pulling ceilings, he thought about the old gas lines they had uncovered at that store fire on 5th Avenue. He didn't need any more of the absurd thoughts that had been put in his head.

When the two probies came back with the hooks Henderson barked out his instructions.

"Wozniak, Hillman, you're with me in the front of the store, start working on getting those ceilings down," As the youngest and newest members of the company theirs was the most physically taxing and exhausting assignment. Tin ceilings were always tough to get down and the ones in this old store were particularly high.

"Hanley, Faiella, Walsh, you guys do the secondary." He was referring to the secondary search, a slow and very thorough check throughout the store to make sure that there were no victims. On very rare occasions bodies had been found buried beneath layers of fire debris, sometimes a day or more after the fire. It was never good PR for the fire department.

Sean and Jim headed into the store followed by Faiella who looked more and more like he didn't want to be there. There was no need for him to be standing on the rig operating the aerial ladder at this job. He'd actually have to go inside the building and get his hands dirty.

"You go left, you go right, and I'll take the middle. Don't fuck it up," Sean said to Jim and Faiella. As the senior man he asserted his role as the guy who would organize the search process. The store was wide and deep, and Jim moved cautiously as he stepped over fallen stock and fire debris. They kept their mask face pieces on as they worked, and they could hear each other's breaths as they worked their way in. No sense taking a beating now. The fire was extinguished, but there still might be some lingering fumes or pockets of carbon monoxide in the place. Jim worked slowly probing with his tool and carefully reaching under counters and around display cases. He was aware of that job out in Queens, a store fire in the middle of the night. It was locked up tight but when they got down into the basement, they found about a dozen illegal Chinese immigrants sleeping on mattresses. You just never know.

Laura had settled down on the couch to eat as Jim was working his way further into the store. A cable news channel was playing on the television and a small bowl of General Tso's chicken along with a glass of white wine sat on the coffee table in front of her. She used chopsticks to pick up delicate portions of rice and chicken in between sips of wine. She thought of Jim's usual frustration with the tiny wooden sticks and how he would generally start out using them only to toss them aside for a fork or spoon. They just couldn't keep up with the pace of his appetite. When she glanced over toward the closet, she saw that he had left an old pair of his running shoes on the floor. They were worn and beaten up and there was a pair of white sweat socks sitting on top of them that were clearly in need of laundering. She had been on him to go out and buy a new pair. But he was like that. He got attached to things.

After dinner she generally liked to watch the news for information that might affect tomorrow's opening bell on Wall Street. But it had been an early day for her and a long one. In a little while she was sound asleep on the couch, the empty bowl and half empty wine glass sitting beside her. She would miss the report about the decline in the Asia market and the one about problems with the proposed telecom merger. She would also miss the breaking news that would come in from the on-scene reporters who roamed around Manhattan in constant search of the latest disaster.

Chapter 13

Jim had nearly reached the back of the store as Laura slept. He was slowly working his way through the aisles, carefully prodding with his tool for any hidden pockets of fire and checking on the oft chance of actually finding someone who had been trapped in the place. It was darker back here. Light from the sidewalk streamed through the shattered picture windows but only managed to reach the front section of the store. The rest of it was engulfed in one large shadow. Brief flashes of light from the emergency beacons of the fire trucks reflected on the old tin ceiling above him. To his right he could see the moving beams from Sean and Faiella's flashlights piercing through the darkness as they searched the adjoining aisles. It was much easier to move around back here than it had been in the front of the store. There were no piles of debris to deal with and nothing had been burnt. With his own hand light, he could clearly read the labels on the containers of antifreeze that sat on the shelves. All of the store items back here were wet and the floor was covered with pools of water. The guys in the engine had used the full range and power of their hose line to make sure that the fire hadn't extended beyond the initial point of origin. He wondered if maybe they had used more water than they really needed. Captain Lopez had a reputation for being nervous at a fire. "The king of overkill" some guys called him.

It happened suddenly. So suddenly that his initial reaction wasn't fear. He was surprised and oddly embarrassed before he felt anything else. Before the shock of it all. Before a taste of utter horror stabbed deep into his gut. What would the guys think if they saw him now? Firefighters weren't supposed to move, or be moved, in this way. For a split second that's all it seemed like. An abrupt slip, a sudden drop. In a heartbeat he was totally out of control, his feet above his head, his arms flailing at his sides, his tools falling from his hands. You never gave up your tools. That had been drilled into him. And now his were gone, dropping away somewhere like the rest of his body. He felt himself flipping backwards and falling, falling for what must have only been seconds but seemed like forever. That was when the fear kicked in and he didn't know where he was falling to or how long it would take before he landed on something.

It ended with a thud. And the pain. The shock wave snapped through his air cylinder, into his back, and through his chest. It reverberated through his body like a powerful punch. For a moment it distracted him from the rumble of the world that was collapsing around him. He was stunned. He was scared. In an instant, the meager light he had been working in was replaced by utter darkness. He could see nothing as the dust and debris surrounded him. His helmet was knocked from his head as he fell and he felt dangerously exposed. The face piece of his mask somehow managed to remain in place, and though it magnified the sound of his deep panicked breaths, it could not shut out the roar of falling timbers and wooden flooring and store shelves that continued to rain down from above. The cascade of debris seemed endless. It continued to flow into the basement with an overwhelming sound, a deep rumble that shook the building and vibrated right through his body.

And then, a silence. For a while Jim could still hear the sporadic crashing of smaller items falling down from the first floor into the basement. In a few minutes even that came to an end and he was surrounded by a hushed stillness. The taste of warm blood flowed through his mouth. Had he bit his lip as he fell? Please, let it only be that. He could still breathe and tried to move. He could not. Something on his left side had pinned him down and he could not move his arm, the weight pressed firmly on his shoulder. Despite the shock and the pain, he summoned what strength he had left. He strained and pushed, desperate to free himself from the tight, claustrophobic grip of whatever it was that held him. But he could only lie there. Helpless.

The gradual decay of several decades and the stress of a few minutes had finally taken its toll. Hundreds of pounds of water from the hose line had added to the weight of the stock and the shelves and the fixtures and everything else in the store and provided just enough force to finally overwhelm the old, dry rotted floor beams. They gave way in the rear of the store. In the dark area, on the left side. Right where Jim happened to be working. No rhyme or reason why there and not someplace else. An indifferent act of fate. It just happened.

Jim tried to think as he laid in the silent rubble. The initial shock of the fall was fading but the pain was not. He began to cautiously probe and test his body in an effort to determine just how badly he was injured. A part of him was afraid to find out. Like if he didn't see something really bad it wouldn't exist. He could move his right arm and leg. That was reassuring. But his left side was still immobile. Whatever it was that was pressing on his shoulder had a tight grip on his left leg as well as his left arm, he couldn't move them at all. But he found that he could wriggle his fingers and toes and, although he couldn't actually reposition himself, he could at least flex the muscles in that side of his body. That gave some sense of relief from the fear of being totally immobilized. If he could move even a little bit he could act. He could try to survive. For that's what he *had* to do right now. They would be coming for him. He had to hang on.

His mask must have at least a half a tank of air still remaining if not more. He had only been working in the store for a short time. He had to control his breathing. Slow it down. Get hold of himself and his fear. Stretch out that air tank as much as possible. Hold on until they get to him. He tried to calm his breathing. One inhalation, hold it, very slowly let it out. Like that breathing technique in yoga Laura was always on about. Laura. Not now, concentrate, concentrate, calm down, and control what you can. Control? In this? He banished the thought from his mind.

He had to communicate. Let them know. He was here. He was alive. He grabbed for the radio with his right hand, just as he had done hundreds of times in the past. It always hung on his left side, beneath his coat. The microphone was merely an inch from his fingers. But he could not touch it. His coat and the radio were both tightly covered by that immovable weight that held down his side. He had to reach them in some way, make a noise, send some kind of beacon. I'm here, I'm here! He began to beat his free hand against a large timber that had fallen on his right. Again and again as hard as he could. But he only managed to make a soft muffled sound as his glove struck the wood. If only he had his tools. They were as buried as he was. He could still taste the blood in his mouth. There seemed to be more of it now and he felt its warm moisture dripping from his mouth and collecting at the bottom of his face piece.

Jim became immediately alarmed when he heard the vibrating sound that suddenly emanated from his mask. The low air pressure alert. Time was running out. He must have been breathing faster or longer than he thought. Or maybe the tank had not been full to begin with. He always checked out all the equipment before the tour. Always Mr. Thoroughly. Not this time. The job had come in too soon.

There was no hesitation when the tank finally ran out. No decision to be made. The tight plastic seal that ran around the edges of his face piece created a suction as he tried to inhale a breath that was no longer to be had. The mask was sucked into his face and created a gagging sensation that left no other alternative. He immediately ripped it from his face with his right hand. He needed to inhale regardless of what might be available to breathe in the tight atmosphere that surrounded him. Like a man popping his head above an ocean wave desperate for a lungful of life.

His first breath was a deep one, followed by a few short, cautious inhalations. The dirt and soot were overwhelming. His nostrils were immediately assaulted by a sharp, irritating scent that left a dry, dusty taste in his mouth. He felt like gagging again but struggled to control himself. In a minute or so he was able to calm down. His breathing was labored and the air was foul. But at least he *could* breathe as he laid there, longing for a voice or a sound, anything that might give him some hope.

Although he could not have known it, the quirk of fate that trapped him in the basement had also mercifully granted something in his favor. Carbon monoxide levels around him were low. Had the concentration been higher he would have been unconscious in a few breaths and dead in minutes. The fire was contained to the front section of the store and had been quickly extinguished. When the front windows were taken out a considerable portion of the toxic fumes had been vented from the building. Jim was surrounded by heavy wooden beams, piles of wet debris, and volumes of dirt but the CO in the air was just sufficient to make him feel tired and confused and a bit dizzy. It muddled his thoughts and slowed down his thinking, but it also had somewhat of a relaxing effect. He eased the strain in his body and stopped resisting the immoveable floor joist that gripped him. As he lowered his head into the dust it cradled around his skull like a soft pillow. He thought he could hear vague sounds, far away. Somewhere above? A high-pitched sound that for a moment reminded him of saws. Saws. He hadn't checked the saws. But he didn't have time. The job had come in too soon. Then the notion disappeared from his mind, and he just laid there and thought of nothing.

It was his father who first appeared. A vision just above him. He was watching Jim, just looking at him with a sad expression on his face.

"Dad, was it like this?" he asked, though no words were spoken.

"It'll be alright," was all he answered and both knew without saying that "it" was something that had happened in a rice paddy. Decades ago, on the other side of the planet. And Jim was saddened, not for himself, but for the knowledge that they hadn't been able to share that when they were together. There was so much that had been left unsaid.

He was having difficulty now holding onto thoughts as the carbon monoxide seeped through his blood stream and fogged his mind. That was when Laura appeared. She was looking off into the distance like she was someplace far away. Jim summoned up enough awareness in his brain to know that she was home. In her apartment. In that place he had left such a short time ago. She was blocks away. Blocks away from where he was now, from what was happening to him now. And he wanted so badly to talk to her. If only he had dialed her number a few minutes earlier. To tell her what? Thank you. Thank you for being there, for dealing with all my nonsense. For listening to all my confusions.

Blocks away. Blocks away. The words formed in his sluggish mind almost like they were physical things that could be touched rather than mere words.

That's when the sounds began. Coming from far above. He ignored them at first but they steadily drifted into his awareness. Very muted echoes but then louder. Much louder. A creaking noise that sounded like large pieces of wood gradually moving and shifting. The sound grew in intensity and came closer. The hopelessness and terror returned and ripped into him as he waited for the force he knew was coming. A force beyond his control, beyond anyone's control. He tensed and prepared. For the fall, for the end. Prepared for the immense weight he knew was above him. Would it be the entire floor, the entire building?

But nothing happened. And the sound continued, closer now, almost directly above him. That's when he saw the light, a bright beam that pierced the darkness and illuminated the shafts of dust that floated through its narrow path. It was moving slowly, first to the left and then to the right. Probing and searching. Like someone was directing it.

Chapter 14

Sean immediately knew what had happened. A loud groan, a sudden cloud of dust, and a deep rumbling of heavy objects sliding and falling, the flooring, the shelves, the entire corner of the store suddenly dropping into the basement as if a trap door had opened up beneath it all. There was a moment of disbelief. This couldn't be happening. And then a second of fear. Was the rest of the store also going down? He immediately froze in his position in the middle aisle, waiting, hoping it would all just stop. He could feel the floor vibrating under his boots. In a minute the enormous roar ended but he could still hear the occasional crash of heavy objects falling into the void. And then it was silent. As the dust cleared he took stock of the situation. A section of the flooring in the rear had collapsed. Over on his left. Over where Jim had been searching.

"Mayday, Mayday, Mayday! Ladder 57 roof to battalion. Chief, the floor in the back of the store has just collapsed!" Sean screamed into his radio.

Thirty-three years on the job and he had never had to transmit such a message on the radio. Not at that job where he discovered nine people lying dead at the top of the stairs of that tenement fire. Not even the time he was momentarily lost in the smoke inside that enormous theatre. It seemed so unreal, like something you'd train for but would never actually happen.

"Battalion to member giving the mayday what is your location?" The chief suddenly tensed up, his heart pumping and blood pressure shooting skyward. The job had been going so well, the fire was out, it had all seemed under control. And now this. The worst thing he could possibly hear.

"This is Ladder 57 roof. I'm in the middle of the store, it looks like there's been a major collapse in the rear," the words shot from Sean's mouth. He was trying to calm himself and speak as clearly as he could, but the fear and sudden jolt of adrenaline made it difficult.

"Battalion to Ladder 57, you get that message from your roof man?"

"10-4 chief. I got three guys in the rear doing searches," Captain Henderson responded. None of his extensive fire ground experience kept him from also experiencing an instant moment of intense anxiety. These were his guys.

"Ladder 57 you got all your firefighters accounted for?" The chief was desperately hoping for a quick affirmative response from the Captain.

"Stand by chief, I'm checking now."

"Ladder 57 to 57 chauffeur. Where are you?"

"I'm in an aisle on the right-hand side" Faiella responded.

"You and Walsh, get back to the front. Now."

"Ladder 57 to 57 irons. What is your location?" Henderson had the two probies right next to him. Once he got Handley, they were good.

"Ladder 57 to 57 irons," he repeated for a second and then a third time. Everyone at the scene hung on the Captain's radio call, desperately hoping to hear a response. But it was only met with a prolonged silence.

Sean felt like he was standing on the edge of a cliff as he anxiously waited to hear his friend's voice, a "yeah I'm ok" or "I'm on my way out," anything to indicate he was safe. That he was still alive. When nothing came, he accepted the stinging reality of the situation.

"57 roof to 57. Captain, Jim was working right by the collapse," Sean informed Henderson. It was no longer possible to hope for a temporary glitch in communication. Jim wasn't in the process of putting down his tool to grab hold of his radio. He wasn't fiddling with the control knob trying to turn up the volume. Wherever he was he could not respond. He was just gone. Suddenly and frighteningly ripped from the scene. As if he had never been there.

Shit! They were almost out of here. Just finish the searches and do some overhaul and they'd be back on their way to the firehouse. Back to where just a short time ago he was complaining to Jim about all the money those baseball players made. And now this. His friend was, what? Lost? Hurt? Worse than that? Sean tried to put all his upset on hold as he worked his way back to the front of the store. This wasn't the time to be thinking like that. It was time to go to work.

There was a frenzy of activity already underway when he got there. All of Captain Henderson's vast experience had immediately kicked in. He was barking out orders, one after another, in a loud, commanding voice, establishing the strong control that the situation so desperately called for. Like his entire career had been leading up to this one moment. A moment that begged for his strong presence.

"Wozniak, Hillman, grab those saws and come with me!" he ordered the two probies.

"Faiella, go back to the truck and get the fan," Most of the smoke had lifted from the store but Henderson wanted to get it in operation to draw out as much of the remaining haze as possible. Every clean breath, every moment now mattered.

As Faiella headed out to get the fan Tyrone and Dave followed Sean and the Captain toward the collapse area. When they got there, they were met by a total mess. There was a large open gap where the floor had been. It was filled with piles of debris and a jumble of items that had fallen down from the store. Sections of the old floor beams peeked out from beneath it all. They looked like they were leaning at an angle against something in the basement. The oil burner? A partition wall? It didn't much matter. Whatever object those beams were lying on top of seemed to be strong enough to hold the weight of all the wreckage above. It was possible that a small void had been created in the space below the beams. And Jim may very well be somewhere in that void. A classic "lean to" collapse the Captain thought as soon as he sized up the situation. He could picture it in his mind. There was even an illustration of one in the book he had written. But it was going to take some doing to unravel. Much of the debris would have to be removed before they could even get to the beams. Then the saws would come into play as they cut through the flooring and thick wooden floor beams. A plan of action formed in Henderson's mind. And along with it a ray of hope.

Out in the street the chief had also gone to work. His report of a missing member caught the immediate attention of firefighters throughout the five boroughs of the city. Additional engine and ladder companies roared through the crowded streets. Specialized rescue and collapse units began rolling in, primed to put their expertise to work. The police halted all traffic on the nearby streets and staging areas were established for the incoming personnel to gather. The utility companies came to the scene to cut off the gas and electric supply to the building. Even the local subways were halted to ensure that no additional vibrations would affect the precarious state of the collapse.

The media began arriving at the scene as all this was happening. Local cable stations with two person crews arrived and competed for space with the numerous reporters from major news networks who showed up in huge vans covered with satellite dishes. There was an air of tension flowing through the now crowded street and the reporters bombarded the firefighters with questions as they walked past. "What's going on? What do you know? Has the missing man been located?" But the guys ignored them as they hustled toward the building, anxious to go to work, eager to do anything that would help resolve the nightmare. One of the brothers was missing. Everything else could wait.

By now there were dozens of firefighters in the store. Captain Henderson and the members of Ladder 57 were working right next to the collapse area poking through the rubble, trying to remove enough debris to get access to the floor beams. They worked quickly and efficiently, the sooner they got to the beams the sooner they could start cutting them and hopefully establish a path into the void that had engulfed Jim. The chief continued trying to reach him on the radio, calling out for him, pausing for a response, and following it up with another transmission, all of which went unanswered. Although he was standing in a safe position out in the street he was as stressed as anyone at the scene. This was his operation, his guys. What had he missed? What could he have possibly done differently so that this wouldn't have happened? He fought off the deep sense of guilt and responsibility that clung to him. He had to function now, do everything he could to resolve the situation.

Occasionally there would be an abrupt halt to the work and men would yell down into the hole at the top of their lungs, calling Jim's name, hoping for some kind of response, a weak voice, a banging sound, anything to indicate he was there. They would stand by, nervously waiting for a sound. After a few moments of silence the work would begin again, digging and lifting and removing the accumulation of objects that stood in their way.

A long line of men snaked through the store all the way out to the street. A debris removal line, firefighters handing off arm-fuls of wreckage to each other, piece by piece, each load getting them that much closer to reaching Jim. When Sean glanced back for a moment and saw the firefighters behind him he instantly flashed back to the World Trade Center and the long lines of cops and firefighters and volunteers who were doing the exact same thing years ago, frantically digging into the mountains of devastation with the hope of freeing survivors. At least for the first two nights. After that it was a recovery operation, the scent of dead bodies directing a daily grind which was occasionally interrupted by dozens of department funerals. Not here! Not now! Sean jumped right back into the work and forced away the memory. They were making progress, it wouldn't be long now.

"Bring the saws over!" Henderson yelled over to Dave and Tyrone both of whom were knee deep in the debris, Dave using his immense strength to pull up heavy pieces of wood, Tyrone quickly raking through the remaining items and handing them off to Faiella who was standing right next to him.

"That's where we're gonna cut" the Captain indicated, point-ing to a section of the floor boards that were still attached to the now reachable beams.

"A small square section, big enough for us to enter. Then we'll work our way through anything that's below that," Henderson ordered. He had been solid as a rock through the whole oper-ation, barking in his usual manner but performing like a pro, organizing, leading, prodding, and providing direction and hope.

In contrast, Captain Lopez was moving about frantically and issuing an endless stream of instructions to the guys in his company. "Will you please just shut the fuck up!" bounced through Sean's mind, the words unspoken but heartily felt. He found Lopez's incessant barrage of orders to be distracting and grating on his nerves. This guy has a harder time fighting off his own anxiety than he does fighting a fire, he thought. This isn't a promotional exam. It's the greatest test of actual performance you'll face in your entire career. So calm the fuck down and start performing! But despite Lopez's somewhat shaky command presence his firefighters were right there and they were ready, standing by with the oxygen and the backboard and the first aid kit. They had gathered anything that might be required before the rattled Captain even thought to ask for it.

The ear-piercing sounds of power saws began ripping through the confines of the store. The noise was overwhelming and blotted out the men's voices and the constant chatter of urgent messages that screeched from the radios. Sean and Tyrone each grabbed saws and started cutting into the thick beams and sections of wooden flooring. Chips of wood and sawdust flew back from the roaring machines as they slowly ate through the slanted wall of timber. The scent of the exhaust from the gas-powered saws filled the air and firefighters scrambled to the side to avoid the barrage of splinters that kicked past. Sean worked intently and concentrated on each of his precise cuts, carefully watching as the spinning saw blade tore through the thick beams, using every bit of his hard-earned experience to work as quickly as possible. He realized that time was just as much an opponent now as the mountain of wreckage they had to work their way through. Tyrone stood off to his left. His background was nowhere near Sean's and he worked with less confidence as he slowly ripped his saw through the wooden floor boards. But he was able to figure out exactly where to cut and as sections of the flooring loosened Dave scooped them up and handed them off to the line of guys next to him.

Faiella stood off to the side, watching and worrying, shaken to his core by the sudden confrontation with the harsh realities of his job. Men got hurt. Sometimes they died. Years of distractions had shielded him from that. Now there were no distractions, no books to write, no urgent phone calls or text messages to attend to. The nightmare sitting in front of him was the only reality.

In a few minutes they managed to finish their task and, once they shut down the saws, an abrupt silence returned to the store. The background noise resumed, sounding so muted after the intense racket of the sawing operation. Voices on the radio, men shouting in the distance, the screeching sound of wooden fragments being dragged away, Captain Henderson ignored it all as he anxiously peered into the opening they had just created. They now had a good-sized hole, about three feet square, just enough to get into and, hopefully, drag Jim out of once they found him. But when he directed his light into the opening, he could see that there was still quite an accumulation of debris lying below. There was a space, no higher than four feet, between the collapsed floor section and the accumulation of refuse that was scattered beneath it. And that gap seemed to get narrower the further you went in.

This was not going to be the simple, let's get in, tie up Jim to the backboard, and drag him out to safety operation he anticipated. Once they entered the small opening, their work was just beginning. They'd have to crawl in, shore up the flooring above them as they proceeded, and then carefully pick their way through all the debris and hope to find the small void that he hoped existed. Because if it didn't Jim had no chance at all. There was no way he could have survived the collapse of all this wreckage on top of him.

Henderson refused to allow any negative thoughts to restrict his thinking and he immediately started to plan his next steps.

He felt for the yellow bag that hung at his side. It held the long vinyl search line that he would deploy out as they moved in, ensuring a guide to the way out from the mess they would be crawling into. Everyone would have to wear their mask, there was no way of telling what the air was like down there. There'd have to be a constant supply of wooden cribbing available so that guys could shore up the spaces they had to crawl through. And, he'd have to keep a tight control on his men, especially the probies. The Captain knew too well from past experience that guys often got lost themselves, or worse, when they became involved in the emotional efforts of trying to recover a fellow firefighter. It was a tight brotherhood, which was a good thing. But those same sentiments could sometimes push them beyond limits they could safely reach for.

Faiella was the first one to enter the hole. Faiella, of all people. Fucking Shakespeare. But not because he was especially courageous or motivated or even an exceptional firefighter. He had no special training or experience to warrant his decision. He just happened to have the misfortune of being the one standing closest to the opening when Henderson issued the order.

"Mask up, let's go!" the Captain said to his men. He had stepped away from the hole to call for someone to bring up the rescue air pack, a device that would be hooked up to Jim's mask and provide a vital supply of air once they found him. Sean and Tyrone had carried their saws away from the opening they had just cut and were standing near the Captain. Dave was helping a guy from another company drag a heavy section of timber away from the hole. And Faiella stood there, alone, right next to the hole, the members of the other companies staring at him. He really had no choice. Peer pressure alone dictated his actions. He was the chauffeur of Ladder 57. A guy from Ladder 57 was missing. Case closed. He slid on his mask facepiece and cautiously stepped down into the opening. Henderson was right behind him, closely followed by Sean. Tyrone and Dave remained near the hole as per the Captain's orders. He had instructed them to pass in the cribbing and to make sure that the search rope didn't get hung up on something as he proceeded into the void. And, more than anything in the Captain's mind, stay the hell out of trouble. He didn't want another one of his men to go missing.

Faiella proceeded to crawl over the accumulation of debris, moving slowly, pushing aside objects that were blocking his way. Fragments of splintered wood were scattered throughout the tight space, the pieces shifting beneath the padded knees of his bunker pants as he crept forward. The diaphragm in his face piece amplified his breathing- deep, nervous breaths, each one a reminder of the limited supply of air stored in his tank. He was already struggling with the thought of just how far he should go, how much he could push, or how hard the Captain would push him, before he'd be too far removed from a safe exit out of this maze. In the silence he could hear Sean and Henderson huffing away right behind him. His movement became increasingly awkward and tiring as he crawled forward. He fought off a sense of claustrophobia in the tight confines as the top of his helmet kept hitting the flooring and wood beams that hung precariously just above his head. He wasn't ready for this. This was above and beyond. Faiella was the chauffeur, the one who usually remained in the street observing the building and operating the aerial ladder. This was the stuff the gung-ho guys did, the rescue specialists with their extensive training and aggressive instincts.

Slowly, carefully, the three men inched their way through the web of broken floorboards and leaning beams, their hands constantly gripping the search line as it stretched further and further away from where they had entered. Now they were some fifteen feet from that small opening, but it seemed far more distant.

They moved together, one right behind the other, as if they were not three separate men but one unit struggling through an urgent search for a man and a desperate race against time. A steady sound of hammering echoed through the void as men worked behind them and positioned the wooden cribbing to keep their passageway from collapsing, an image that each of them struggled to rid from their minds as they continued forward.

By the time he was twenty feet in, Faiella had just about reached his limit. He lost all sense of how long he had been moving through this mess or how much time he would need to escape it. He had been breathing very rapidly. How much longer before the tank just ran out? He stopped and turned around to direct his flashlight behind him, desperate to leave. But he could see that Henderson and Sean were still moving steadily toward him, still crawling forward with purpose and showing no sign of giving up. They were going to push on. With the two of them blocking the way it wouldn't be possible for him to leave even if he tried. There was no escape from this nightmare. It felt like he had just been casually sitting at his locker in the firehouse. That was only a few hours ago but from here, stuck in the chaos of this disaster, it seemed light years away. Alarmed and frustrated by a complete inability to alter his fate he turned again and continued moving forward, the search rope tightly gripped in his left hand.

And that's when he spotted it. An opening, just ahead, right next to the foundation wall in the rear of the building. The endless jumble of debris just seemed to end at the edge of a small crevice. He swept his light back and forth to be sure of just what he was seeing. And it was what he thought. A void. The gap they had been searching for, hoping for. Somehow a small space had formed beneath the utter wreck of all that had collapsed around it. If Jim was anywhere in this mess that was where he should be. But it wasn't going to be easy to reach it. The flooring above him got lower and lower the further you went. This was going to be an even tighter space to move through.

"Capt, I see something! Looks like there's an opening, back by the rear wall!" he yelled out, his words muffled by his face piece, his fear put on hold for the moment by the sudden, unexpected discovery.

"Let's get over to it. Keep your hands on the search rope," Henderson replied, ever the professional. They were close now and in the moment of excitement he knew it would be tempting to forget about just how dangerous a position they were working in. They had to stay focused, they had to stay organized. He checked the pressure gauge that hung from the mask strap on his right shoulder. Half a tank left. They still had time, but they had to get busy.

A burst of adrenaline shot through Faiella giving him a surge of energy. He suddenly felt sharper, stronger, his fears temporarily assuaged. He crawled quickly, the barker right on his heels. But he no longer needed the Captain's prodding. Now there was a sense of purpose, a feeling that they were on the very edge and soon it would all be over. He moved through the final area of debris, quicker now, all the while getting closer and closer to the back wall. The passageway became much narrower, the beams no were no more than three feet above him and kept striking the air tank on his back. He had to stretch out on his gut to fit through. For the first time he thought not of himself but of Jim, the guy who was trapped, the man they were trying to save. They had just been sitting by their lockers, speaking to each other. He mentioned the book. Wanted a signed copy. He wasn't like a lot of the others. The guy never complained, never ridiculed anyone, or anything. He was supposed to be getting married soon.

Now Faiella was no longer afraid. He was no longer thinking like an aspiring writer or even a firefighter. He was just a guy on the verge of helping someone who was in desperate need of help. Someone he had known and worked next to for years. Someone with rapidly dwindling chances that he could save if he acted quickly. That was the only reality, his only responsibility.

He was breathing heavily when he finally got to the edge of the crevice. It was dark and deep and he reached in with his flashlight, scanning to the right and to the left, hoping to see something. He was directing it to the right when the beam of light reflected on something that stood out in the dark sooty hole. A helmet. His helmet. Faiella could make out the white 57 numerals on the front piece of Jim's helmet. It was lying in a corner and covered with dust. This was it. He had to be right here. Closer, he had to get closer. Faiella could almost reach out and touch the helmet. He yelled out for him, calling his name again and again at the top of his lungs, hoping he might be heard through his mask. If he could reach the helmet he could reach Jim, and he moved deeper into the void, constantly straining, probing, and reaching with every fiber of his six foot three inch frame.

But Jim was no longer lying there. He was sitting. On a stoop. In a distant neighborhood far, far away. Distant, but somehow strangely familiar with scents of summer and horses and the sounds of strollers and peddlers. Just sitting and staring down at the flagstone sidewalk in front of him. And when he looked up, he saw her. As he knew he would. Her eyes were pale blue and happy. It was like she could smile with those eyes even if you couldn't see the rest of her face. As if such a thing were even possible.

Deep in the void he waited, calmly, patiently, knowingly. Trapped by debris but freed of all doubt. For, finally, he knew.

It was real. It was all real.

And it always had been.

Author's Note

I do not actively believe in reincarnation. However, there are entire cultures that base their metaphysical beliefs on the concept. I'm sure that each of us has at some point given thought to the big questions of life. Where did we come from and where are we going? Are our present circumstances the only realities we will ever experience or is there something beyond? One could get lost in such conjecture. The possibilities give more substance to the relatively short existence we are blessed with. And since no one has ever come back from death to tell us what it's all about, I guess a philosophy based in reincarnation is about as good as any.

There have been many cases of children who recall past experiences. A four-year-old who remembered a life in which he worked as a Hollywood agent, the five year old boy who recollected living as a girl and dying in a fire, and numerous children in Myanmar who retain images of previous lives lived as World War II Japanese soldiers.

Studies have indicated that in most situations children lose such recollections around the age of six. However there have been rare cases of adults who retain these images. Those individuals are blessed, or cursed, with the ability to recall unexplained memories throughout their lives.

Acknowledgements

My sincere thanks to my editor, Carlos Balazs, designer, Sienna Whalen, and to Apprentice House Press for taking on this project. Thanks also to the many individuals I had the opportunity to work with over the course of a 33-year career as a New York City firefighter. That job truly changed my life and much of this novel is drawn from my experiences with them.

Last and certainly not least, my appreciation to my family for their warmth and encouragement. To Kevin and Erica, I am so proud of the people you are. To Suzanne Chazin, my wife and favorite author, thanks for the guidance and example you set.

About the Author

Thomas Dunne is a retired Deputy Chief and a 33 year veteran of the New York City Fire Department. He is the author of *Notes From the Fireground*, a memoir of his experiences in the city. His writing has appeared in the *New York Daily News* and he has published numerous magazine articles. His work as an FDNY firefighter along with a background of growing up in Brooklyn have provided him with a unique perspective of urban living. He still lives near New York and is currently lecturing throughout the country. His website is www.chieftomdunne.com

.

Apprentice
House Press
Loyola University Maryland

Apprentice House is the country's only campus-based, student-staffed book publishing company. Directed by professors and industry professionals, it is a nonprofit activity of the Communication Department at Loyola University Maryland.

Using state-of-the-art technology and an experiential learning model of education, Apprentice House publishes books in untraditional ways. This dual responsibility as publishers and educators creates an unprecedented collaborative environment among faculty and students, while teaching tomorrow's editors, designers, and marketers.

Eclectic and provocative, Apprentice House titles intend to entertain as well as spark dialogue on a variety of topics. Financial contributions to sustain the press's work are welcomed. Contributions are tax deductible to the fullest extent allowed by the IRS.

To learn more about Apprentice House books or to obtain submission guidelines, please visit www.apprenticehouse.com.

Apprentice House
Communication Department
Loyola University Maryland
4501 N. Charles Street
Baltimore, MD 21210
Ph: 410-617-5265
info@apprenticehouse.com • www.apprenticehouse.com

Lightning Source UK Ltd.
Milton Keynes UK
UKHW022005010223
416337UK00006B/166